**Get swept away by
Joanna Fulford's
stirring trilogy
*Victorious Vikings***

***No man could defeat them.
Three women would defy them!***

In

DEFIANT IN THE VIKING'S BED

...ilsson is enslaved by his
...s revenge on the woman
...y Astrid will become *his*
slave—and will pay the price in his bed!

**The thrilling trilogy continues
with ...nn's story, coming soon**

Securing ships and weapons,
powerful Viking ...inn must take a bride
in return. The fie... Lara may have to walk
meekly to th... o...; but she'll fight their
unwanted ... ction ...each step of the way!

And concludes with Erik's story

When adventurer ...rik is forced to reunite
with his estranged wife, Katlin, the warrior
will discover all her secrets—including the
passion that still burns strong between them…

AUTHOR NOTE

While researching ninth century Norway I found an invaluable resource in *Heimskringla*. It's good for historical background and even better for the larger-than-life individuals who inhabit its pages. Characters like Halfdan Svarti, Gandalf of Vingulmark and the berserker, Hakke, are a gift for the novelist. I'd never have invented better names than theirs, or imagined half the things they actually did.

While I try to be historically accurate, it can be convenient to have leeway where the facts aren't known. I deliberately departed from the source only twice: Hakke lost a hand and later fell on his sword when the wound became gangrenous. I've given him a swifter end, albeit for selfish reasons. The second deviation concerns the spelling of his name. Originally it was Hake, but this seemed too fishy, even for a villain, so I toned it down with the extra letter.

Writing this trilogy was great fun: Vikings have forceful personalities and strong opinions. I've learned to listen to my characters and know when to back down. Trust me: it's a mistake to argue with an axe-wielding berserker who doesn't like your game plan.

DEFIANT IN THE VIKING'S BED

Joanna Fulford

First published in Great Britain 2013
by Mills & Boon, an imprint of Harlequin (UK) Limited.
Harlequin (UK) Limited, Eton House, 18-24 Paradise Road,
Richmond, Surrey TW9 1SR

© Joanna Fulford 2013

ISBN: 978 0 263 89856 9

Harlequin (UK) policy is to use papers that are natural, renewable and recyclable products and made from wood grown in sustainable forests. The logging and manufacturing process conform to the legal environmental regulations of the country of origin.

Printed and bound in Spain
by Blackprint CPI, Barcelona

Joanna Fulford is a compulsive scribbler with a passion for literature and history, both of which she has studied to postgraduate level. Other countries and cultures have always exerted a fascination, and she has travelled widely, living and working abroad for many years. However, her roots are in England, and are now firmly established in the Peak District, where she lives with her husband, Brian. When not pressing a hot keyboard she likes to be out on the hills, either walking or on horseback. However, these days equestrian activity is confined to sedate hacking rather than riding at high speed towards solid obstacles. Visit Joanna's website at www.joannafulford.co.uk

Previous novels by the same author:

THE VIKING'S DEFIANT BRIDE
(part of the *Mills & Boon Presents...* anthology,
featuring talented new authors)
THE WAYWARD GOVERNESS
THE LAIRD'S CAPTIVE WIFE
THE COUNTERFEIT CONDESA
THE VIKING'S TOUCH
THE CAGED COUNTESS
REDEMPTION OF A FALLEN WOMAN
(part of *Castonbury Park* Regency mini-series)
HIS LADY OF CASTLEMORA
CHRISTMAS AT OAKHURST MANOR
(part of *Snowbound Wedding Wishes* anthology)

**Did you know that some of these novels
are also available as eBooks?
Visit www.millsandboon.co.uk**

For my former writing tutor and mentor, Paul Kane,
who set me on my way and regularly saved me
from myself. Thank you, Paul.
I couldn't have done it without you.

Chapter One

~~~

Leif Egilsson pulled his dagger free and silently lowered the body of the dead guard. Across the wide clearing in front of him he could see a large camp fire around which a dozen men lounged at their ease, laughing and talking among themselves. Their war gear was piled a few yards off. Behind them was pitched an imposing tent, no doubt sheltering the prince and his closest henchmen. Hard by was a smaller shelter with two guards posted at the entrance. Leif noted their presence with satisfaction.

'That's where Hakke will be holding her, my lord,' he murmured.

Halfdan Svarti nodded. 'We'll go in fast and hit them before they know what's happened. In the meantime, you and your men find Lady Ragnhild and keep her safe.'

'Depend on it.'

The two men retraced their steps into the trees a little way to where fifty armed warriors waited. Halfdan surveyed them keenly.

'Take no prisoners. This time we end it once and for all.'

They heard him in wolfish anticipation.

Leif met his brother's gaze. 'Ready?'

Finn smiled. 'Does Thor hurl thunderbolts?'

'He does today.'

'I'm glad to hear it, Cousin,' said Erik. 'Life has grown dull of late.'

Beside them a grizzled campaigner stroked the haft of an axe. 'You speak true. There hasn't been so much as a skirmish for weeks. Skull Cleaver is thirsty.'

'She shall drink her fill, Thorvald,' said Leif.

The older man laughed softly. It drew answering grins from those who stood nearby. There followed the muted chink of mail and the sinister whisper of blades unsheathed. Leif smiled, tightening his grip on Foe Bane's hilt, and then briefly touched the amulet that he wore around his neck.

'Let's do it.'

They moved forwards to the edge of the thicket. Halfdan raised his sword aloft and then, with a deafening roar, the whole force broke from cover and hurtled upon the enemy.

Astrid sat bolt upright, her startled gaze meeting Ragnhild's. 'What was that?'

'I'm not sure. It sounded like...'

The rest was lost, swept aside by a deafening war cry and then confused alarm: shouting, running feet and then the unmistakable clash of steel. Astrid leapt to her feet and ran to the entrance of the tent, pushing aside the hangings to peer out. Her eyes widened.

'Merciful gods! Where on earth did *they* come from?'

Ragnhild hastened to join her and then she too stared in dismay at the throng of fighting warriors. 'Whose men are those? Can you tell?'

'No, but they're definitely enemies of Prince Hakke, which means...'

'They might prove friends to us?'

'Let's hope so, my lady.'

Astrid prayed that her words were true and that they might not find themselves even worse off than before. It was hard to see how, but then, nothing was certain. This might mean deliverance or doom. Hakke would not yield up his prisoners easily. Indeed, he might rather slay them than lose them. She swallowed hard. They had no weapons with which to defend themselves; even their belt knives had been confiscated when they were captured. Possibly the prince had not wished to leave temptation in their way. He was right: Ragnhild would have used it on herself before agreeing to his demands and Astrid didn't blame her. Nor would she have chosen to linger among the present company after her mistress's demise. Some things *were* worse than death.

Leif parried the blow aimed at his head and laid on with a will, driving his opponent back several paces. The defender fought desperately, recovered again and came on, his expression a feral snarl. A wicked thrust was deftly deflected. The blades slid and locked. Leif brought a knee up hard, heard a grunt of pain and saw the man stagger. A second later Foe Bane sank deep in his opponent's gut. Leif tugged the sword free and darted a swift look around. His gaze fell on a familiar figure some twenty yards off; a warrior whose helm bore the crest of a hunting hawk. He was yelling furious orders at his troops. As the latter piled into the fray the warrior looked round and as his gaze locked with Leif's, anger became malevolence.

'You!'

'As you say, Hakke.'

'This will not be forgotten. Not this, nor the battle at Eid.'

'I hope not.'

'All will be paid for, Leif Egilsson.'

Before they could say more one of Halfdan's men stepped into Hakke's path, compelling his attention. Other fighting pairs jostled in. The prince spied his opponent and backed off, lost to view behind the mêlée. Leif hesitated, sorely tempted to go after him. However, his promise to the king could not be ignored and reluctantly he turned away. The others would have to deal with it. He had a more pressing mission.

The sounds of conflict drew nearer and then the view from the tent was entirely blocked by fighting men. There followed a cry of mortal agony and blood sprayed across hempen fabric. Both women gasped, leaping out of the way as the guard's lifeless body fell through the opening. Then the hangings were torn aside and a tall figure blocked out the light; a figure clad in chainmail and whose fist wielded a blood-stained sword. He was flanked by several other mailed warriors. The two women paled and retreated, brought to bay at the rear of the tent.

As the intruder advanced Astrid stifled a scream, her heart pounding like Thor's hammer. Her attention flicked from the naked dripping blade to the darkening gore streaked across the chainmail byrnie and thence to the steel helmet that partly concealed his face. He halted a few feet away and for the space of a few heartbeats his gaze swept both women, cool and assessing. Then he lowered the sword.

'Don't be afraid. No harm shall come to you.'

The sensation of relief was so strong it made her feel light-headed. With an effort she mastered it and faced him.

'Who are you?' she demanded. 'What do you want with us?'

'I want nothing, lady, other than to ensure your safety. The rest my lord will explain himself.'

'And who is your lord?'

'King Halfdan.'

Both women regarded him in astonishment. Ragnhild's hand tightened on Astrid's arm. 'Halfdan?'

'Aye, my lady.'

'Oh, the gods be thanked.'

Astrid too let out the breath she had been holding, hardly able to take in such a swift reversal of their former ill fortune. Turning to Ragnhild, she saw the same expression mirrored in the other woman's face.

'The king is here?' Ragnhild continued.

'Nothing could have kept him away, my lady. Your safety and well-being are most dear to his heart.'

'As his are to mine.' She paused. 'To whom do I owe thanks for bringing such happy news?'

'Leif Egilsson, at your service.'

'I shall remember that name.'

'My lady does me honour.'

Just then they heard more voices outside, one much louder than the rest, demanding to know Ragnhild's whereabouts. Moments later the newcomer strode into the tent, a big man, dark of hair and beard, whose face might have been hewn from rock. He paused and as his gaze came to rest on Ragnhild its expression softened. That look was enough. Ragnhild ran to him and was swept into a close embrace.

'I thought I'd never see you again, my lord.'

'No man shall ever take you from me.' He glanced down at her. 'Did the brute hurt you?'

'No, I am well.'

'I thank Odin for it.'

Astrid looked on smiling, her heart full, happy for Ragnhild and for an outcome so different from the one they had earlier expected.

Presently the reunited couple left the tent, no doubt wanting a little space alone for private speech. Halfdan's men grinned and watched them go; then took themselves off in other directions.

'A happy turn of events,' said Astrid. Then she turned to Leif. 'But for your timely intervention it might not have been. I too am grateful.'

He paused to make use of the door hangings and wipe his sword clean; then sheathed it. 'No thanks are necessary. It was a matter of unfinished business.'

'I see.'

'Now it is done.'

'Perhaps there will be peace at last.'

He unfastened the chin strap and removed his helmet. 'Perhaps.'

Astrid caught her breath, wondering for a moment if Baldur the Beautiful had not just assumed human form. A mane of pale gold hair framed a face remarkable for its strong chiselled lines and planes. His eyes were somewhere between blue and grey, like the sea just after a storm, but much harder to read. Realising she was staring, she dragged her mind back to the conversation.

'If it comes about I shall know whom to thank.'

He smiled faintly. 'You have the advantage of me, lady.'

'I am Astrid, companion to Ragnhild.'

The blue-grey gaze surveyed her from head to toe and back again. 'A pretty name and most aptly bestowed.'

His expression was both hard to interpret and mildly disconcerting. Had he paid her a genuine compliment or had she detected a faintly mocking undertone? Perhaps it was a little of both. Whatever the truth of it she was keenly aware that everyone else had left the tent; that now she had his undivided attention. While male attention was nothing new, it always made her feel uneasy and resurrected unwelcome memories, so she tried to avoid it. This man didn't make her afraid as Hakke and his mercenaries had done but there was something about him that disturbed her all the same, and on an entirely different and unfamiliar level. She decided to parry.

'It is I who am fortunate in having so kind a mistress.'

'Your mistress is about to become a queen or I miss my guess.'

She smiled. 'I think your guess is accurate, though perhaps not hard to arrive at.'

'True.'

'I believe theirs will be a most happy marriage.'

'That will make them both lucky and exceptional.'

'Why should it be exceptional?' she replied. 'Plenty of marriages are happy.'

'It may be so but it is entirely outside my experience.'

'Then how can you judge?'

'I was referring to the latter part of your statement, not the former.'

'Oh.'

The conversation lapsed into an awkward silence made more difficult by the weight of that steady blue-grey gaze. A slow flush of warmth crept upwards from her neck and throat. It was time to bring matters to a conclusion.

'Speaking of my mistress; I should rejoin her.' She paused. 'Will you take me to her?'

'As you wish.'

He drew the hangings aside and stood back to let her pass. She brushed past him and stepped outside. There she checked abruptly, wide-eyed as she took in the number of the slain. The earth was dark with their blood; its thick metallic reek hung on the still air. Mingled with it were other smells, equally rank. She swallowed hard, trying not to breathe too deeply.

'Battle isn't pretty, is it?' he said.

'Hardly.'

'And yet you do not scream or swoon.'

'Is that what you were expecting?'

'Had you done so, I wouldn't have been surprised. Now I am.'

She wondered what he would have done if she had swooned. The possibilities were vaguely disconcerting, like his smile now. Quickly she looked away. 'The reality of battle is worse than I imagined.'

'One grows used to it.'

'I think I could never grow used to it.'

'A woman shouldn't have to.'

Astrid had no intention of arguing the point. Instead she looked around, seeking Ragnhild, and located her some little way off, in conversation with Halfdan and some of his men.

Her companion followed her gaze. 'Shall we join them?'

'Certainly.'

He placed a hand under her elbow to steer her around the worst of the carnage. The touch transferred unsettling warmth through the sleeve of her gown. She glanced up quickly and saw him smile. The previous awkwardness might never have happened. Aware of him to her fingertips, she looked away and tried to fix her attention on where they were going. They joined the others a few moments later.

The king's expression was sombre. Astrid felt a twinge of apprehension and directed a quizzical look at Ragnhild. Her friend lost no time in explaining.

'Hakke isn't here, Astrid.'

'No, curse him,' said Halfdan. 'When he realised he was heavily outnumbered he slipped away in the confusion. We went after him but some of his men had horses waiting nearby; a second string. I should have foreseen that.'

'Easy to be wise after the event,' replied Leif.

'Since we'd left our own mounts back in the wood the fugitives had a head start. The man's more slippery than a greasy weasel.'

'But far more treacherous, my lord. We need to put him under ground.'

'I have men out looking for him now.'

'He'll be heading for his ship. The coast is only a few miles off.'

'My thought exactly.'

'With your leave I'll take my own force and join the pursuit.'

Halfdan nodded. 'Do it; and may the All-Father bring you better luck.'

Leif bowed to Ragnhild and Astrid and then bade them a brief courteous farewell. With that he turned and strode away. As she watched his retreating figure, Astrid experienced an unwonted sensation of regret, knowing she wouldn't forget him. He, on the other hand, being bound upon his quest, would already have dismissed her from his mind. Not that it mattered. They were unlikely to meet again. Drawing her mantle closer, she followed Halfdan and Ragnhild towards the waiting horses.

Leif and his companions reached the coast in time to see the ship heading towards the open sea. Anger mingled with frustration, emotions he was not alone in feeling, to judge from the flinty expressions around him.

'Hakke will return to his lair and lick his wounds awhile,' said Finn, 'but he'll be back.'

'And in force, no doubt,' added Erik.

'Well, there's nothing we can do about it now,' replied Thorvald.

The others were silent, each man inwardly acknowledging the truth of that statement. They had ridden hard, sparing neither themselves nor their mounts, only for this. Leif restrained the urge to curse, knowing it would serve no purpose.

Eventually Finn glanced his way. 'It'll be dark soon. What do you want to do?'

'We'll make camp here tonight.'

'I was hoping you'd say that. My stomach thinks my throat's been cut.'

'Looks like Hakke's crewmen were before us,' said Erik, eyeing the charred remains of a fire on the strand beyond. 'He really had every eventuality covered, didn't he?'

Thorvald followed his gaze. 'They were certainly waiting awhile. They've even left us some wood.'

'Thoughtful to the last,' replied Finn.

'No, they probably pissed on it before they left.'

In spite of himself Leif grinned. 'Most like. Even if they didn't it won't be enough to keep a fire alight for more than half an hour.' He turned to the others. 'Aun, Harek, Bjarni, Ingolf and Trygg—start looking for some more wood. The rest will take care of the horses.'

As the men moved to obey he went down to inspect the abandoned campsite. Contrary to suspicion the remaining firewood was dry. However, when he tested an ember in the makeshift hearth it was barely warm. They were going to have to start again. Brushing a smear of soot from his fingers, he straightened and went off in search of kindling.

Within an hour they had another fire going and a pile of wood to feed it. The company settled down to eat, breaking out cold rations from the saddlebags. However, conversation was muted, the result of fatigue and disappointment that their quarry had escaped and, once a guard detail was organised, most of the men elected to turn in.

However, although he was tired, Leif found sleep elusive. Hakke's escape was a serious blow, and likely to have far-reaching ramifications. It might have been prevented had it not been for the need to safeguard the women. He sighed, knowing the thought unjust. They were not to blame and certainly did not deserve to be left to Hakke's mercy. Lady Ragnhild was an acknowledged beauty, daughter of a jarl and a queen in the making. However, it was not she who lingered in his thoughts.

He couldn't have said exactly why Astrid should have left a deeper impression. True she was pretty, yet he'd seen other young women as fair; women who had tried much harder to please. He smiled, but its mockery was directed inwards. He couldn't detect anything remotely flirtatious in her manner. On the contrary, he suspected that her gratitude towards him was in no way influenced by liking. Nor could he entirely blame her. She had been courteous: he had been…abrupt. The subject of marriage was one he avoided when possible since he found it impossible to be impartial. Such discussions always awoke his cynicism, but then, he had nothing to go on except personal experience. Nevertheless, it occurred to him that, since Halfdan's marriage to Ragnhild was a foregone conclusion, both he and Astrid would be bidden to the feast. That aspect at least was not displeasing. Perhaps he could make amends…

The idea gave him pause. His contact with women in recent years was about money for favours rendered. Astrid fell outside that category which made things potentially tricky. It surprised him that he should even want to see her again: usually his female acquaintances didn't linger in the mind. The fact that she had might be due in part to the circumstances of their meeting. In part. There was something about her that he couldn't quite explain, some quality that drew him in spite of himself. Her presence at the feast would make the occasion more interesting and, he decided, much more enjoyable.

Chapter Two

Lady Ragnhild's marriage to King Halfdan was a splendid affair attended by music and feasting. Both bride and groom looked blissfully happy and had eyes only for each other. Astrid, looking on, thought that was how it ought to be, even though it rarely was. Too often marriages were made without any thought for the personal inclination of the participants. It made her glad for Ragnhild. So fair and kind a lady deserved the love of a good man. Halfdan would treat her well. Having almost lost her, he would know how to value what he had.

The only thing to mar events was the news of Hakke's escape to Vingulmark, the seat of his power. He still had strong support there, including that of her uncle. A wily politician, he must be gnashing his teeth over recent events, as must the prince. Robbed of a bride and defeated in battle, his anger would be great indeed. He would seek revenge for that, and for his brothers' deaths. Hysing and Helsing might have fallen in battle but their passing was the excuse that would fuel another uprising, sooner or later. Unless Halfdan pre-empted it...

'You seem preoccupied,' said a voice behind her, 'though I have no expectation that your thoughts were of me.'

Her pulse quickened as she turned to see Leif at her shoulder. The chainmail byrnie was gone now, along with the dirt and gore of battle, and he was clad in a tunic of dark green wool richly embroidered with gold thread at the neck and wrist where the linen of his shirt was just visible. Round his neck he wore an amulet in the likeness of Thor's hammer. The tooled leather belt round his waist held a fine dagger. He was altogether a most imposing figure.

'No, they weren't,' she confessed.

'I am crushed.'

She laughed. 'It would take more than that to crush you, my lord. However, I am sorry to have dashed your hopes.'

'I'm not convinced that you are sorry.'

'In truth, not very,' she replied, 'but I didn't want to hurt your feelings as well.'

His eyes gleamed. 'I suppose I asked for that.'

'I was thinking about Prince Hakke and what

he might do next. I feel sure we have not heard the last of him.'

'I'm afraid you're right.'

'Will he be able to raise another army?'

'I'm sure he'd like to but, in reality, I think it unlikely. King Gandalf's force took a hammering at Eid. The survivors will not seek another confrontation with Halfdan if it can be avoided.'

'So we're safe.'

'I wouldn't go that far; at least not while Hakke lives.'

'It was unfortunate that he managed to escape.'

'Yes, most unfortunate.'

Astrid's eyes widened a little. 'I did not mean to imply blame.'

His lips twitched. 'I am relieved. I should not like you to think less of me.'

'Oh, I could not think less of you.' As soon as the words were out she winced inwardly, wondering if her tongue had suddenly become disconnected from her brain. She hurried on, 'What I meant was that I could never be induced to think less of you, because of the great service you have rendered my mistress and me.'

He eyed her askance. 'I am relieved.'

Astrid could hardly fail to miss the note of irony and wondered if he were really offended.

'Forgive me. I expressed myself badly.'

'My pride will doubtless recover—in a month or two.'

Unable to help it, she smiled. 'Oh, I think it will be much sooner than that, my lord.'

The smile was both mischievous and unwittingly beguiling, like the look in those big violet eyes. All at once Leif found himself staring, realising that she was a lot more than pretty. Intelligent too. It was a rare combination. Perhaps that was why she aroused his curiosity. He took two cups of mead from a passing servant and handed Astrid one.

'Tell me how you came to be into the queen's service.'

'My uncle placed me in her father's household five years ago. Sigurd Hjort was an ally back then. It was an advantageous situation for me, given my mistress's connections. She and I subsequently became good friends.'

'Your uncle?'

'He is my guardian now. My father died some years ago.' She sighed. 'My uncle was ever an ambitious man and it suited him to have a foothold in two camps.'

'Two camps?'

'Vestfold and Vingulmark.'

'I see. Well, he isn't the first man to hedge his bets thus.'

'No. In any case I was glad to be out of the way. He is not an easy man to be around.'

'Do I know him?'

'Possibly. He is Jarl Einar of Ringerike.'

Leif's cup paused in mid-air. He had miscalculated; he had supposed her to be of good birth, though possibly a poor relation placed in an advantageous situation. He could never have guessed that her family was among the foremost in Vestfold.

'An influential man,' he said.

'He has influence,' she agreed, 'and wealth, and yet it seems the more he has the more he wants.'

'It's a common complaint.'

'So I believe. At all events he holds jealously to what is his. Most of his lands lie just beyond the territory ceded to King Halfdan. Tensions remain high in the region.'

'I know it. I too have lands there.'

'You have?'

'They were granted by the king in recognition of my family's service to him.'

'I see.'

'It makes us near neighbours in that sense.'

'I have not returned there since and have no wish to do so. Nor do I share my uncle's political sympathies. My loyalty is to Queen Ragnhild.'

'That's understandable in the circumstances, but it may not be an easy position to maintain.'

'By that I suppose you mean that I am technically still in my uncle's control.'

'Just so.'

'He is too busy to concern himself with me.

He resembles my late father in that respect. Only sons were of real interest.'

'But daughters are useful for strengthening alliances. Nieces too.'

It was the bald truth and unwelcome withal. 'I'll cross that bridge when I reach it.'

'Does the thought displease you?'

'In principle, no. However, much would depend upon the man.'

'Of course.'

'Are you married, my lord?'

His expression changed. 'No, I'm not married.'

Astrid was aware of having made a false step, and that he might have interpreted it to mean that she had an ulterior motive in finding out. Mortified, she retracted hurriedly. 'I didn't mean that the way it sounded. It was said out of curiosity alone.'

'It is no matter.' He paused. 'As it happens I did have a wife at one time but the marriage was not a success and it ended a year later.' *To say that it was not a success was a massive understatement*, he thought, *and the mere mention of it threatened to curdle the wine in his stomach. The spectres of the past were best left alone.*

Divorce was not uncommon but she could well imagine that it wouldn't be easy either. 'That is unfortunate.' She paused. 'Do you have any children?'

'Not any more. My son died in infancy.'

Gods, this was getting worse. 'I'm so sorry.'

'It was long ago. Now I follow the whale road.'

'The call of adventure?'

'Something like that. At all events it suits me well. I shall not take another wife.'

The reply was lightly spoken but it also held a warning, one she would do well to heed. At the same time, and for reasons she could not explain, it saddened her too.

'However,' he continued, 'that does not mean I am incapable of enjoying the company of a beautiful woman.'

'I'm sure you must have known many such.'

'Some.' He paused, surveying her steadily. 'What of you? Are you betrothed?'

'No.'

'Why not? There can have been no lack of suitors.'

There were several answers she might have given, all concerned with deep inner reservations and each more complicated than the last. Instead she sought refuge in evasion. 'My uncle has more important matters on his mind.'

'He is remiss.'

'Perhaps he is holding out for a king, and I shall make as splendid a match as my mistress.'

Although the tone was flippant, she wouldn't have put such a notion past her uncle. Indeed she wouldn't have put anything past him.

Leif's eyes gleamed. 'What king in his right mind would refuse such an offer?'

'Kings marry for political advantage. I fear I cannot offer any such.'

'Kings are still men. Leaving politics aside, it seems to me that you have much to offer.'

Astrid swallowed a mouthful of mead. This conversation was straying into dangerous territory again. 'You exaggerate my appeal there.'

'I was speaking for myself.'

'I regret that I can offer nothing, my lord.' And particularly not to one who was clearly not over the loss of his wife and had just said he had no intention of remarrying.

'Not so.'

Before she could reply, another man appeared at his shoulder. Facially he bore a startling resemblance to Leif, although his hair was a little darker. They were much of a height too. Evidently good looks ran in the family.

The newcomer acknowledged her with a bow and then murmured something to Leif. She saw him frown.

'Pray excuse me for a moment.'

Relief washed over her. 'By all means.'

As the two stepped aside for private speech, Astrid saw the opportunity to extricate herself and took it, slipping away into the crowd of revellers. The tenor of the recent conversation had left her in no doubt that it was a wise move. Leif was both handsome and charismatic, a dangerous combination and one that had not failed in its allure since she knew perfectly well that she wasn't indifferent to him. It was also quite clear that what he sought was a little light amusement. She guessed that such a man would have plenty of willing takers too. However, she wasn't going to be one of them.

When Leif turned round a minute or so later Astrid was gone. Swiftly he scanned the crowd but could discern no trace of her. At once he was conscious of both disappointment and regret. After the recent conversation he did not suppose it had been done on purpose to increase his interest. All the same, it had, and to a degree that surprised him. However, it was evident that she would not fall easily into his arms either. This evading action was an unwitting challenge, and one that would be met.

'Pretty girl,' said Finn. 'Who is she?'

'The queen's companion.'

'Thor's teeth, she *is* out of the usual field. Are you sure you know what you're doing?'

'I always know what I'm doing.'

'Even so, it's dangerous ground, Brother. You risk getting burned.'

'I'm grateful for your concern, but you of all people should know that your fears are unfounded.'

'It's because I've been through the same mill that I mention them.'

Leif returned a wry smile. 'I know.'

'Someone has to watch your back.'

'There's no one I'd rather have at my back. However, this challenge I handle alone.'

'Ah, like that, is it?'

'It is.'

'Well, well. She has lit a fire under you, hasn't she?'

'Mind your own business.'

Finn merely laughed. 'I take that to mean yes, then.' As he eyed Leif his expression grew speculative. 'Never tell me the lady is proof against your good looks and charm. I won't believe it.'

'She likes me well enough, although she doesn't know it yet.'

'I have every confidence in your powers of persuasion. In the meantime, there are other, more willing subjects present. The dark-haired beauty over there hasn't taken her eyes off you all evening.'

Leif followed the direction of his brother's gaze and located the woman in question. She returned an inviting smile. He studied her a second or two longer and then looked away.

'I leave that one to you.'

'Don't say later that I didn't offer you the chance.'

Finn left him and headed across the room. A

few minutes later he was deep in conversation with the object of his attention. Leif watched them for a little while and then drank down the rest of his mead, wondering at his own behaviour. The dark beauty had been ripe for the taking, but he felt only indifference—even though, just a few days ago, he would have considered her worthy of his most assiduous attention. He turned away and went to look for another cup of mead.

Astrid lay awake for a long time, unable to shake off the implications of the discussion that evening. Far from attempting any amorous subterfuge, Leif had made his position quite clear. His interest in her had nothing whatever to do with marriage. If she offered him any encouragement now it would result in her being a mistress, not a wife. Not that she had the least desire to be either of those things. Once, long ago, the thought of marriage to such a man would not have displeased her. Since the married state was inevitable, all girls wanted a handsome, virile bridegroom. Back then it would never have occurred to her to question any of that. Now she did question it. Not that her doubts would carry any weight even if she had voiced them. In any case pleasing her would be the very last consideration when her uncle eventually found her a husband, and nor would she be consulted. Her husband could be old or ugly or cruel, or all three, and it would make no difference to

Jarl Einar. He would see her wedded and bedded regardless, and by force if necessary.

Old resentments woke and she tried to imagine a world in which a woman might be free to make her own decisions about such things; a world where she wasn't subject to the will of powerful men. It was an agreeable fantasy. In the meantime, any dalliance with Leif would be disastrous. They had already spent longer together than was wise and she didn't want him to take that for encouragement. Moreover, she never wanted him to think of her in terms of a possible conquest. His opinion shouldn't have mattered. They were mere acquaintances and parting wouldn't be long in coming once the festivities were done. The knowledge was attended by relief, but mixed with a twinge of regret. Leif was handsome and personable and somehow larger than life. She suspected that he wouldn't be easy to forget.

Chapter Three

~~~

Two days later the first group of guests departed. Now that the wedding celebrations were over the rest would be gone soon enough and life would settle back into its familiar routine. Once Astrid would have felt content with that, but now it induced very different thoughts. Chief among them was restlessness. It had no apparent cause but it was no less strong for that. Perhaps it was a natural consequence of the recent excitement and festivity; one felt the lack when it ended.

She turned away but, unwilling to return to the hall or the bower, headed in the opposite direction instead. A walk might help dispel her present mood. She was so absorbed in thought that she didn't notice the man until she was almost upon him. When she realised who it was she would have retraced her steps—but by then it was too late.

Leif smiled. 'This is a pleasant surprise.'

She eyed him askance. 'A surprise, my lord?'

'All right, I admit I followed you. Or rather I watched to see which way you were going and then took a short cut.'

'Why?'

'I missed your company.'

'I find that hard to believe.'

'It's true. Besides, we never got to finish our conversation the other night.'

'I believe we did.'

'If I have offended you I'm sorry for it.'

'Forget it.'

'I wish it were that easy. As it is I've thought of nothing else.' He paused. 'We need to talk, Astrid.'

Her pulse quickened. 'Everything needful has been said.'

'No, it hasn't.'

He surveyed her steadily, waiting. She sighed. Since he wasn't going to be dissuaded the quickest way to end this might be to let him say his piece. 'Very well.'

'I apologise if my manners have seemed rough; it is the result of having spent too long among fighting men. I am out of practice when it comes to gentler speech.'

'Yes, you are, but it is no matter.'

'Well, some things are best spoken directly.'

'Speak, then.'

'In a few days' time I leave for my estate in Vingulmark. The place has been left in the hands of a steward and there are many matters requiring my attention.'

The news created a flood of unexpected emotions. After this they really would not meet again. She realised she was going to miss him rather more than she'd thought. 'Yes, I can see that.'

'Come with me.'

She stared at him. 'What?'

'Come with me, Astrid.'

'You must be crazy.'

'Perhaps. What I do know is that I don't want to leave you behind; that I want you with me.'

His arm slipped around her waist and then he was very much closer. She could feel the warmth of him, breathe his scent. The pulse became a drumbeat. She felt his lips brush hers, light, tentative. The touch sent a shiver through her that was not entirely to do with fear. The kiss became a little more assertive, more seductive, coaxing her mouth open, allowing his tongue to tease hers, persuasive and infinitely more dangerous, awakening sensations she had never known existed. His hold tightened and the kiss became intimate. She could feel the start of his arousal. Desire was replaced by something very like panic and she tensed, turning her head aside.

He drew back a little to look into her face.

'What are you afraid of, Astrid? You cannot believe I would hurt you.'

She shook her head, not in agreement but in denial, knowing instinctively that he had the power to hurt her very badly. She wasn't the woman he really wanted.

'Well, then, what is it?'

'I won't go with you to Vingulmark.'

'Why not?'

'How can you ask that?'

'You know how I feel about you, and I think you are not indifferent to me.'

'You're wrong.'

'You're a poor liar, Astrid.'

'It's not a lie.'

'No? Then look at me and tell me you feel nothing.'

Her gaze met his and yielded. 'I confess I do like you, and I have enjoyed your company, but there is no future in this. You know that as well as I.'

'All I know is that I haven't been able to put you out of my mind since first we met. When I'm awake I think of you; when I sleep you fill my dreams.'

'I cannot do what you're asking.'

'You have no reason to be afraid. I would treat you well; whatever you desire you shall have if it be in my power to give it.'

'Will you offer me honourable marriage, Leif?'

'In my experience there is precious little honour to be found there, and I will not deal in false promises.' His gaze never wavered. 'I have already intimated as much.'

'So you did, and I am grateful for that honesty.'

'I don't want your gratitude, Astrid. I want you, but I would not have any pretence between us. If you come with me it will be with your eyes open.'

'They are open and I'm not coming with you.' *You love someone else*, she thought.

'You don't have to make up your mind now. Take some time. Think it over.'

'There is nothing to think over. I will not be any man's whore.'

With that she stepped away from him and hurried away down the path. For a moment or two he watched her go, strongly tempted to fetch her back and at the same time knowing he wouldn't. What he wanted from her could not be compelled. It still surprised him that he did want her that much. His offer had been an impulse and yet he couldn't regret making it, even if she had turned him down flat. Realistically he ought to have been better prepared for that. It was also ridiculous to feel quite so disappointed by her refusal.

Astrid reached the buildings a short time later, barely registering the lathered horses or the group of men outside the hall. She had no wish to see anyone until she had recovered her composure so she ducked around the corner and headed for the bower. The encounter with Leif had left her shaken for many reasons, not least because he was right; she was not indifferent to him. His kiss lingered still. The strength of the attraction she had felt in that brief embrace was profoundly shocking and it could only lead to disaster. Thank all the gods that good sense had prevailed.

On reaching the bower she bathed her face and tidied her hair, by which time she was calmer and better able to face the world. She was about to leave when the door opened to admit Ragnhild. When she saw Astrid she smiled.

'I hoped I might find you here.'

'Forgive me. I went for a walk...'

'Then you will not have heard.'

'Heard what, Highness?'

'Your uncle is but lately arrived.'

Astrid stared at her in dismay. 'My uncle? What is he doing here?'

'I imagine he will tell you that himself. He wishes to speak with you.' Ragnhild paused. 'I wanted to prepare you first.'

'I thank you. It was a kind thought.'

'He is in the hall.'

Astrid paused on the threshold, surveying the newcomers uneasily. There were half a dozen of them, all slaking their thirst with ale. However, she had no problem locating the burly figure of her uncle. Although only just above the average height, he was powerfully built, reminding her of nothing so much as an old bear. Foreboding grew. Then, taking a deep breath, she went in.

Her uncle failed to notice her until his companion gave a discreet cough alerting him to her presence. He looked round. Cunning dark eyes subjected her to a cool and thorough appraisal. Then he nodded in grudging approval.

'Well, well. The cygnet has become a swan.'

She dropped a polite curtsy. 'Your visit is an unexpected surprise, my lord.'

'No doubt.'

'May I ask what brings you here?'

'You do.' He drained his cup and tossed it to a servant. 'I am come to take you back to Vingulmark.'

Her stomach lurched. 'My lord?'

'I have found a husband for you. You're to be married.'

It was like being punched and, for a moment or two, speech was impossible. The piercing gaze fixed her.

'Why do you stare at me, girl?'

There were many things she might have said, all of them angry and all of them unwise since their utterance would only create a public scene. Instead she strove for self-control.

'Forgive me. I…I was just taken by surprise, that's all.'

He grunted. 'No doubt. Possibly you thought I had forgotten the matter entirely.' Without waiting for a reply he continued, 'I will admit it should have happened sooner, but I have been occupied with other things. However, it has turned out well enough. Your future husband is connected to the most influential family in Vingulmark.'

Astrid licked dry lips. 'May I know his name?'

'Of course. You are to marry Jarl Gulbrand.'

She controlled resentment and a sensation of rising panic. Her uncle had spoken the truth. Gulbrand did indeed have a noble name: he was related to the royal house. He was also Prince Hakke's cousin and, like his cousin, he had an unsavoury reputation, on the battlefield and off it.

'When is this marriage to take place?'

'Next month.'

'But that's barely two weeks away.'

'Time enough. We leave tomorrow.'

'I cannot go so soon. I have duties here.'

The dark eyes narrowed. 'Your duties here are over. Be ready to leave first thing in the morning.'

It was dismissal. Astrid made her escape from the hall, her mind reeling. Ragnhild caught up with her outside.

'I'm so sorry, Astrid. It has come as a shock to me too.'

'Is there no way this can be prevented?'

'I wish there were, but your uncle is your guardian, not I.'

'Might not the king intervene?'

'He has no more jurisdiction in this than I do.'

Astrid blinked back angry tears. 'Then I am well and truly lost.'

When Leif looked around the hall that evening he could see no sign of the one he sought. He wondered if she were avoiding him but then decided it was unlikely, since Ragnhild wasn't present either. No doubt Astrid was keeping her company. All the same, it was frustrating and, if he were honest, disappointing too. Her absence cast an unexpected pall over the proceedings. Until then he hadn't realised how much he had been hoping to see her; to speak with her; to try and persuade her...

'What in the name of Tyr One-Hand is *he* doing here?'

Finn's voice roused him from his reverie and he followed his brother's gaze across the hall. Seeing Jarl Einar, he frowned. The jarl's estates in Vingulmark might be close to Leif's own lands, but that was the sole extent of their neighbourliness. While there hadn't been open hostility as such, it was well known that many of Einar's associates were connected with the royal house of Vingulmark. The defeat at Eid must have come as a blow. He could not have foreseen that, or the subsequent turn of events, when he placed his niece with Sigurd Hjort and his family all those years ago.

'Good question,' he replied.

'I doubt it bodes any good.'

'He won't start any trouble here, be assured of that.'

'All the same,' said Finn, 'he's not a man I'd choose to turn my back on.'

'You were wise not to,' replied Erik. 'All the same, Leif is in the right of it. Einar isn't here to cause trouble. He's come to fetch his niece.'

'Fetch her where?'

'Back to Vingulmark. Seems she's to be married.'

Leif was suddenly still. 'Married?'

Erik nodded. 'That's right.'

'How would you know?' demanded Finn.

'Ingolf heard some of Einar's men talking.'

Finn glanced at Leif. 'It looks as if your hopes there are dashed, then.'

Leif casually reached for his cup. 'It does rather, doesn't it?'

'Never mind. Plenty more shingles on the roof, eh?'

'As you say.'

Erik eyed him speculatively. 'Fancied her yourself, did you?'

It was an understatement, but Leif wasn't about to confide the fact. Instead he shrugged. 'You win some, you lose some.'

'True enough. Besides, Finn's right. The world is full of pretty women.'

Finn smiled. 'Do you remember that redhead in Alfheim who...?'

Leif barely heard him, his mind still trying to assimilate what he'd just heard. He hadn't seen that coming. Nor would he have anticipated his own reaction. He had hoped to have more time to achieve his goal; that Astrid might somehow be persuaded. Not only was he out of time, but the goal was unattainable as well. It engendered a series of unwonted emotions. He smiled in self-mockery. He'd lost. It happened. He just hadn't expected it to matter quite as much.

The following morning Astrid left with her uncle and his retinue. Leave-taking had been hard, particularly from Ragnhild.

'I shall miss you, Astrid.'

'And I you, my lady.'

The queen embraced her and, lowering her voice, murmured, 'If ever you need me you know where I am. Don't forget that.'

'I won't forget.'

Ragnhild stepped back and smiled. 'I wish you a safe journey. May the gods be with you.'

With that the departing group left the hall. Outside, in a cool grey dawn, the horses were saddled and waiting. With a heavy heart Astrid mounted and, having settled herself in the saddle, looked around her, committing the scene to memory, certain that she would never see this place or her friend again. It was then she saw Leif. He was some yards off with a group of other casual bystanders. For a brief interval the blue-grey gaze met hers and she saw him incline his head in acknowledgement. Her present resentment was displaced by sadness and a strange and fleeting sense of loss. Summoning up the shreds of self-control, she replied with a like greeting. The courtesy didn't pass unnoticed.

'What is your interest there?'

Astrid started, hearing her uncle's voice and then annoyance temporarily superseded sadness. She controlled it.

'I have no interest there. I did but acknowledge an acquaintance.'

It was a lie on both counts, she realised. However, it seemed to satisfy her uncle. He grunted and turned his horse's head.

'Come. It's time to go.'

With that the cavalcade rode away.

Leif watched them go, his face impassive. The men beside him followed suit.

'Seems like everyone's leaving all of a sudden,' said Harek.

Bjarni grinned. 'The fighting's over. The feasting's over. There's not much to stay for, is there?'

Leif silently endorsed the point, though for rather different reasons. Harek eyed him quizzically.

'So, what now, my lord?'

'We leave for Vingulmark,' replied Leif.

'Right. When?'

'As soon as we've collected our gear. Tell the others.'

As they took themselves off to do his bidding, Leif lingered a few moments more. The riders were almost out of sight now. He permitted himself a wry smile and then turned away. Bjarni was right: it was over. Now it was time to move on.

Chapter Four

Astrid recalled little of that journey afterwards, only the increasing sense of isolation and dread of the future. Along with that was anger. Was it wrong to want to control her destiny instead of being used in the furtherance of political ambition? Was it wrong to resent being used as a brood mare by a total stranger? Jarl Gulbrand's reputation and that of his kin did nothing to allay her doubts.

The only bright spot in the gloom was Dalla. The servant woman had looked after her when first she was brought to her uncle's hall six years earlier, prior to her attendance on Ragnhild, and was the only person to have shown her any kindness there. Apart from the addition of a few more wrinkles, Dalla was unchanged, greeting Astrid with unfeigned pleasure and helping her settle in.

'I know you'll not be with us long, my lady.'

'No, not long,' replied Astrid. 'More's the pity.'

Dalla eyed her shrewdly. 'Well, I trust we can make you comfortable while you are here.'

'I'm sure of it and I'm so glad to see you.'

'And I you, my lady. Who'd have thought it, eh?'

'Who indeed?'

'I felt certain that Lady…forgive me…*Queen* Ragnhild would have found a handsome husband for you by now.'

For no good reason Leif came to mind, the memory vivid and disturbing. Astrid sighed. 'Unfortunately the queen is not my guardian.'

'I'm sure there was no lack of willing suitors. You've grown to be a beauty and no mistake.'

'Much good may it do me.'

'There now. All may yet be well.'

Astrid wished she could share that optimism.

As Leif had anticipated there was much to occupy him on his arrival in Vingulmark, starting with a thorough shake-up of the existing regime. In the absence of a controlling hand the steward and some of the servants had grown slack. Leif had swiftly disabused them of the notion that matters would continue that way. With Finn and Erik to back his plans, along with thirty others used to a life of action, the old regime was swept aside overnight. When they understood that retribution followed carelessness and sloppy work, the slackers fell quickly into line. Moreover, no one knew when their master or his kin might appear and were thus unwilling to take chances. Within the space of a few days the place became as active as an anthill.

Leif lost no time in familiarising himself with the whole estate. For part of each day he rode out with Finn or Erik, accompanied by a few of his men. While much of the land was arable there was a large area of woodland too, a fact which Finn noted with approval.

'The hunting ought to be good hereabouts. With your leave I'll take some men tomorrow and investigate.'

Leif nodded. 'Be my guest. We could do with some fresh meat in any case.'

'My thought exactly. Do you want to come along?'

'Not this time. I've got other things to attend to.'

'Fair enough,' said Finn.

'Incidentally, be sure to hunt within our boundary lines. We don't want trouble with the neighbours.'

'Jarl Einar?'

'Amongst others.'

'As you wish.' Finn followed his brother's gaze to the stream that marked the northern limit of the estate. 'Speaking of Jarl Einar, do you suppose he'll send us an invitation to his niece's wedding?'

Their companions grinned.

'I seriously doubt it,' said Bjarni. 'Anyway, would you really want to stick your head in a hornet's nest?'

'Not even for a free drink,' replied Ingolf.

'Quite right. We'd be about as welcome as pox in a whorehouse.'

The men laughed and, as the group rode on, the talk turned to other things. Leif took no part in it, being otherwise preoccupied. His brother's facetious question had proved oddly unsettling. In spite of being kept busy from daylight till dusk ever since his arrival, Leif still hadn't been able to put Astrid entirely out of his mind. She lingered there on the edge of consciousness, only to return in force at those odd moments when he was forking hay or mending a fence and he had let his thoughts drift. She returned at night too after he'd retired, her violet eyes holding sleep at bay. Then he'd remember that brief stolen kiss and the scent and taste of her...

'Are you all right?' asked Finn.

Leif looked up quickly. 'Of course. Why?'

'You seemed miles away.' His brother grinned, jerking his head towards the northern boundary. 'Miles *that* way, perhaps?'

The reply was succinct and deeply insulting. Finn laughed out loud.

* * *

Astrid avoided her uncle as far as possible and, for the first few days after her return, kept to the bower and immediate environs. However, confinement grew tedious and she began to take a walk each day, re-familiarising herself with the place. Her uncle permitted these excursions but there were always a couple of his men in sight too. His trust only extended so far. It did nothing to improve her mood. Preparations were already underway for the wedding: her uncle was planning a great feast in honour of the occasion and, no doubt, to impress the noble guests who would attend. Three whole hogs were to be roasted, along with haunches of venison and dozens of chickens. The slaughterers were already busy. Her uncle's fish traps would provide carp, tench and pike. The bakers had been ordered to make scores of loaves; the brewers gallons of ale and mead.

However, it wasn't the thought of all the food which made Astrid feel queasy. It was the wedding night that preyed continually on her mind and the thought of that unwanted intimacy. She closed her eyes, seeing the barn, the empty stall and her cousin with his breeches open to reveal the swollen jutting spear within. She had stared at it in horrified fascination. He grinned. *'Wouldn't you like to feel this inside you?'* Appalled, she had shaken her head and backed away but he grabbed hold of her arm. *'Come now, you know you want to.'* Swiftly she'd bent her head and sank her teeth into his hand. He cursed but his hold slackened and she tore free of him and ran. She never spoke of it afterwards. It would have caused uproar and it would have been her word against his in any case. All the same, she avoided her cousin whenever possible and when it wasn't she made sure they were never alone. Disgust was harder to shake off, but as time went on, the incident was relegated to the back of her mind.

She wasn't entirely sure why it had returned now, except perhaps that, like her marriage, it had involved coercion. She was a grown woman who knew the facts of life, and marriage was one of them. That was all very well when there was mutual consent, but being treated as a chattel was something else, and every instinct rebelled against it. Not that her uncle would care for that. He had the authority to determine her fate and he would make her submit one way or another. She would be forced to marry Gulbrand. There was no other choice now.

No other choice? For perhaps the hundredth time she relived that last conversation with Leif. *If you come with me it will be with your eyes open.* Having taken a high moral stance over that and spoken about honourable marriage, the same institution was about to be used by her uncle to prostitute her to Gulbrand. How amused Leif would be if he knew. Tears prickled behind her eyelids. He would not promise what he wasn't prepared to deliver and, possibly, their time together might have been fleeting. *I follow the whale road.* All the same, she suspected now that a few months with him would be worth a lifetime with Gulbrand. *If she had to choose again...*

The sound of distant hoofbeats brought her back to reality and she stopped in surprise to see a column of horsemen approaching. There had to be fifty at least. They were too far away for her to make out details but their presence made her uneasy. Could Gulbrand have arrived early? While she didn't much care for the implications, it was important to find out. Stepping into the lee of the brew house where she could watch unnoticed, she waited.

The column drew nearer, light glinting off helmets and spears. This was the retinue of a nobleman, and one of some importance. *It had to be Gulbrand.* Astrid's stomach knotted. The sound of horses' hoofs and jingling harness grew louder and details began to come into focus. She frowned, her gaze fixed on the man in front. *Hakke!* Despite her relatively secluded position she stepped back quickly, not wishing to attract his notice. *What in the name of all the Aesir was he doing there?* She wasn't naïve enough to suppose it was merely on account of her forthcoming marriage to his cousin.

As the leading riders drew rein in front of the

hall Hakke dismounted and Jarl Einar hurried forwards to meet his guest. The two men exchanged a few words and then went inside together. Feeling much disturbed Astrid stayed out of sight and took the long route back to the bower.

She was passing the back of the weaving shed when a servant stepped out in front of her. Astrid checked mid-stride to avoid a collision. The man bowed.

'Beg pardon, my lady.'

Her heart leapt towards her throat as she recognised the voice. *It couldn't be. She must be imagining things.* Her startled gaze scanned the plain homespun garb but the face under the hood was unmistakable like the smile greeting her now. She returned it, albeit somewhat tremulously.

'Leif! What are you doing here?'

'I came to see you.'

She glanced furtively over her shoulder, hoping they were not observed. 'You must be mad.'

'Perhaps. All I know is that I can't get you out of my mind. I had to come.'

'You took a terrible chance.'

'Not so terrible.'

'How on earth did you know where to find me?'

'I've been watching the place for a couple of days, waiting for an opportunity to speak with you.'

'It's too dangerous for you to be here.'

'Would it be a matter for concern, then, if I were caught?'

'Of course it would. How can you ask that?' She took another swift look around but there was no one else in evidence. Relief mingled with a raft of other emotions.

'I needed to know.' He stepped closer, letting his hands ride her waist.

Her heartbeat accelerated. 'Please, just tell me what you came to say and then get out of here while you still can.'

'Do you want to marry Gulbrand?'

'My wishes were never consulted when my uncle arranged this match. The alliance is dear to his heart.'

'You haven't answered the question.'

A lump formed in her throat and she looked away.

'Astrid?'

'No, I don't want to marry him.'

'Then don't.' He paused. 'My offer still stands.'

'This isn't fair, Leif.'

'Fairness doesn't enter into it, not with men like Einar and Gulbrand. They'll have you bound fast—if you allow it.'

'You make it sound like a simple choice.'

'It is a simple choice, but only you can make it.'

She took a deep breath, trying to order a maelstrom of conflicting thoughts, torn between fear and wanting. Not so very long ago she'd believed this chance lost for ever, and regretted her decision—yet now he'd come back to offer her a lifeline and she was hesitating. It made no sense. Either she was going to trust him or she wasn't. He had been honest with her so far. Now she needed to be honest with herself.

'Then I choose you.'

For a moment he was quite still. If she hadn't known better she would have said he was surprised. Then he bent and kissed her, a gentle salute that set every nerve tingling. 'I am honoured.'

'What now, Leif?'

'Now I must make arrangements to get you safe away from here.'

'Where will we go?'

'To my estate in Agder.'

'Overland?'

'Only as far as the coast. We'll take a ship from there.'

'If we are overtaken…'

'We won't be. Your uncle will have no idea where you've gone.'

'It isn't just him, Leif. Prince Hakke arrived today, along with a large escort.'

He frowned. 'Hakke, here? Are you certain?'

'Quite certain. I'd know him anywhere.'

'That's something I could have done without.'

'I don't like it either. The wedding isn't for another five days yet. Why should he be so early?'

'Keep your ear to the ground and see what you can find out.'

She nodded.

'As soon as all the arrangements are in place I'll get word to you,' he continued. 'Two days at most.'

'I'll be ready.'

He stayed just long enough for a parting kiss and then left her. Astrid watched until he was out of sight among the trees. Then the enormity of the decision she had just made set in. It felt terrifying—and yet, oddly, it also felt right. If she were offered a chance to retract and change her mind she wouldn't do it. Her imagination didn't extend quite as far as sharing Leif's bed. She would cross that bridge later.

When Leif returned to his own hall he lost no time in finding Finn and Erik. First and foremost he needed to take them into his confidence. They heard him in silent astonishment.

'You're planning to steal Gulbrand's bride?' said Erik.

'That's right.'

Finn regarded his brother in grudging admiration. 'I've got to hand it to you, Leif. When you think of a wild idea there's no limit to your imagination, is there?'

'There will be nothing wild about it. On the

contrary; it will need to be planned and executed with meticulous care.'

'More likely we'll be the ones executed with meticulous care.'

'Why so?'

'The royal house of Vingulmark is still smarting over its defeat at Eid and the deaths of two princes of the blood. Hakke is robbed of a bride and now you propose to do the like to Gulbrand.' Finn paused. 'Are you serious?'

'Never more so.'

'I thought you'd given up on this one.'

'So did I but, as it turns out, I can't.' Leif still didn't know exactly why and so further explanation was impossible.

Finn sighed. 'I don't suppose there's anything that I can say to change your mind, then?'

'Nothing.' Leif paused. 'I'll understand if you want no part of this.'

'I'm your brother. I'm already part of it.'

Erik nodded. 'We're kin and kin stick together. Besides, we swore an oath as sword brothers.'

'That we did,' replied Finn. 'So if you have a plan whereby we can sneak past Einar's men, snatch the woman, defeat Hakke's fifty guards and get away to Agder with a whole skin we'd really like to hear it.'

Leif gave them a wry smile. 'As a matter of fact I've given some thought to that.'

'Oh, good. For a while there I was afraid we'd have to improvise.'

Chapter Five

Much to Astrid's relief she was not bidden to attend her uncle or his guest that day or the next and the two men remained closeted together for much of the time. It suited her well enough. Since her conversation with Leif she had been living in a state of suppressed nervous tension and dreaded that her uncle might intuit something amiss. Let him think she was resigned to the match with Gulbrand. If things went according to plan she would be away and clear before anyone knew she was gone.

She hadn't let herself think further ahead than that; to try and imagine what her life might be like afterwards. If anyone had told her that one day she would be a kept woman, and by choice, she'd have been shocked beyond measure. Now it seemed the only possible course of action. If she had to belong to a man then she would choose Leif and trust that her faith wasn't misplaced.

When she had given her consent to this she had half expected a triumphant smile from him but it hadn't happened. His reaction was not of a man taking a whore into his keeping but rather of a nobleman paying court to a lady. Would he treat her with the same consideration in bed? This was a part of the agreement that her mind had glossed over but reality was about to catch up. She would have to give herself to him and, possibly, feign enjoyment. That last sat ill with her because she didn't want to practise deception with Leif. Perhaps time would help there. Perhaps when she became accustomed to him and her new role—

Her train of thought was broken as the door opened to admit Dalla. 'Here's such a to do, my lady. More of Prince Hakke's men arriving and the servants running around like witless chickens.'

Astrid's stomach lurched. 'More of the prince's men?'

'Two ships' crews just sighted. They'll be here in minutes.'

'Is Gulbrand with them?'

'I don't know, my lady.'

'Can you try and find out?'

'Of course.' Dalla shook her head. 'It looks as though your uncle intends this wedding to be memorable.'

Astrid frowned. Her uncle never did anything without a reason, and even a wedding didn't seem to account for such a huge influx of men. The impression was reinforced when, ten minutes later, the newcomers arrived. She and Dalla watched from a distance as the column approached. It bristled with spears. Every man there wore mail and was armed to the teeth besides.

'Mercenaries,' murmured Astrid.

'What are they doing here?'

'I don't know but I'd be prepared to swear it has nothing to do with the wedding celebrations.'

'I'm inclined to think you're right.'

Astrid watched with misgivings as row upon row of warriors marched in. No green boys these, she decided. They were men grown, seasoned fighters by the look of them, the kind who'd kill without a qualm. She estimated at least a hundred. Their leader was a burly hatchet-faced individual whose dark beard was plaited and interwoven with a strip of red cloth.

'That's Steingrim out in front,' said Dalla. 'The one-eyed brute on his right is Thorkill. They've been here before.'

'Not the sort you'd want to meet on a dark night.'

'Not the sort you'd want to meet at all, my lady. Their kind will kill and maim because they enjoy it.'

Hearing the servant give voice to her former

thought Astrid's frown deepened. 'With these and the men Hakke brought with him before he's got a small army. What's he up to?'

'Nothing good, I'll wager.'

'See what you can find out, Dalla.'

It was late afternoon before the servant returned. Her expression only increased Astrid's apprehension.

'What did you learn?'

'You were right; their arrival has nothing to do with the wedding. They've been brought here for a hall burning.'

'What?'

'Some of them were openly talking about it earlier. They were virtually straining at the leash.'

The feeling of foreboding increased. 'Whose hall, Dalla?'

'Leif Egilsson and his kin. It seems the prince intends to settle a score.'

Astrid paled. 'When?'

'Tonight.'

For a second or two Astrid was speechless. Such a possibility had never occurred to her. Only now was the extent of Hakke's malice apparent. It filled her with disgust. Mingled with that was concern for Leif, and it went deeper than she'd realised.

'This mustn't be allowed to happen.'

'How can you stop it, my lady?'

'By getting a message to the intended victims first.'

Dalla raised an eyebrow. 'That's quite a risk to take for a group of strangers.'

'Leif Egilsson once did me a service and I am not one to forget such things.' It was a partial truth only but it would have to serve. The rest was too complex to explain, even to herself.

'If the prince or Jarl Einar found out…'

'They won't find out, not if the matter is handled with care. One man could slip away unnoticed and take a message.' Astrid paused. 'All I need is someone who can be trusted.'

'I know of one person—the stableman, Ari. He keeps himself to himself but he's reliable. He might be prepared to go.'

'There's no time to lose. Go and ask him.'

As the maid hurried away, Astrid glanced through the open doorway where afternoon was merging into early evening. She let out a long slow breath. She had to keep calm. Nothing would be served by panic. If she could get a message to Leif all might yet be well. It would mean some disruption to their plans but surely that was not insurmountable, unless of course he decided to cut his losses and leave without her. That was a possibility. He didn't seem to be the kind of man to renege on a promise but it was a question of risk. It would be simpler to save his skin rather than hers. After all, it was nothing to him if Astrid

had to wed Gulbrand. A man like Leif would have
no trouble finding another mistress either. She bit
her lip. *Would he keep faith with her? Would he
come for her?*

Twenty minutes later Dalla returned. In response to Astrid's quizzical look she nodded.

'He's agreed to go.'

Relief rose like a tide. 'The gods be thanked.
I'll make sure he's amply rewarded for this.'

'Let's hope the warning arrives in time,' said
Dalla.

Leif reached for a loaf and broke off a size-
able chunk. A day in the open air had given him
a keen appetite. Quite apart from the usual chores,
he'd also had to put his other plans in train as
well. That he'd been able to do so was due in no
small part to his brother and cousin and a well-
trained crew. If anyone was surprised by the sud-
denness of their forthcoming voyage it was never
mentioned, and the men set about their preparations with a minimum of discussion and the speed
born of long practice. Arrangements had also been
made to leave a few reliable men in charge of the
estate. Everything was in place. All he had to do
now was fetch Astrid.

Her decision to come with him still carried
with it an element of surprise. He had been quite
open about what the relationship would be but she

had still elected to go with him rather than marry Gulbrand. It was a courageous choice in many ways. It also raised interesting questions. Was this just the lesser of two evils? He preferred to think that wasn't the case, that he hadn't imagined the spark between them. The answer would be evident soon enough, a thought that filled him with a sense of anticipation. He couldn't recall anything he'd wanted half as much. Did a woman's value increase in proportion to the risk involved in winning her? If so, their relationship was likely to be a protracted affair.

The torches flared in a sudden draught and he looked up as the oaken door of the hall swung open to admit Trygg.

'A messenger has just arrived, my lord. Man by the name of Ari. Says he brings important news.'

Leif frowned and lowered his cup. 'Admit him.'

'What in Hel's name does a messenger want at this hour?' demanded Finn.

'Good question.'

The question was uppermost in other minds too and around the table conversation died as their shield companions exchanged quizzical glances. Before anyone could say anything more Ari came in and hastened across the hall to the high table.

'My lord, I am sent by Lady Astrid to deliver a warning.'

'What warning?'

'That Steingrim and a large contingent of men are on their way here.'

Conversation died and all eyes turned towards the speaker. Leif's expression lost all traces of good humour.

'Steingrim comes here?'

'Aye, my lord. They mean to attack tonight and to kill all they find.'

The men remained silent and for several moments the only sound was from the crackling logs in the hearth.

Leif's eyes glinted. 'How did your mistress find out about this?'

'Steingrim's men were openly discussing it.'

'How many men has he got?'

'Two ships' crews of his own, my lord, but Thorkill has brought a third.'

The news elicited murmurs of angry disbelief. Leif's jaw tightened as he assimilated the implications. In that he wasn't alone.

'Hakke doesn't give up, does he?' said Finn.

Erik frowned. 'We should have killed the treacherous bastard when we had the chance.'

'We'll get another,' replied Leif. 'If not we'll make one. In the meantime, we're going to be outnumbered five to one.'

'Unpromising odds. What are we going to do?'

'We've got no choice but to go.' Leif thought rapidly. 'We'll split up though. Steingrim can't follow without dividing his force.'

Finn nodded. 'That'll make it easier to take them on when we're ready.'

'We'll each choose the time and place for that,' replied Leif, 'once we've recruited extra swords.'

As the implications sank in, the faces around him were expressive of quiet appreciation.

'I'll round up my men and head for Alfheimer,' said Finn. 'We have friends there.'

'I'm for Hedemark,' said Erik. 'King Sigelac owes us a few favours. It's time to call them in.' He shot a look at Leif. 'You?'

'My estate in Agder.'

'Agder? But didn't you once say you'd never...'

'I know, but needs must. I'll find swords enough there.'

'No doubt.'

'Send word when you can.' Leif paused. 'In the meantime, let's arm and make ready to depart.'

Leaving the remains of the meal on the table, the men hastened to obey. Finn paused, looking round the hall, taking in every detail from the carved pillars to the smoke-darkened rafters, his expression compounded of anger and resentment. 'This place was hard won, yet Steingrim will burn it to the ground in one night.'

'A hall can be rebuilt,' said Leif, 'and we'll live to fight another day.'

'When we do, I'll cut Steingrim's throat myself.'

'I'll hold you to that.'

With a short space of time the company was armed and ready to ride. Leif embraced Finn in a bear hug and then did the like to Erik.

'Go well, Cousin. We'll meet again soon if the gods so will.'

Erik nodded and clapped him on the back. 'May Odin smile upon our endeavours.'

He and Finn mounted their horses and, raising a hand in salute, rode away. Leif turned to his shield men. 'Go and ready the *Sea Serpent*. Take her round the headland to Gulderfoss. I'll meet you there.'

His men regarded him in surprise.

'Where are you going?' demanded Thorvald.

'There's something I have to do first. I won't be long.' He looked at the messenger. 'Ari, you come with me.'

With that he turned his horse's head and rode away into the darkness. Thorvald stared after him for a moment; then looked at the others.

'All right. You heard him. Let's get going.'

Leif reined to a halt and surveyed the looming shapes of the buildings that made up Jarl Einar's holding. Most were in darkness save for the great hall illuminated by flaming cressets. Ordinarily he would have expected to hear the sound of carousing from within but tonight the place was unnaturally quiet. He looked at his companion.

'Find Lady Astrid and tell her to meet me in the usual place.'

Ari looked round furtively. 'It's dangerous, my lord. If you're found here...'

'This is the last place anyone will be expecting to see me. Besides, the inhabitants are otherwise engaged tonight.'

'But, my lord...'

'Do it, and be very discreet if you value your life.'

As the servant rode away in the direction of the buildings, Leif dismounted and tethered his horse to a tree. Then, loosening his sword in its sheath, he took a circular detour and made his way towards the rear of the weaving shed, making use of deep shadow for concealment. The quiet intensified. The place might have been completely deserted. Hakke must have sent every available man to accomplish his mission tonight. Had he gone with them? Had Jarl Einar? Somehow he doubted it, which meant that the two of them were holed up somewhere waiting for Steingrim to report back. Leif smiled grimly. Unwittingly they had just made it easier to get Astrid out. By the time anyone knew what was happening the birds would have flown.

As Ari briefly reported the success of his mission, Astrid felt intense relief. Hakke's plan had failed. At most his men would burn an empty hall.

Leif and his men would live to fight another day. However, the leaving had other, more immediate, implications. With an effort she controlled her voice.

'Did Jarl Leif send any message for me?'

'Aye, my lady. He's waiting to speak with you now. In the usual place, he said.'

Her heart leapt. *He hadn't abandoned her. He'd kept faith.* Handing Ari a small pouch of coin, she dismissed him with her thanks. Then, taking a swift look around to make sure the coast was clear, she hurried towards the weaving shed. She reached it a short time later and stole silently along the wall to the far corner.

'Leif?'

The word was scarcely more than a murmur but it did not fail in its effect. A tall figure detached itself from the depths of the shadows.

'I'm here.'

Pale moonlight gleamed softly on mail byrnie and silver arm rings. The relief at seeing him there was so strong it almost hurt. Mixed up with that was heart-thumping excitement. 'You did come.'

'Did you doubt it?'

'I hoped you would but I didn't know if it would be possible.'

'I always keep my promises.' He paused. 'Besides, I owe you a debt of gratitude for the timely warning. You took quite a chance.'

'I'm just relieved that it arrived in time.'

'Time enough. My men are safe away.'

'I'm glad of it.'

'Now we must be gone too.' His hands came to rest on her shoulders. 'Do you still want to come with me?'

The touch thrilled through her. His closeness diminished fear. 'Of course.'

'It isn't too late to change your mind.'

'I won't change my mind.'

'Then let's get out of here. My horse is tethered in the trees behind the barn.'

He took her hand and led the way, retracing his original route. As they passed the bower Astrid felt a fleeting regret that she hadn't been able to say goodbye to Dalla, but there was no time for delay now. Every moment they lingered carried an element of risk so she hurried along beside Leif, occasionally looking round to make sure their flight was undetected. The holding was silent, almost eerily so. She shivered, just wanting to be away from the place now.

Leif paused in the shadow of a building and glanced down. 'Are you all right?'

She nodded. 'I'm fine.'

'Come, then.'

They ran across the intervening space to the edge of the trees. Astrid breathed a sigh of relief. Leif squeezed her hand, a strong warm clasp that reassured and excited too.

'Not far now.'

A voice behind them said, 'Far enough.'

Astrid's heart leapt towards her throat and she cried a warning as half-a-dozen armed men detached themselves from the shadows. Leif whipped round, reaching for his sword hilt. The blade had barely cleared leather before the first club swung at him. He ducked. The blow aimed at his head connected with his shoulder instead, jarring the length of his arm. He struck out and heard a grunt of pain. One of the attackers reeled backwards. The rest closed in, clubs swinging. He defended himself valiantly but there were too many of them.

Astrid screamed in helpless horror as he went down beneath a rain of blows. He hit the ground and lay still. Appalled, she stumbled towards him, dreading what she would find. Before she reached him strong hands seized hold of her, pinning her arms. She fought it struggling furiously wanting only to get to Leif, but the grip was unyielding. Then she heard the same voice speak again.

'Take him to the hall. Bring the woman too.'

Chapter Six

Astrid continued to struggle but resistance was futile; her captors were roughly twice her size and strength and the hands that held her might have been made of steel. Half carried, half dragged, she was propelled across the open ground towards the hall. The doors opened to a blaze of torchlight that revealed the group of men inside. The feeling of sick horror increased and she estimated thirty at least; thirty who had never left and had never intended to leave.

Conversation stopped as the newcomers entered and the weight of attention turned their way. The two captives were dragged before the high table and Leif flung to the floor. He lay still. In the light of the torches Astrid could see the wound on his head and the blood darkening his hair and running down his face. Had they killed him?

Anger mingled with fear and again she tried to free herself but the grip on her arms was inflexible. Thirty pairs of eyes looked on in amusement. She ignored the grinning faces. There was only one man here whose opinion she had to worry about: with pounding heart her gaze went to the high table where her uncle sat.

Jarl Einar surveyed the unconscious form on the floor for a moment and then turned to the man beside him.

'Well, well. You were right after all. In truth, I didn't think he'd come.'

'You should have more faith, especially since the trap was so well baited.'

Astrid's attention flicked to the speaker, seated at her uncle's right hand. A cold lump formed in the pit of her stomach as she recognised Hakke. Like many of those present he was physically impressive with the lean muscular build of the warrior. However, the richness of his clothing set him apart. Garnets glowed like blood in the gold brooch that held his cloak. Black hair fell over his shoulders. He might have been handsome, save for the thin-lipped mouth and steel grey eyes. Their gaze rested on Astrid for a moment.

'Very well baited indeed.' He smiled but the expression stopped well short of his eyes. 'I am in your debt, my lady.'

Astrid glared at him. 'Tell these oafs to let me go.'

He ignored that. 'Pray come and sit next to me.'

The words were not an invitation. Astrid's captor escorted her to the designated place and shoved her on to a chair. Her cheeks flushed with indignation and she threw him a venomous look. His smile widened. She'd have liked to slap it off his face but knew better than to try. Losing her temper would achieve nothing and might make things worse for Leif. She threw another anxious glance his way. Still he didn't stir. Misgivings grew. How badly was he hurt?

Hakke looked at the prisoner and spoke to his men. 'Remove his weapons and mail shirt. Then strip him to the waist and bind him fast.'

The task was performed with ruthless efficiency.

'Fetch a bucket of water and bring him round.'

Jarl Einar regarded his companion in surprise. 'Wouldn't it be easier to leave him unconscious?'

'No, I want him to be fully aware of what's happening to him.'

Although he smiled, the prince's tone sent a shiver through Astrid. Nor was there any trace of compassion in the steely eyes. The churning sensation in her stomach grew stronger and her hands clenched on the arm of the chair.

Moments later a man returned with a bucket. He dashed the contents over Leif. The injured man groaned and stirred. Astrid bit her lip, torn between anxiety and relief that he wasn't dead. She darted a look at the men who stood around him.

She didn't recognise any of them—they weren't attached to her uncle's retinue. Nevertheless, it took no more than a second to know what they were: sea wolves who fought only for gain and whose loyalty was to the highest payer. Their attention was currently on the prisoner, their expressions feral, each face lit with cruel anticipation.

A second bucket of water brought Leif to consciousness. For a moment or two he was disorientated, unaware of anything save a crashing headache and pain in his face and ribs. Slowly he became aware of more details: the soiled rushes pressed against his cheek, the smell of stale food and dogs. He tried to move his limbs but couldn't.

'Get him up on his knees.'

The voice sounded vaguely familiar but he couldn't quite place it. Then calloused hands seized his arms and hauled him up. He winced as his injuries protested.

'It's good to have you back with us, Jarl Leif,' the voice continued. 'I should hate you to miss any of this.'

Leif frowned, and looked in the direction of the speaker. With a jolt of recognition he knew who it was.

'Hakke.'

The prince smiled. 'Indeed. May I say I've been looking forward to this for some time.'

'We all have,' said Jarl Einar.

Leif's gaze flicked that way and his gut tightened as the implications began to dawn. Then, with a sense of shock, he saw who was sitting next to Hakke. For a moment his gaze locked with Astrid's. She looked pale but, as far as he could tell, she seemed unharmed.

The focus of his attention didn't go unnoticed. 'You have good taste, my lord, I'll say that for you,' said Hakke. 'But then, a big fish requires special bait.' He smiled at Astrid. 'You have played your part to perfection, my dear.'

She opened her mouth to speak but Leif was before her. 'What part? What are you talking about?'

'Your interest there hasn't gone unnoticed. A beautiful woman is a reliable lure, in this case outstanding. Well done, my lady. Without you we could not have brought him here.'

Leif frowned, his gaze locking with Astrid's. 'What does he mean?'

She paled a little more. 'It means nothing, I swear it.'

'It means you have been tricked, my lord, and easily too,' said Hakke. 'Still, you are not the first to fall for a pretty face and I don't suppose you'll be the last.'

Leif glared at him. 'It's a lie!'

'And yet here we are.'

The outwardly pleasant tone belied the enormity that lay behind those words. It fuelled Leif's anger. Such treachery was impossible, inconceivable. He looked again at Astrid.

She shook her head. 'You mustn't believe him, Leif.'

Hakke raised an eyebrow. 'You are too modest, my lady. After all, it was your message that brought him here tonight.'

Her face went as white as bleached linen as the extent of the game became apparent and, along with that, her unwitting part in it. Her anguished gaze met Leif's. In it she read anger and something frighteningly like doubt. Surely he couldn't have swallowed those lies? He must know she would never have done such a thing; that they were using her for their own ends.

She shook her head. 'That's not—'

'Not what he was expecting,' interrupted Hakke.

Leif's head thumped painfully. His mind was in turmoil, fighting against Hakke's words. Astrid could not have done this. She wanted to leave; to escape an unwelcome marriage. There had to be another explanation.

'Your presumption with regard to the Lady Astrid will be dealt with in due course,' Hakke went on. 'In the meantime, I have other bones to pick with you, my lord, beginning with the deaths of my brothers.'

'They fell in battle,' replied Leif, 'and died with swords in their hands.'

'They fell because of Halfdan Svarti's greed. He wants Vingulmark and doesn't care what he has to do to take it.'

'Had you and your brothers not ambushed him and tried to kill him he might not have been so eager for that confrontation.'

'We did but defend what was ours.' Hakke's eyes glinted. 'Speaking of which, you have lately robbed me of my bride.'

'The bride you kidnapped and intended to force into wedlock.'

'Ragnhild was mine.'

'Yet she was only too happy to be saved from that fate,' said Leif.

Hakke's gaze grew colder. 'Nothing is going to save you from yours, I promise you.'

'Then kill me and have done with it.'

'I have no wish to kill you, my lord. Far from it. I wish you to live for a long time yet, and each day that you live you will think of me.'

The knot in Leif's gut tightened. 'What do you mean to do?'

'I am delivering you into Jarl Einar's safe keeping, as his bondsman.'

'Never!'

'Perhaps we need to put you in the right frame of mind for your new role.' Hakke snapped his fingers. 'Fetch the shears.'

A servant returned with the blades. They were the type kept for clipping sheep, sharp-edged and with wicked points. He handed them to one of the men standing guard over Leif. Hakke nodded.

'Crop his hair in the manner befitting a slave.'

The words were greeted with a mocking cheer that drowned out Astrid's cry of protest. In rage and desperation Leif fought his bonds but they yielded not a whit. Seconds later his captors flung him face down on the floor and a boot between his shoulders held him there. A large hand grabbed hold of his hair, yanking his head back. Then the shears went to work. By the time they had finished all that remained of the flowing mane was an inch of golden stubble. The audience thumped the table in approval.

Hakke nodded. 'Now the collar.'

'No!' Again Astrid's voice was drowned out. She tried to rise but a strong hand on her shoulder pulled her back again. Through welling tears she watched as the thick leather collar was fitted around Leif's neck and riveted shut.

Hakke rose from his chair and strolled across to his prisoner. For a moment or two he surveyed him in silence. Then, unhurriedly, he threw back his cloak and reached for the coiled whip at his belt, shaking it free. The onlookers whistled and cheered.

Astrid turned to her uncle. 'Stop this, I beg you.'

He eyed her coldly. 'I'll do no such thing. His

punishment is more than merited. Besides, it will help you to understand what it means to cross me.'

The whip descended, leaving a bloody welt across Leif's naked back. He writhed but made no sound. Astrid's knuckles whitened.

Hakke delivered a dozen more strokes and then paused, surveying the man at his feet. 'If it were solely up to me I'd flog you until your bones showed through your flesh,' he said. 'However, Jarl Einar wants you fit for work tomorrow.' He cast the whip aside and looked at the waiting men. 'Chain him in the kennel with the other dogs.'

They hauled Leif to his feet and dragged him from the hall. Astrid looked on, her face ashen. Jarl Einar turned to the man behind her chair.

'Take her to the women's bower and put a guard on the place.' Then he looked coldly at his niece. 'I'll deal with you later.'

Leif's captors shackled his ankle to a great wooden stake and then departed, locking the gate behind them. Several large hounds growled at him but he ignored them, gritting his teeth against the pain in his back and ribs. The bruises on his face were tender now, and one eye was half closed. Cold struck up from the earthen floor where the stench of hound vied with urine and faeces. For a while anger held it at bay but as time passed the chill grew more pronounced, along with a growing sense of dread as the true extent of his pre-

dicament hit home. His men would be concerned
by now. They would likely guess where he'd gone
and why, but, even suspecting something had gone
wrong, they couldn't do anything to help him.
Their numbers were too few. The longer they
delayed the more precarious their own position
would become. When Steingrim found the hall
and farm abandoned he'd head for the anchor-
age. The only sensible choice for Leif's crew was
to sail without him. That way they could escape
the intended slaughter and go to Agder to raise
the force they needed. Of course, that would take
time. Mentally he visualised it all. It would take
weeks, perhaps months, to organise, and that was
before they liaised with Finn and Erik, always
assuming Finn and Erik were successful in their
mission. If not… Leif let out a ragged breath. He
ran a hand across his shorn head, feeling congealed blood among the stubble. Anger surged
and his fingers closed on the rim of the leather
collar. Exerting all his strength, he tried to force
the ends apart. The rivets held fast. Eventually,
with a curse he gave it up.

It occurred to him then that this was just a
taster of what his enemies had in store for him. In
his mind he could hear Hakke's mocking voice: *I
wish you to live for a long time yet, and each day
that you live you will think of me.* He would do
all in his power to prevent any chance of rescue.
Nor would it be too hard. Hakke still had numer-

ous allies, men who would be only too pleased to witness the downfall of an enemy. All he had to do was to move his captive elsewhere and keep on moving him at regular intervals so that the trail grew cold and was lost. Leif felt a chill in the pit of his stomach and for the first time experienced something close to fear.

He closed his eyes and suppressed the emotion. It wouldn't help him. He had to think. His enemies had set a clever trap, but to do it they had needed information. How had they got it? Astrid's image loomed large at the forefront of memory. Only the two of them had been privy to his plans, unless she had told someone else. Had the scene in the hall been an act on her part? The thought of possible duplicity in her cut like a blade. *You mustn't believe him, Leif.* As though in response he saw Hakke's mocking smile. *And yet here we are.* Someone was lying and, like it or not, all the evidence appeared to be pointing one way. Doubt flickered into being. Leif's jaw tightened. In that moment he knew that, no matter what it took or how long, he was going to discover the truth. And if Astrid had been complicit in this there was going to be a reckoning.

Chapter Seven

That night was the longest Astrid could ever remember. All she could think about was Leif, about his rage and pain, and his possible belief that she had been involved in the plot against him. Somehow she must show up the prince's lies for what they were. In the meantime, Leif must be suffering physical and mental torment. Such a cruel and public humiliation smote at the heart of a man, especially one who was proud and strong. He would not take easily to his allotted role; he would have to be starved and beaten into it, diminished by slow degrees until he lost all will to fight and his spirit was broken. The very idea broke her heart too. Hakke's revenge would not be swift, but it would be thorough.

Astrid shivered. Her mother's brother, Jarl Einar, had been a shadowy figure in her life, more often spoken of than seen since he was often away, fighting in various wars. It wasn't until after the deaths of her parents that he had come to play a larger role. She and her older sisters had been removed from their home and taken to his hall. Magda and Gunnhild were twins, then fifteen years old, and he lost no time in finding them husbands from among his political allies. Nor had he offered them any choice in the matter. Tears and pleas availed them nothing. Both were married off regardless, to older men whose first wives had died and who were certainly not averse to young and attractive replacements. Thirteen-year-old Astrid was alone.

'You will make a better match than either of your sisters,' Jarl Einar told her, 'for you are prettier than they. When you are older I shall marry you to a prince or a king.'

A few weeks later he placed her in the care of his ally, Sigurd Hjort, where, under the tutelage of his lady, she would learn about wifely duty. It was there that she had met Ragnhild. The two had become fast friends. Being both beautiful and spirited, Ragnhild had had many admirers, among them Hakke of Vingulmark. When his suit was refused, he kidnapped her, thinking to wed her by force, only to be robbed of his prize. Leif had played a leading role in that episode. Now Hakke intended to make him pay. Astrid shivered. No matter what happened she must protect Leif. Protect him and help him escape.

It seemed that others had anticipated her thought. The following morning Jarl Einar sent one of his men to summon her to the hall. Astrid made no demur, being quite certain that her burly escort had been told to use force if necessary. Besides, she needed to find out what her uncle was planning. She might even get a glimpse of Leif. The thought filled her with hope and painful longing.

In the end it was a disappointed hope. There was no sign of Leif anywhere and she reached the hall a few minutes later. Save for a few servants, her uncle was alone. He watched in silence as she approached. Taking a deep breath Astrid looked him in the eye.

'How did you know Leif would be here last night?'

'I didn't know for sure; I guessed, based on information received.'

'From whom?'

'You've been kept under close watch since your arrival, and my men are vigilant. They do not tolerate traitors either.' His hand closed round her arm and he drew her with him out of a side door, marching her across the open area of ground beyond. In front of them was an ancient oak tree. As the distance narrowed and Astrid saw the figure hanging from one of the lower branches the bile rose in her throat.

Her uncle had no trouble reading her expression. 'I see you recognise the traitor.'

'Ari was no traitor. He was guilty only of doing what I asked him.'

'And by his actions he betrayed me,' replied Einar. 'He has paid the price.'

She looked away, sick to her stomach, understanding now just how naïve she had been, and knowing the guilt of it would never leave her. In that instant she also understood the meaning of hatred.

'The only reason he was given a relatively quick death,' he continued, 'was that he helped deliver Leif Egilsson into my hands.'

Astrid looked up quickly. 'What have you done with him?'

'He's cleaning out the pigsties, under close supervision, of course.'

Astrid clamped down hard on a surge of anger and disgust. 'I want to speak to him.'

'You will not speak to him again. You will not so much as look in his direction. Do you understand me?'

'Why? Will you beat me for disobedience?'

'Not you, girl: him.'

Sickened, Astrid looked away. A large hand closed on her chin, forcing her head round.

'He will be beaten while you watch. For a second offence I'll have him beaten harder, and stop his food for a day or two. Am I making myself clear?'

It was only too horribly clear. She nodded dumbly.

He leaned closer until his face was only inches from hers and then bellowed, 'Am I making myself clear?'

Astrid swallowed hard. 'Yes, Uncle.'

'I hope so.' He released his hold. 'Just to make sure, he will be watched and so will you, until you both leave.'

'Both?'

'That's right. He is to be relocated after the wedding.'

'But…'

'Did you think he would remain here indefinitely; that his allies would mount a rescue attempt perhaps?'

It was exactly what she had been hoping and the words acted like a deluge of icy rain. 'Where… where will you send him?'

'That need not concern you. Suffice it to say that his friends will never find him. Leif Egilsson will remain a slave until his death, and that will not be soon.'

'He will never submit, no matter what you do to him.'

'He has got off lightly thus far, but this is just

the beginning. By the time we're done with him he'll be little better than a miserable animal.'

Astrid shuddered inwardly. She wanted to shout defiance, to say that they would never succeed, but she bit the words back. In his present mood her uncle might well consider them a challenge to be met, with possibly dire consequences for Leif.

'You, on the other hand, are going to be married as planned,' Jarl Einar continued. 'Gulbrand will keep you on a short leash, my girl. Be assured of that. He needs heirs and you will provide them.'

'I won't marry him.'

'Oh, yes, you will. It is arranged.'

'I don't care.'

'But you care for Leif Egilsson, don't you?' Jarl Einar's voice became silky. 'So unless you wish to see his tongue cut out and his nose slit you'll do exactly as you're told.'

Astrid choked back fury and lowered her gaze, knowing she didn't dare to test this further. It was defeat and they both knew it. 'I'll do whatever you wish.'

'That's better. Frankly, I'd have you off my hands tomorrow but Prince Gulbrand has business requiring his attention so he cannot be here until the end of the week. In the interim you will follow all my instructions to the letter.'

Leif wiped the sweat from his brow and shovelled another load of slurry into the cart. With

every movement his bruised body protested, but
the least pause drew the attention of his guards
and brought down a rod across his back. The two
men had evidently been ordered to punish infrac-
tion but not too harshly. Hakke wanted his enemy
alive. Leif worked steadily, trying to ignore the
growling in his stomach. He had been working
since dawn but, thus far, he had been given no
food or drink. Nor had he seen any sign of Astrid.
She had been much on his mind since his cap-
ture. In spite of what had happened, he was still
reluctant to believe that she had betrayed him. It
seemed so out of keeping with what he had seen.
He wanted to give her the benefit of the doubt,
to hear her side of the story. Somehow he had to
find an opportunity to speak with her.

However, none presented itself that day. He was
kept busy until evening. Then, tired and filthy, he
was given water to drink and chained in the kennel again. When the hounds were fed he was given
a plate of scraps as well: a chunk of stale bread
and a piece of hard and mouldy cheese. He ate it
ravenously, oblivious to the dirt and the stench
around him. The meagre quantity of food barely
took the edge off his hunger but, he guessed, that
was all part of the intent. He tried not to think of
the long-term physical effects of such a regime.
Instead he focused his mind on Astrid.

If he closed his eyes he could see her clearly;
could remember the feel of her in his arms, the

details of her fine-boned face and pale gold hair, the way her lovely eyes sparkled. Eyes the colour of spring violets. Surely the warmth, the sincerity he had seen there could not have been feigned. Experience had taught him of the pitfalls in relationships between the sexes; that what seemed strong and sure could evolve over time into something poisonous and rotten. After that he confined his later relationships to those that satisfied physical need and preserved emotional distance. Then he met Astrid. She had seemed different from the rest. It wasn't beauty alone but a deeper attraction that drew him, a glimpse of something he had thought lost and hadn't realised he still wanted. For a moment he saw his wife's face and the look it had worn in the early months of their marriage; a gentle loving look for him alone. The feeling had been returned. Other women had ceased to exist for him then. When he'd looked at them since, it was not with any expectation of finding warmth or tenderness in their eyes. Such emotions were not to be trusted in any case. Yet Astrid had seemed different; had made him hope. Just what he had hoped for was unclear. He'd thought himself past such folly and it disturbed him to discover that he wasn't, or not entirely. Had Astrid seen that weakness in him and exploited it for other ends? Had he been deceived in her from the start? Uncertainty was worse than knowing. He needed answers.

* * *

Astrid was bidden next day to attend her uncle at the stables. She received the summons with mingled loathing and trepidation but knew she didn't dare refuse. When she arrived it was to see two horses, saddled and waiting. Jarl Einar gestured towards the smaller animal.

'Mount up. We're going for a ride.'

She eyed him dubiously, wondering where this tended. It was the first time he had shown any inclination for her company and she didn't suppose that this was about a desire to make amends. Yet he never did anything without a reason. However, refusal was out of the question so she gathered the reins and mounted the horse. As her uncle followed suit she risked another glance at his expression but it revealed nothing. When he was settled comfortably he turned the horse's head.

'Come.'

They turned away from the stables towards the outlying farm buildings. Jarl Einar held his horse to a walking pace but he made no attempt to speak to his companion until the pigsties came into view. Then he fixed Astrid with a piercing stare.

'Do you remember what I told you?'

'I remember.'

'And do you also recall the penalty for defiance?'

'Yes.'

'I hope so.'

Misgivings increased and her fingers tightened on the reins. As they approached the pigsties, she saw three men already present. Two were strangers, her uncle's men. The third was Leif. He was naked to the waist and begrimed with filth, but dirt could not conceal the mass of dark bruises or the welts on his flesh. Of necessity his ankles had been unbound, but his wrists were manacled, the length of chain between just enough to enable him to work. As he turned to toss another load of muck on to the waiting cart, she drew in a sharp breath. His face was bruised and swollen, one eye half closed. Blood from the cut on his head had congealed into a dark ridge in his shorn hair. He might have looked pitiful and dejected but those words seemed entirely inappropriate for that lean and powerful figure, however battered: instead he looked as a captured lion might, angry, predatory and dangerous.

Jarl Einar reined to a halt and gestured for Astrid to do the same. Then, leaning casually on the saddle pommel, he addressed the guards.

'Has the slave been working well?'

'Well enough, my lord,' the man replied. 'If he shows any sign of slacking we give him a taste of the rod.'

'Good. Keep him at it. I want the job finished today.'

'It'll be finished, my lord, I guarantee it.'

Jarl Einar turned to Astrid and smiled. 'Is it

not satisfying to see our plans fall out so well, my dear?'

Her stomach wallowed but she forced an answering smile. 'Most satisfactory, Uncle.'

'I think we might have him clean the kennels next. It will teach the churl to know his place. What say you?'

'An excellent idea.'

The shovel paused and Leif shot a look her way, a look that was expressive of shock and disbelief. Jarl Einar raised an eyebrow.

'Do not dare to raise your eyes to my niece, clod. She is far beyond your touch. Your aspirations there were laughable.'

He glanced meaningfully at Astrid. Recognising the cue she assumed an expression of cold hauteur. 'As if I would ever have lowered myself thus.'

'I am sorry you had to pretend, my dear, but the end has certainly justified the means.'

'As you say, Uncle.'

'Now you can forget about this and think instead about your wedding.' Seeing Leif's expression Jarl Einar's smile widened. 'Yes, churl, five days hence my niece is to wed a prince, a man worthy of her hand.'

Astrid stiffened, forcing herself to maintain a haughty expression. 'It cannot come soon enough for me.'

'Patience, my dear. Your bridegroom will be

here soon enough.' Jarl Einar glanced at Leif. 'I think we will let the slave remain here until then. I'm sure Prince Gulbrand would like to see him.'

'I'm sure he would.'

'So be it. After that I shall have the scum relocated: somewhere remote, I think.'

'Send him where you like,' replied Astrid, 'as long as I never have to see him again.'

'You may depend on that, my dear.'

Leif eyed him with contempt. Then his gaze went to Astrid. It almost undid her, until she remembered what would happen to him if she failed in this. Lifting her chin, she looked away, feigning indifference.

'This grows tedious. Shall we continue with our ride, Uncle?'

'Presently. Meanwhile, I don't care for the churl's demeanour.' Jarl Einar looked at the guards. 'He must be taught to show respect to his betters.'

The first man strode forwards and struck Leif across the shoulders. Astrid stifled a cry, aware of her uncle's gaze and that this was also part of the test. Biting her tongue, she willed herself to silence as the rod descended several times more. Leif staggered. Astrid tasted blood.

Jarl Einar held up a hand. 'Enough! Now get back to work.'

Only with the greatest effort did Astrid refrain from looking at Leif. If she had her expression

would surely have given her away. Instead she
contrived to look bored. It seemed to satisfy her
uncle though.

'Come, Niece. Let us be gone.'

They rode on for a little way in silence. Jarl
Einar looked at Astrid and nodded.

'Not bad. However, I shall look to see this performance repeated as occasion requires.'

She lowered her gaze to conceal the anger and
hatred there, and adopted an expressionless tone.
'Whatever you say, my lord.'

'Quite so,' he replied.

Leif retrieved the shovel and resumed work,
barely aware of his smarting shoulders. All he
could think about was Astrid, or the woman he
had thought was Astrid. The person he had seen
just now was a total stranger. Her expression, her
speech, her manner, everything was different.
That woman cared nothing for him. Her coldness
and her disdain were unmistakable. The revelation
that her marriage to Gulbrand was going ahead
with her willing consent made him see it had
never been in doubt. It was the final piece of the
puzzle that had been teasing him since his cap-
ture. Now it all fell into place. His gut knotted as
the realisation of how far and how neatly he had
been tricked was borne forcibly upon him. All the
beatings he had received were as nothing to what
he felt in that moment.

For a little while it was hard to think at all and he was actually glad of the hard physical labour. He moved mechanically, shovelling and lifting, unheeding of hunger or thirst or fatigue, just needing to be doing something to take his mind off the truth.

It wasn't until the evening when he was chained in the kennel again that his thoughts came crowding in. Pain gave way to rage, part of it directed at himself. Had experience taught him nothing? The only women one could rely on were whores; a man knew where he was with them. You took them, you paid them and there it ended. Emotional involvement made a man vulnerable, weak and foolish. As moon-struck foolish as he had allowed himself to become. He grasped the collar around his neck and tried again to force the ends apart. His muscles bulged with the effort but the rivets remained fast. A cry of fury and frustration tore from his throat.

A soft laugh carried towards him on the evening air and his head jerked round to see Hakke watching him from the gate.

'Never mind,' he said. 'You'll get used to it, in time. The shackles too, I expect.'

'Keep looking over your shoulder from now on,' replied Leif, 'because one day, when you least expect it, I'm going to be there.'

Hakke evinced interest. 'And how do you propose to do that? It looks like a tall order from where I'm standing.'

Leif made no reply. His tormentor smiled.

'We both know it isn't going to happen,' he went on. 'In a little while you will be relocated, you see. Your friends will never find you. I'll make very sure of that. You will spend the rest of your days in chains.'

'No, I will cut out your heart instead.'

'Empty boasting. All the same, I admire your courage, really I do. For that reason I may let you attend my cousin's wedding—in the proper capacity, of course.' Hakke paused. 'Would you like to witness the bedding ceremony as well? I can arrange it.'

Leif gritted his teeth but made no reply.

'No? Gulbrand will pleasure her well. Three times at least I shouldn't wonder, and every night thereafter. My cousin is singularly well endowed; inventive too, and possessed of a lusty appetite in bed. Lady Astrid will have no cause for complaint there.'

When Leif still made no reply Hakke smiled faintly.

'I'll leave you with the thought. Sleep well, Leif Egilsson.'

Leif heard the sound of his retreating footsteps and swore softly. It was hard to remain silent in the face of Hakke's taunts and harder still to forget them. He wasn't entirely sure that it had been mere baiting. The thought of Astrid sharing another man's bed ought not to have mattered now, but somehow it still did. Mentally she was not so easy to dismiss. He also knew that Hakke knew it. Leif wouldn't put it past him to make good the threat either. Equally disquieting was the knowledge of his imminent relocation. His enemies would choose somewhere that would render escape impossible and rescue increasingly unlikely. He clenched his fists and heard the chain clink softly. The sound only reinforced the present hopelessness of his predicament.

Chapter Eight

Ari's death had not only appalled Astrid, it made her horribly aware that Dalla's safety might also have been compromised. However, the old servant was stoical.

'If your uncle knew about my part in this matter I'd already be hanging alongside Ari,' she said.

'I pray you are right. I'm sorry to have put you at risk.'

'Such baseness should be beneath a man of your uncle's standing.'

'He enjoyed it,' said Astrid. 'Just as he will enjoy seeing me married to Gulbrand.'

'Is it certain?'

'Most certain. I dread it, but I have no choice now. If I defy him in any way Leif will pay for it.' Tears pricked behind her eyelids. 'I saw his face when I said those things, Dalla. It was like a knife in my heart.'

'You did what you had to. Jarl Einar would not have hesitated to carry out his threat otherwise, and if not him, Hakke.'

'I know, but it sickened me all the same.'

'*They* sicken me,' replied Dalla.

'If Leif does not escape soon I fear he will never do so, but I have no idea how to achieve it. He is under guard by day and chained at night. If I go anywhere near him the consequences could be disastrous.'

'You're right. It would be just the excuse your uncle wants.'

'If only there was some way of getting word to his men, but I fear they will be long gone by now.'

'Do we know that for sure?'

'It seems most likely.'

'A way might be found. There are those hereabouts who have good reason to hate your uncle.'

'Even assuming they could be trusted, I can't ask anyone else to take such a risk.'

'It's Leif Egilsson's only hope.'

'I know it.'

'Well, then.'

'I can't send another man to his death.'

'You won't have to. Enquiries could be made discreetly. News travels fast and a hall burning will not have gone unremarked. I have relatives nearby who will know what happened to the jarl's crewmen.'

'All right, but be very careful, Dalla. I would not have any harm come to you.'

The servant nodded. 'I'll be careful. In the meantime, you must seem to go along with your uncle's plans. Let him think you're becoming resigned.'

Resigned was the last thing Astrid felt, but she could see the sense of the proposal. 'I'll do it if it keeps Leif safe.' She paused, thinking hard. 'There may be something else I can do for him as well.'

'What is that?'

'Hakke wants Leif kept alive. It may be possible to use that as leverage to get him better food, maybe clothing too.'

'If you suggest it your uncle will refuse.'

'I was thinking of something more subtle.'

'Such as?'

As Astrid explained her companion smiled. 'It might just work.'

'We'll have to see, won't we?'

Astrid's opportunity came sooner than expected because that evening she was bidden to the hall and tasked with pouring ale for the noble guests. It was a function of the women to do so but up till now Astrid had been exempted from the duty. Given the present company she suspected it was intended as another humiliation. The very thought of spending any more time with her uncle was repellent but it was also necessary now, just as it was necessary to strike the right attitude. She couldn't appear entirely resigned to her fate just yet: her uncle would smell a rat immediately. Instead she adopted a sulkily submissive demeanour that she hoped would serve the purpose. Then, grabbing a jug of ale, she went to refill the drinking horns at the top table. Prince Hakke eyed her speculatively for a moment and then turned to Jarl Einar.

'It seems that your niece is learning obedience at last.'

'She will be completely obedient, my lord,' replied her uncle.

'I know. Gulbrand will see to that.'

The two men chuckled heartily. Astrid schooled her expression to neutrality and continued pouring ale, aware of Hakke's steady gaze.

'Have you fed the slave yet?' he asked.

'Not yet.' Jarl Einar summoned a servant. 'Fetch a plate of scraps and be quick about it.'

A minute or two later the woman returned with a platter on which reposed a small piece of bread and two thin strips of fat and gristle. Jarl Einar nodded approvingly.

'Take it out to the slave cur.'

Astrid concealed her dismay and overlaid it

with a satisfied smile. Then she resumed her task.
Her uncle frowned suspiciously.

'Something amuses you, girl?'

'Why, yes,' she replied.

A large hand closed round her arm and dragged
her closer. Ale slopped from the jug but he ignored
it. 'What?' he demanded.

Astrid allowed her tone to become sarcastic.
'You said that you wanted Lord Leif to live for a
long time, and yet you feed him too little to keep
him alive.'

'He'll live. He'll just be a lot thinner, that's all.'

She achieved a sneer. 'No, he'll be dead soon
enough, and I'm glad of it.'

The grip on her arm tightened until she winced.
'Let him starve. I care not.'

'No!' Hakke's voice cut across them. 'I want
him alive. There will be no easy escape for him.
Put some more food on the plate.'

For a moment or two it seemed as though Jarl
Einar might argue. Then he appeared to think better of it and shrugged. 'As you like.'

'Your slave will still die of cold or disease,' said
Astrid, 'and you're too stupid to see it.'

Jarl Einar released his hold on her arm and
slapped her hard. She gasped, holding her burning cheek.

'That's for impudence. Next time I'll give you
a good thrashing.'

Hakke laughed. 'No need. You may rely on Gulbrand for that.'

'I'm glad to hear it,' her uncle replied. 'She needs breaking to bridle.'

'I almost envy my cousin the task.'

His gaze grew speculative again, mentally stripping her. Astrid's skin crawled. However, she remained silent and presently her uncle dismissed her with a wave of his hand. Nothing loath, she left them. Her cheek hurt but it was worth it to get Leif some more food.

The following day Dalla sought out her mistress to say that while there was much talk of a hall burning no one seemed certain about what had happened to the intended victims. It was reported that they had fled before the attack and taken ship.

'Then it's over,' said Astrid. 'Leif is truly lost.'

'I saw him earlier, from a distance, of course. They've set him to digging a new waste pit now, along with the other slaves.'

Astrid bit her lip. She might have succeeded in getting him more food but nothing could relieve the humiliation and drudgery of thralldom. Conscience smote her because, indirectly, she was the reason for his downfall. If Leif hadn't kept faith with her he'd still be free. Each passing hour brought them closer to separation and then she wouldn't be able to help him in any way. Worst of all, he would continue to think she had been part of the plot against him, a misapprehension that she wanted to correct. It mattered, even though their acquaintance was brief. Not for anything would she have him think her false.

Soon Prince Gulbrand would arrive and when he did... She repressed a shudder. Her sisters had wept when they learned who their future husbands were, but her dominant emotion was not sadness. It was rage, and all the stronger for being impotent. There would be no escape for her any more than there would be for Leif.

The subject of her thoughts worked on, seemingly unaware of the curious glances directed at him from his co-workers. No one spoke though, and that suited him well, since it permitted him time to think. The past few days had brought unexpected changes: instead of being chained in the kennels he was locked in a shed at night. It was empty of everything save a sleeping mat but it was reasonably clean. He had been given a tunic too. It was a rough and dirty homespun cast-off of the kind that the other slaves wore, but better than nothing. Moreover, the amount of food had increased. Seemingly his enemies really didn't want him to die just yet.

He thought back to his last conversation with Hakke. Far from breaking Leif's resolve, the baiting only increased it. He would not spend the rest of his days in bondage. Somehow, some time he would escape. It might not be soon but one day he would break free and eventually he would be reunited with his kin and his shield companions. When that happened he would return with a force and avenge himself most bloodily on Jarl Einar and Hakke. After that he would turn his attention to Astrid. She would be married by then so it might take him a while to find her, but eventually he would succeed. He'd make it his mission. His revenge there would be of a rather different kind but it would be no less thorough. Then he'd walk away and forget her. She, on the other hand, would remember him for the rest of her life.

The sound of horses' hooves impinged on his consciousness and he glanced up to see a large group of horsemen approaching. As they drew nearer it became clear that they were warriors, mercenaries from the look of them, led by a nobleman on a chestnut stallion. Leif frowned. The man looked vaguely familiar, though the pace made it difficult to see details. The riders barely spared a glance at the group of thralls but sped by in a cloud of dust and were eventually lost to view.

'Trouble there,' muttered the slave beside him.

'Why? Who was that?'

'Jarl Gulbrand. Nasty piece of work by all accounts.'

'How do you know him?'

'Seen him here before, several times. He's to marry Jarl Einar's niece.'

Leif's hand clenched round the shaft of the spade. 'They're well suited to each other.'

'If you ask me, she doesn't know what she's letting herself in for.'

'Then she'll find out, won't she?'

He turned away and viciously jabbed the spade into the ground again, his mind in turmoil. The thrall was right: she had no idea what she was letting herself in for. But, by Odin, she would find out soon enough. The thought gave Leif a momentary savage pleasure. Underneath it was something rather different and much harder to define. *Would you like to watch the bedding ceremony? I can arrange it.* His jaw tightened. Clearly what he felt wasn't jealousy because he no longer cared, but it might just be some residual notion of possessiveness. He'd get over it soon enough.

Astrid's heart lurched and she regarded Dalla in mounting horror. 'Jarl Gulbrand here already? Are you quite certain?'

Dalla nodded. 'He rode in not half an hour ago with a large retinue of men.'

'Merciful gods! It wasn't supposed to be till the end of the week.'

'He must be eager to see his new bride.'

Astrid took a deep breath to steady herself. 'What am I going to do?'

'Smile and speak him fair,' replied Dalla. 'Whatever happens, you must not incur his displeasure for any reason. If you do there will be a reckoning later, depend on it. And perhaps not for you alone either.'

'Leif.'

'Exactly. Hakke and his kinsman will use any excuse to humiliate him further. It might even go beyond that now Gulbrand is here. You cannot give them a reason.'

'You're right. I know you are. It's just that I don't know how far my acting abilities will stretch.'

'Do your best. In the meantime, you need to change your clothes. You must seem to do your future husband honour.'

Astrid nodded, knowing she was right. Thus, with Dalla's help, she donned one of her best gowns, a soft mauve, richly embroidered at the neck and sleeves. A fine girdle rode her waist. Her pale gold hair was combed and re-braided with matching ribbons.

The maidservant stepped back to admire her handiwork. 'You look beautiful.'

'I hope it will serve.'

'It will serve.'

With a heavy heart, Astrid sat down to await the summons that she knew was coming.

It was perhaps an hour later when a servant came to announce that Jarl Einar desired her presence in the great hall. When she arrived she paused a moment on the threshold, regarding the gathered company with misgivings. There were at least thirty of them, currently refreshing themselves with cups of ale. Her uncle was standing by the hearth, along with Hakke and a couple of others she didn't know. Gathering all her courage, she advanced to join them.

Seeing her approach Jarl Einar surveyed her critically and then, surprisingly, smiled faintly. He turned to the man beside him.

'My lord, may I present my niece, Lady Astrid?'

Gulbrand's dark gaze swept her from head to foot. Then he too smiled, revealing cruel white teeth. 'I see that the rumours of your beauty have not been exaggerated, my lady.'

Like his cousin he was tall and powerfully made. He resembled Hakke too, in terms of the thin-lipped mouth and aquiline nose, but she saw this man was older, by at least ten years, and his waistline was beginning to thicken. Silver strands were clearly visible in the jet-black hair receding from his forehead, and in the thick black beard that adorned his chin. The small black eyes held a predatory glint.

'I am glad now that my business was concluded early,' he went on.

Astrid managed a smile. 'You do me honour, my lord.'

Evidently her response found favour because her uncle smiled along with the rest. Then he turned back to his guest. 'We are delighted to see you so soon. In truth, we were not expecting to.'

'I was keen to see my bride.'

'Keener still to make her your wife, I'll wager,' said Hakke.

Gulbrand grinned. 'You are in the right of it, Cousin. What man would not be keen to take so fair a lady to his bed? Nor shall she find me wanting there. I mean to get heirs.'

An icy lump formed in the pit of Astrid's stomach. Once they were married he could take her whenever he wished regardless of her inclination. He could do whatever he liked. She would be little more than a chattel. The thought filled her with rage.

'She will give you many sons, my lord,' replied Jarl Einar.

'That she will.'

'I have no doubt that she will do her utmost to please you in every way.'

'Well, there's no reason why you should wait another week, is there?' said Hakke. 'Why not bring the wedding forwards?'

Astrid's heart leapt towards her throat and she darted an indignant look his way. He returned a malicious smile.

'Good idea,' replied Gulbrand. 'I would have this knot tied as soon as possible.'

Jarl Einar beamed. 'It shall be as you wish, my prince. Shall we say two days hence? That will give us time to make the necessary arrangements and to prepare a suitable feast.'

'That will suit me very well.' He threw a sideways glance at Astrid. 'Very well indeed.'

'Then it's settled. In two days it shall be. My niece will hold herself in readiness.' He laid a hand on her shoulder, an apparently affectionate gesture that only increased her apprehension. 'In that regard, would you excuse us for a moment? There are one or two things we need to discuss.'

He led her apart until they were out of earshot then drew her round to face him. 'Jarl Gulbrand is pleased. You have done well. Perhaps you will be able to win his affections.'

She had no wish to win his affections, always assuming he had any, but it would have been a serious error to say so. She met her uncle's gaze steadily. 'I will do what I must, my lord.'

'That's true. After all, you know the consequences of failure. Nevertheless, you will remain in the women's bower from now on, unless it pleases his lordship to have you with him, in which case you will be informed. Do you understand?'

'I understand.'

'Good.' He eyed her coolly. 'You may go.'

Astrid returned to the bower, seething inwardly. If she were a man she would have seized a sword and run him through, and his confederates with him. As it was, there would be no escape. Two days would pass swiftly enough, and then Gulbrand would take her to wife. In her mind's eye she could see Hakke's taunting smile and knew he had guessed at her true feelings. Furthermore, he enjoyed the knowledge with the cruelty of a cat that toys with its prey. Anger surged afresh, all the worse for being entirely impotent. Mingled with it was cold dread. Not so long ago she had been dreaming of escape. How quickly dreams turned to ashes.

Chapter Nine

Astrid would willingly have remained secluded but it seemed her future husband had other ideas. She didn't dare to refuse his company, but the strain of pretence increased, particularly as he lost no opportunity to touch her. In other circumstances it might have been considered a flattering degree of attention, but underneath it she sensed the keen predatory nature of the man and it repelled her. As the eve of their wedding arrived her spirit sank under the weight of dread. Only the thought of Leif enabled her to bear it. She would do whatever was necessary to protect him. She owed him that. It was little enough and, very soon now, even that little would be removed. Gulbrand would take her to his own estate and she would likely never see Leif again.

She retired early that night, a request that no

one tried to deny her. Gulbrand smiled. 'Aye, go and get some rest, my lady. We've a busy day ahead of us tomorrow.'

'And precious little rest at the end of it, I'll warrant,' replied Hakke.

'It's not sleep I'll be thinking of.'

'Nor would I.'

The men laughed. Astrid's face grew hot with embarrassment and indignation. However, she forbore to reply and took her leave with all the grace she could muster, only too aware of the looks that followed her from the room. The bower was a sanctuary after the loud voices and raucous laughter in the hall. It was the last time she would ever sleep here. Tomorrow night she must share Gulbrand's bed, must submit herself to his will… For a moment panic reared its head and she fought tears. They would avail her nothing now.

Leif woke with a start, knowing that something was wrong, or at least different. The inky darkness inside the shed made vision impossible so he propped himself on one elbow, listening. In the distance he could make out the sound of carousing from the direction of the hall but he knew that wasn't what had disturbed him. From outside he heard muted voices and then the sound of scraping metal. His heartbeat quickened and he got to his feet. Was this another trick of Hakke's? If his enemies thought to take him by surprise they were going to be disappointed.

Moments later he felt cool air against his face as the door opened and then a man spoke quietly.

'Jarl Leif? Are you there?'

His heart missed a beat. 'Thorvald?'

'Aye, my lord.' The speaker turned away and murmured to someone behind him. 'We've found him.'

For a moment or two Leif was overwhelmed by a resurgence of hope so strong it hurt. Then practicality reasserted itself. 'I'm chained, Thorvald.'

'Don't worry. We've come prepared.'

Leaving their companions on guard, three of them entered the hut, closing the door behind them. Moments later the small space was bathed in soft light from a small lantern. Leif blinked, waiting for his eyes to grow accustomed to the brightness. His men surveyed him closely. When they saw what had been done to him and saw the collar around his neck, their expressions became taut with rage. However, there was no time to waste on words and they addressed themselves to the chains instead.

'We found this on the guard after we cut his throat,' said Thorvald. He produced a small key.

'It's for the ankle lock,' replied Leif.

His companion inserted the key and the anklet opened easily. They turned next to the shackles on his wrists but, having no key for those, used an iron bar to prise apart the links in the connecting chain.

'We'll strike off the bracelets later, Chief,' said Snorri, 'but at least you'll have freedom to move in the meantime.'

Leif nodded, and rose to his feet, surveying the broken chain with grim satisfaction. Then they left the hut and rejoined the group outside. Thorvald handed Leif a sword belt. He buckled it on and drew the blade from the scabbard.

'How many we?' he asked then.

'Not enough to save you,' snarled a familiar voice behind them.

He whipped round to see three of Hakke's henchmen. The prince's guards were doing night rounds to check on the prisoner. Leif just had time to register the swords in their hands before they attacked. He smiled grimly and went for the tallest one, countering a vicious thrust on the way. He followed it with a rain of blows, all of them potentially lethal. However, his opponent was quick and able, meeting and parrying each move, his eyes alight with battle lust. Leif felt it too, a fierce, hot urge to kill fuelled by hatred and determination. He wanted to take his time, to inflict a cut for every humiliation suffered, until the ground was soaked in his enemy's blood. Then to cripple and kill—slowly.

With an effort he controlled his anger, knowing he couldn't afford to prolong this. They were some distance from the hall but the noise might carry that far. In spite of the carousing he'd heard earlier, there might be some light sleepers and that would mean reinforcements on the way. Setting his jaw, he laid on with a will, seizing the initiative, looking for the opening he needed. His foe met him head on, trading blow for blow. He was fit and agile, a seasoned warrior.

Leif feinted, giving ground, inviting his opponent in. Then, closing his left fist around the length of hanging chain, he swung it hard. The end smashed across the man's face, splitting his cheek like a ripe plum. He snarled, reeling sideways, half blinded by blood. Leif came on. The wounded man threw up his arm to parry the next blow but it was too little too late and the descending blade severed his arm at the wrist. For a moment he stared in horrified disbelief at the bloody stump where his hand had been. He never saw the thrust that killed him.

Leif pulled his sword free and glanced down at the corpse with fierce and silent exultation. A few yards off lay the lifeless bodies of the other two guards. They had been slain quickly and with no attempt at finesse.

'We need to get out of here, Chief,' said Thorvald.

'So we do,' replied Leif, 'but first there's something I have to collect.'

* * *

Astrid didn't know what had woken her, only that something wasn't quite right. The quality of the darkness was less dense which meant it was the time between night and dawn, the time when sleep is deepest and the world silent. Except that it wasn't, or not entirely. She lay still, listening. Then she heard it again, the soft sound of leather on wood, the quiet tread of footsteps across the floor. Dalla going out to the privy? No, not going out, returning, and not just Dalla either. Yet there were only the two of them in the place.

'Dalla?' she whispered.

A hand twitched aside the curtain that separated her sleeping place from the others and someone stepped into the room, a large dark shape silhouetted against the lighter gloom.

'Who's—?'

The question was abruptly cut off as a wad of cloth was shoved into her mouth. She tried to scream, but the only sound that emerged was muffled gurgling. Panicking now, she struck out, her fists connecting with hard muscle. She struck out again and landed another blow. Strong hands seized her wrists in a hold as inflexible as iron. In moments she was securely bound. In the process she caught a whiff of stale sweat and dirt, rank and feral. Then an arm of steel dragged her out of bed and carried her, kicking and struggling, down the passage to the communal room beyond. When they reached it her captor altered his grip just long enough to throw her over his shoulder. With that she was carried from the bower.

Outside several more armed men were waiting. Having accomplished their aim, the whole group melted back into the gloom. They moved swiftly and silently. Torn between fury and fright Astrid stopped struggling until it might do some good. She had no idea of direction, only of cool air and the smell of damp earth. She glimpsed tree trunks and then horses. Minutes later she was slung across the front of a saddle like a sack of meal. What followed was a confused impression of a man's leg, galloping hooves and jolting motion that jarred every bone in her body. It seemed to go on for a long time.

Eventually the riders pulled up and her captor dismounted. He dragged Astrid off after him. She caught the sound of lapping water and made out the dark bulk of the waiting ship before he swung her into his arms and bore her up the gangplank.

'Make for the island.'

As she heard him speak her stomach lurched and she realised then whose prisoner she was.

Leif dumped her in the stern and left her there, making no attempt to untie her or remove the gag. Since her hands had been bound in front of her, she managed the latter herself, but the knotted cord round her wrists resisted every effort to undo it. Nor did anyone else offer to help. Indeed, beyond one or two curious looks, the men ignored her. She heard them cast off the lines and then the splash of oars. With a growing sense of apprehension she felt the ship begin to move.

Around them the sky began to lighten and black faded slowly to grey. Astrid could make out details now, both of the ship and the rowers. However, her gaze moved away from them to the tall, lean figure standing by the mast. As if sensing himself watched, he turned slowly to face her. Astrid caught her breath. The short-cropped hair revealed all the familiar planes of his face on which the bruises stood out in sharp relief. He still wore the irons on his wrists and the leather collar round his neck but, far from diminishing him as badges of slavery, they lent him an altogether different quality. It was barbaric, predatory and dangerous. As his gaze locked with hers she felt her mouth dry. There was no trace of friendliness or warmth in those blue-grey eyes, only cold anger and the silent promise of retribution.

For the duration of the journey Leif spoke no word to her and nor did any of his men. She might not have been there at all. Neither was she offered food or drink. Her body felt stiff and cramped from sitting in one position and her wrists ached from the rope. The hard light of day made her painfully aware that her sole garment was a linen shift which reached only to mid-calf leaving an indecent amount of lower leg on view. It increased the feeling of vulnerability. She had no idea where Leif was taking her—only that, wherever it was, it didn't bode well. With every stroke of the oars her apprehension increased.

It was mid-afternoon, as far as she could guess, when the ship entered the fjord. Rugged hillsides dotted with spruce trees rose out of the dark waters. As they progressed the hillsides became sheer cliffs and she could see a few small rocky islets, deserted save for gulls and terns. The only sounds were the cries of the birds and the lapping water. They might have been at the uttermost end of the earth.

Their destination was an island, larger than the rest, and screened by spruce trees and clumps of bushes. As they approached she could see a mooring place and, through the trees, glimpsed the low roof of a building. Her heart sank. The rowers shipped oars and the ship glided in to a wooden jetty. A couple of men jumped ashore and then their companions threw them the lines to make the ship fast. The deck became a hive of activity as the rest of the crew prepared to go ashore.

Astrid watched it all but didn't move. Then a man's shadow fell across her and she looked up quickly. With hammering heart she saw Leif standing over her. Leaning down, he seized hold of her arm and hauled her to her feet. Astrid stumbled, wincing as her cramped muscles protested.

'Where is this place?' she demanded.

'It's called Long Isle.'

The name meant nothing and she had no time to ponder it anyway as he led her across the deck to the side of the ship.

'What is it?'

'Your new home for a while, my lady.'

'I don't understand.'

'You will, soon enough.'

Neither the tone nor his expression was calculated to inspire confidence and, irrationally, she hung back, resisting the hand on her arm. Leif said nothing. Lifting her with insulting ease, he called to a crewman on the jetty. Astrid gasped as she was tossed across the intervening space and deftly caught again. Leif vaulted the gunwale and joined them. Taking possession of his struggling burden once more, he set off along a narrow pathway through the trees. It led to a clearing on which was situated a large *hov* and several smaller ones. It was towards one of the latter that he headed now.

As they reached the threshold he set her down and then threw open the door. One glance at the baskets and sacks beyond revealed a storage shed. Before she had time to examine it further he drew the dagger from his belt and cut her bonds. Then a hand in the small of her back propelled her into the shed. The door slammed behind her and she heard a heavy bar drop into place.

She ran to the door, beating on it with clenched fists. 'Leif? Leif! Let me out of here!'

He made no reply. The only sound was of retreating footsteps.

Astrid leaned against the rough planks, listening. 'Damn it!'

For a while indignation kept apprehension at bay but, as time went by, it returned and more strongly than before. The warlord who had kidnapped her was a stranger. His coldness and indifference were frightening. There was no discernible trace in him of the man she had known. His treatment of her revealed that he no longer thought of her in those terms, and if so, there was only one reason for it: the act she had put on to satisfy her uncle had been entirely convincing to Leif. She shivered inwardly. Betrayal, real or perceived, was an unpardonable crime, and it carried dire penalties. His bringing her here could only have one purpose.

Another hour went by before the shed door opened again, only this time it wasn't Leif who stood there. The stranger halted on the threshold, a big, burly individual almost as wide as the doorway.

'You're to come with me.'

'Come with you where?' she demanded.

'The chief wants to speak to you.'

Her heartbeat quickened. The thought of having to face Leif filled her with dread but it was inescapable. Indeed any attempt to avoid it would only compound her guilt in his eyes. The only possibility now was to adopt a bold face.

'Very well,' she replied.

'This way.'

At first she thought they were heading for the largest of the *hovs* but he skirted it instead. As they passed she heard men's voices from within. Perhaps Leif wished for a more private conversation than would be possible there. Her escort brought her to a smaller building behind the central *hov*. Like the others it was made of wood and had a shingled roof. The stout wooden door was open. Astrid hesitated on the threshold, but her companion pushed her firmly across it and closed the door behind her.

For a few moments she and Leif faced each other in silence. He had changed his clothes since their last meeting, the dirty homespun replaced by a shirt and a tunic of dark blue wool, girded at the waist by a leather belt. The iron bracelets were gone from his wrists now and the leather collar from his neck. He had bathed too, since every last trace of filth was gone. Only bruises and cropped hair remained to tell of his ordeal.

The blue gaze swept her from head to foot, cool, appraising and unnerving, a reminder of just how scantily she was clad. In the relatively confined space he looked bigger than she remembered and, just then, utterly intimidating. Unwilling to let him see it she lifted her chin.

'Why have you brought me here, Leif? To hold me to ransom?'

He drew nearer, his gaze never leaving hers. 'I have no doubt that the thwarted bridegroom would pay a great deal to get you back. However, I have no interest in gold or silver.'

'What, then?'

'Don't you know, Astrid?' He halted in front of her. 'I'm sure you do, whatever you may pretend.'

Her mouth dried. 'Revenge.'

'Quite so.'

'I understand why you wish for it, but the people who sought your downfall are not here.'

'Do you now deny your part in it?'

'I do deny it.'

'You colluded with my enemies in every possible way, even to agreeing to be the bait in their trap.'

'I knew nothing of what was planned, Leif. I swear it.'

'You cheating little bitch. You betrayed me and now you lie to save your own skin.'

'I'm not lying. The first I knew of treachery was when the prince's men surprised us that night.'

'No, you were in on it from the start. You never

had any intention of leaving Gulbrand.' The blue gaze bored into hers. 'You never had any intention of rejecting so exalted a marriage in order to become my mistress. I only wonder that I was so simple as to believe it.'

'I did intend to leave! I never wanted to marry him.'

'A likely tale.'

'It's the truth!'

'You are a stranger to truth. If anything, you are more treacherous than the others.'

Tears pricked her eyelids. 'You cannot believe that.'

'You cannot imagine that I don't.' His lip curled contemptuously. 'You took as much pleasure in my humiliation as they did.'

'You're so wrong.'

'Perhaps you're going to try and tell me that I imagined what I saw; what I heard.'

'You did not imagine it, but you interpreted it wrongly. I was forced to say those things.'

He uttered a low and savage laugh. 'There really are no depths to which you will not sink, are there?'

'If you believe that, then why didn't you kill me at the first opportunity?'

'Because I don't want you dead, my sweet.' The tone became chillingly soft. 'I have a very different plan for you. Don't you want to know what it is?'

Her heart thumped so hard she was sure he

must hear it but she continued to meet his gaze. 'You want to tell me.'

For a moment something like grudging admiration flickered in his eyes. 'Very well. We are going to exchange roles, you and I.'

Astrid stared at him in shocked and speechless silence. However, he had no trouble reading her expression at all. He smiled; an expression that stopped well short of his eyes.

'From now on you belong to me—body and soul. You will do whatever I command.'

Anger momentarily displaced fear. 'I will not!'

'What will it take to convince you that I mean it, Astrid? A shaven head and a collar round your neck, with a beating thrown in for good measure?'

'You're just low enough to do that, aren't you?'

'Don't be in any doubt about it.'

At that moment she wasn't in any doubt, and didn't care to push the matter either. Holding down the lid on simmering indignation, she forced herself to remain still and continued to meet his gaze. 'And just what duties would you have me do, my lord?'

'You will undertake all routine domestic chores,' he replied. 'You will clean my quarters, wash and mend my clothes, prepare food as required, fetch water and chop firewood. From time to time I may require you to carry out additional tasks as occasion arises.'

Her jaw tightened. 'I see.'

'And at night you will share my bed and you will do whatever it pleases me to command.'

Astrid felt as though all the air had been driven from her lungs. 'You can't mean it.'

'I assure you I do mean it. By the time I send you back to Gulbrand he's going to know how thoroughly I have pleasured you, my sweet.'

'You mean to send me back?'

'Eventually.'

As the ramifications sank in and the full extent of his revenge became apparent, she felt sick. That had nothing to do with the thought of being returned to Gulbrand. It was about understanding for the first time just how deeply Leif hated her.

He strolled past her to the door. For a moment or two she thought he was leaving her to sweat awhile over what he'd just said, until she heard the soft thud of the bar dropping into place. As its significance dawned she turned quickly. What she saw in his face then caused her stomach to lurch.

'What do you think you're doing?'

'I thought I'd just made that clear.'

Astrid paled. 'Don't even think about it.'

The blue-grey eyes surveying her now were the colour of a winter sea. 'I mean to do a lot more than just think about it, my sweet.'

Chapter Ten

Unhurriedly he advanced on her. Astrid's throat dried and she retreated, darting frantic looks around for a weapon, anything with which she could defend herself. Edging round the hearth, she grabbed a piece of firewood and hurled it at him. He dodged it, and the second piece. The third found its mark, but it might as well have been a cushion for all the effect it had. Still he came on. The room seemed to shrink around him. Astrid backed further off, desperately seeking other missiles and finding none. Once she tried to dodge around him to the door, but he countered the move, staying between it and her while still pushing her inexorably in the direction of the bed. She could see it out of the corner of her eye…the bed, the wooden chest, the pile of war gear…the sheathed sword.

She raced for it, grabbed the hilt and drew the blade free. The point swung round just in time to stop Leif in his tracks. Astrid glared at him.

'Get away from me!'

'Are you going to kill me, Astrid?'

'If I have to. Now back off.'

He shrugged and stood off a pace. 'It won't do you any good. There's no way off this island except the way you came.'

'I'll swim if I must.'

'I believe you'd try at that.' The blue-grey gaze locked with hers. 'First, though, you still have to get past me.'

'Get out of my way.'

'No.'

'I don't want to injure you, but I will if I have to.'

'You overestimate your ability.'

'Do I so?'

Astrid swung the sword and he sprang aside so that the blade went wide.

'You'll have to do better than that if you're planning on reaching the door.'

'I'll carve my way out if need be.'

She swung again and he dodged. Chips of wood flew from the window shutter and she heard him laugh. Gritting her teeth, she came on but he danced out of the way, evading the blows with ease so that the blade found only empty air.

'You'll tire before I do, my sweet.'

'We'll see about that.'

Instead of swinging she thrust. This time the point came much closer. Leif's eyes glinted. That was all the warning she got. As the momentum of the next lunge carried her forwards, he dived and the pair of them crashed to the floor. Wood slammed against her back. Breathless, half pinned by his weight, she twisted, trying to lift her arm. A hand like a vice closed round her wrist and tightened relentlessly until the weapon fell from her grip. Astrid writhed and kicked, her free hand clawing at his face. He caught that wrist too and then one large hand imprisoned both while the other grasped the hilt of the sword. Seconds later the edge of the blade was against her throat, its touch every bit as cold as his eyes.

Astrid glared back. 'What are you waiting for, Leif?'

'I told you, you're not going to die; at least not in the way you think.' He rolled on to his feet and stood over her. 'Get up.'

Slowly she obeyed. The blade hovered over her breast, forcing her to retrace her steps. When she reached the end of the bed she stopped.

Leif nodded. 'That's better. Now take off your shift.'

'No.'

The point of the blade came to rest against the base of her throat. 'I said take it off.'

'Never.'

The blade pressed a little harder. A bead of blood welled at the tip. Leif's gaze locked with hers. 'Do it.'

She made no move to obey. 'You'll have to kill me first.'

'Death before dishonour, Astrid? Is that it?'

The violet eyes blazed anger. 'No: death before any man will do that to me again.' It was stretching the truth but this was war.

He frowned. 'What are you talking about?'

'I was twelve years old the last time a man decided to have his way with me. He had thrice my strength and no qualms about hurting me either. I fought then and by all the gods I'll fight now.' She leaned a little closer to the sword point and the bead of blood became a trickle. 'So, use the blade if you will, Leif, and then take me after. I won't know or care but your revenge will be complete and you can boast about it to your men afterwards. Perhaps you'll even let them take turns as well before you return my corpse to Gulbrand.'

For the space of several heartbeats he didn't move or speak. Then, slowly, he lowered the sword, his expression a grimace of disgust. Without a word he turned away and strode to the door, unbarred it and flung it wide. Moments later he was gone.

Trembling now, Astrid sank down on the end of the bed and let out a long breath. He was terrifyingly strong; the marks of his grip clearly visible on her wrist. He could have done anything he liked and she wouldn't have been able to prevent it. He could still do anything he liked. She had only her wits to defend her. Her words had been a partial truth only but they had carried weight. She hadn't missed the expression of disgust on his face just before he left. No doubt the tale of her past had only reinforced his opinion of her. Not only was she treacherous in his view, she was soiled goods to boot. Did he find the thought distasteful? Was he disappointed to think that he wasn't going to have a virgin? She hadn't thought him hypocritical, but the evidence tended that way. Once she would have felt badly about using subterfuge with him; now she couldn't regret it. In a battle any weapon was better than none. Of course, whatever personal benefit attached to that it was attended by disadvantage too, because he would now feel justified in treating her with contempt. Punishment had been deferred, not abandoned.

It was almost an hour before Leif returned. For a moment he paused in the doorway, blocking out the light. Astrid rose at once and moved away from the bed, eyeing the naked sword in his hand. She was also keenly aware of her present state of undress and of the piercing gaze directed her way. Had he returned to finish what he'd started?

Leif said nothing at first. Instead he crossed the

room and, retrieving the fallen scabbard, sheathed
the sword and laid it aside. Then he turned to the
wooden chest by the far wall. Throwing back the
lid, he reached inside, drawing out what looked
like a length of brown cloth. He doubled it over
and then, using his dagger, cut a long slit along
the centre section of the fold and a shorter verti-
cal one in front of that. Then he tossed the fabric
at her feet.

'Put it on.'

Astrid eyed it disdainfully. She'd never worn
anything so outlandish in her life. 'What's this?'

'What does it look like?'

'I'm not wearing that.'

He raised an eyebrow. 'Perhaps you'd like some
help to get dressed.'

Hurriedly she bent and picked up the fabric,
then passed her head through the slit he had made.
It formed a shapeless, sleeveless over-gown that
reached to her ankles. A leather belt landed at
her feet.

'Use that.'

Wordlessly she fastened it around her waist,
holding the makeshift garment together. For all
her scorn, and in spite of its clumsiness, it did at
least cover her, and she felt marginally less vulnerable. She still had no shoes, nor did he consider
the point worthy of remark.

He surveyed her critically for a moment.
'It'll do.'

'I'm sure you find it most pleasing.'

'A naked slave would please me far more, though you might find it humiliating.'

'Why, you…you…'

He raised an eyebrow, waiting. Astrid subsided into furious silence wanting, but not quite daring, to test him on the point.

'Very wise,' he said softly. He nodded towards an empty bucket by the door. 'Now, go and fetch water and be quick about it.'

Astrid bit back the words she would have liked to utter, knowing it would be a serious mistake. Hefting the bucket, she headed out of the door and looked around. A grassy path led towards the fjord. She followed it and presently came to the rocky shore. Stones dug into feet and she winced, stifling a curse and mentally calling Leif all the vile names she could think of. Lowering the bucket into the water, she let it fill, looking surreptitiously around her. So far as she could tell the island looked to be about two hundred yards long and perhaps half of that at its widest point. Her captor had no need of chains or ropes or guards: she wasn't going anywhere and he knew it. Nor was there anywhere to hide that he wouldn't find her inside ten minutes flat. He could not have chosen a more secure location in which to hold her while he enacted his revenge. With a heavy heart she hauled up the bucket and began to retrace her steps.

* * *

On her return Leif held out a broom. 'Now you will sweep the floor. When you've done that you can clean out the hearth and fetch firewood.'

'I will not.' Astrid dumped the bucket down. 'If you need someone to perform these menial tasks you should find a serf. I will not be treated thus.'

The reply was a sharp rap across the backside with the bushy end of the broom. He hadn't put any serious effort behind it but the twigs acted as miniature whips nevertheless, causing Astrid to jump and stifle an exclamation.

'It'll hurt a lot more next time,' he said.

The violet eyes darkened. She wanted to hit him; she wanted to scream; to hurl abuse at his head and name him for the brute he was. His expression suggested that he was very much hoping she might. The thought of what would happen then was mortifying. Without another word she grabbed the broom and began to sweep the floor.

Leif settled himself comfortably in a chair and stretched his legs in front of him. Astrid's jaw tightened. The swine was enjoying this, no doubt intending to wring every possible drop of pleasure from the situation, every last obnoxious inch of him gloating over her humiliation. An intimidating presence at the best of times, his silent scrutiny was downright unnerving now—not that she was about to give him the satisfaction of showing it. Nor would she utter any further complaint about the menial nature of the work, though she sensed he was waiting for it. Waiting and hoping. He would thoroughly enjoy beating her. Much as it went against the grain, the only sensible option right now was to obey.

By the time she finished her chores it was early evening. The smell of food drifted on the air, a sharp reminder that she hadn't eaten anything since the previous day, and her stomach growled in response. However, pride held her silent. Whatever happened she wasn't going to beg.

Having seen all the tasks performed to his satisfaction, Leif rose from his chair. 'Stay here until I return.'

'Where else did you think I might go?' she retorted.

He raised an eyebrow, surveying her coolly. 'You are impudent, slave. Do it again and you won't enjoy the consequences.'

'Ah, yes. You will beat me, will you not?'

'Soundly, and since you have no idea how much I should enjoy it, you would be well advised not to test the matter.' He paused to let the effect of his words sink in. 'In future you will speak when you are spoken to and not before. When you do address me you will say "my lord". Is that clear?'

Her hands clenched at her sides but, unwilling to give him an excuse to make good his threat, she held her temper. 'Very clear, my lord.'

'I hope so.'

With that he turned and left her. As she watched his departing back Astrid muttered an imprecation. It served no purpose other than to afford a temporary vent for her feelings. After that there was nothing to do but wait. The temperature was dropping with the sun and the air growing cool, so she sat down by the hearth, trying to draw some small comfort from the fire.

From the central *hov* she could hear conversation and laughter. The smell of cooking was stronger now, her appetite keener, but she held out little hope of getting anything to eat. There were many ways to punish; many ways to enforce obedience. In that moment she didn't know which was worse; starvation, or the thought of what might happen when her captor returned.

Leif finished his food and, having replenished his cup, leaned back in his chair, letting himself relax for the first time since his arrival. It was the first chance he'd had to take in the swift reversal of fortune that had given him back his freedom. He'd been lucky and he knew it. Without the loyalty of his men his fate would have been very different. He had no idea how they'd managed to find him; just then he was only thankful that they had. Truly he was favoured by Odin.

The All-Father had delivered another gift into his keeping, and with it the means of gaining his revenge. That ought to have been a very simple matter. Astrid was completely in his power: she was his for the taking. So why hadn't he? He wasn't entirely sure of the answer. It was partly concerned with her courage. Not only had she fought him tooth and nail, she'd even had the nerve to use his sword against him. The recollection drew grudging respect. However, it was the accompanying outburst that had maximum impact, along with the pain he'd glimpsed in her eyes. *I was twelve years old the last time a man decided to have his way with me.* What he had been about to do was no different, and the words acted on him like a bucket of icy fjord water. Until that moment he hadn't understood how close he'd been to losing control; to losing all sense of himself as a man. It was as if the cruelty of his erstwhile captors had stripped him of humanity, and left only a wild beast in its place. It was exactly what Hakke had set out to achieve.

Leif's fingers tightened round his cup. He'd thought himself stronger than that, indeed above such actions. It disturbed him to discover how close the beast had come to deposing his better self. Astrid's reaction had not been feigned, and the thought of being forever equated with that first brutal rape filled him with disgust. It also brought him to his senses, and he'd left abruptly. He'd never forced a woman in his life, and no amount of anger could justify doing that either.

After he'd cooled off he'd realised that in part his behaviour was a response to shattered illusion, to being shown that the relationship he'd hoped to have with her was never going to happen. That disturbed him. Disappointment never featured in his dealings with women any more, or it hadn't until then. It was deeply disconcerting to realise that he wasn't as immune to female charms as he'd imagined, and that his actions were not solely about revenge. There were other ways of bending Astrid to his will. She would resist of course, as she had earlier. In spite of himself, the recollection brought a smile to his lips, but then, he'd have been less than human if he hadn't enjoyed that little show of defiance.

An hour crawled by, then two, and weariness began to make itself felt. Astrid wanted nothing more than to sleep but she didn't dare. Leif already had too much advantage to give him more. She shivered, and not on account of the chill either.

The sound of a footstep brought her head up at once and then the door opened. She scrambled to her feet, heart pounding. Leif stepped into the room and thrust a wooden platter towards her.

'Here.'

She took it and glanced at the contents: the heel of a loaf and a piece of fish. It was plain enough fare, but it was fresh. Half suspecting a trick, she looked quizzically at Leif.

'Eat, slave. I don't want you fading away.'

It was tempting to retort in kind but she resisted the urge and addressed herself to the food instead, before he could change his mind. He watched her for a moment or two then closed the door and dropped the wooden bar into place. The soft thud filled her with foreboding. It was like being caged with a large and angry lion. Suddenly her appetite wasn't as keen but she forced herself to eat anyway. Notwithstanding his taunt, it was only common sense. Even so, she dragged it out as long as she dared and then set the platter down.

Leif divested himself of his belt and dagger and laid the weapon aside. Then he pulled off his tunic and shirt. The firelight revealed the bruises on his ribs, the black fading a little now to a mottled yellowish green. They did not in any way detract from the suggestion of power in the hard-muscled arms and torso. If anything they enhanced it. Any lingering thought of holding him off by main strength evaporated immediately.

He crossed to the side of the room and opened the wooden chest, drawing out a rolled mat. Shaking it out, he laid it on the floor at the foot of the bed.

'You will sleep there tonight.'

Astrid remained silent, every nerve alive to the man, hardly daring to hope that he meant it.

Slowly he finished undressing. She swallowed hard. Leif naked was infinitely more intimidating. Under her anxious gaze he unsheathed the sword and set it down within easy reach, then climbed into bed.

She hesitated, keenly aware that he was watching her. Then, seeing that there was nothing else to be done, she lay down on the mat. He had not offered her a blanket, and she certainly wasn't about to ask for one, even though away from the immediate influence of the fire the night chill was becoming pronounced. For some time she lay quite still, straining to catch every sound from the bed. However, Leif settled quickly and soon she heard only the sound of soft breathing. Relief washed over her, and she closed her eyes.

Thereafter she dozed intermittently. The floor was hard and the sleeping mat offered little in mitigation. It was also much colder now, and she awoke shivering. Cautiously, she sat up, wrapping her arms around herself, and glanced towards the fire. It was reduced to a bed of glowing embers, but they would offer some residual heat. For a little while she hesitated but there was no sound from the bed so eventually she decided to risk it. As quietly as possible, she got up and decamped to the hearth. It was a little warmer so she lay down once more and curled up to conserve heat. She didn't dare add more logs to the fire for fear of waking Leif. The gods only knew what he'd do if she disturbed his sleep. A beating would likely be the least of it. Closing her eyes, she prayed for sleep to come.

In fact, like most fighting men, Leif was a light sleeper. His senses filtered out the familiar sounds of the night but anything unusual roused him at once. The soft rustling of the reed mat brought him to consciousness, and instinctively his hand reached for his sword. However, the sound moved away from the bed. In the dull glow from the fire across the room he could just make out Astrid's form. On hearing her lie down, he drew back his hand and let himself relax again. It made no difference to him if she slept by the hearth. The thought that she felt cold was accompanied by a twinge of something very like guilt. He repressed it. Cold was the least of her worries. Then, drawing up the covers, he turned over and addressed himself to sleep.

Astrid eventually dozed off from sheer fatigue and was woken some time later by a foot nudging her ribs.

'Get up, slave. It's past dawn.'

She looked up to see Leif standing over her. He was fully dressed now and ready to face the day. She sat up hurriedly, stifling a groan. Every part of her felt stiff and sore and chilled. His expression was no warmer.

'Put that mat away. Then go and fetch more wood and make up the fire.'

She got to her knees and began to roll up the sleeping mat, but her cold fingers fumbled the task.

'Hurry up. I don't intend to wait all day.'

Yesterday the acid tone would have brought an equally acid reply to the tip of her tongue. Today it reinforced the knowledge of her predicament and, combined with a poor night's sleep, served only to lower her spirits. She finished the task as fast as she could and got awkwardly to her feet.

'Give me that.'

Mutely she handed him the mat. As he took it his fingers brushed her hand and she saw him frown. Then he jerked his head towards the door. It was still fast. As she struggled to lift the wooden bar there was a muffled exclamation of impatience behind her.

'Thor's blood! Come out of the way, wench.'

She stepped aside and watched as he freed the bar and set it down against the wall. Astrid reached for the latch but a large hand closed on hers, holding the door shut. Cold eyes looked down into hers.

'From now on when I rise I shall expect to find the fire lit, water to wash in and food ready. Do you understand?'

She swallowed hard. 'Yes, my lord.'

He was standing so close that their bodies almost touched, so close she could feel his warmth. None of that was reflected in his manner, however. His anger was almost palpable.

'You won't get another warning, slave. Now go.'

To her horror she felt tears prick the backs of her eyelids and swiftly lowered her gaze lest he should notice. Such a display of weakness would only increase his triumph.

He stepped back then and let her pass. Astrid opened the door and, bracing herself against the cool morning air, hurried out. Leif watched her go. Contrary to her belief, he had not missed the sudden telling brightness in her eyes as he rebuked her. It had actually taken him by surprise. That she should be on the verge of weeping ought to have pleased him enormously but somehow it didn't, any more than the icy touch of her hand beneath his. The sensation it provoked was entirely different. If she had wept openly or pleaded or whined he'd have known how to react. As it was, he felt strangely wrong-footed, and it did nothing to improve his mood.

Feeling a need to distance himself for a while he issued Astrid with a list of instructions and then took himself off. Male companionship would put things back in perspective. When he arrived in the main *hov* he was greeted by Thorvald.

'Some of the men were wondering if we might

go hunting soon. A haunch of venison or roast boar would make a nice change from fish.'

Leif nodded. Now that he was back he needed to turn his thoughts to the practical matters attendant on the well-being of his crew. 'Why not?'

'Tomorrow, then.'

'Aye, tomorrow.'

A hunt would be a welcome distraction: it would help put his recent experiences behind him and it would give him something to think about besides Astrid. The treacherous little witch had got further under his skin than he'd imagined. Fortunately he knew his enemy now. Whatever charm she might once have held for him was broken.

'Everything all right, Chief?'

Thorvald's voice broke into his reflections. Leif summoned a smile. 'Of course.'

'If we leave early we'll have the best part of the day to hunt.'

'We'll divide the force. It'll increase the chances of success.'

'As you say. Are you planning to leave a contingent on guard?' Thorvald paused. 'I was thinking about the woman.'

'She's not going anywhere.'

'True.'

'She can remain here until we return.'

'If you don't mind me asking, Chief; what are you intending to do with her?'

'Eventually I shall return her to Gulbrand. Why?'

'Strikes me it would be a more fitting revenge if you didn't send her back.'

Before Leif could reply Snorri entered the hall with Bjarni and Ingolf. They greeted their jarl respectfully and then looked at his companion.

'Well?' asked Bjarni. 'Is the hunt on or what?'

Thorvald grinned. 'It's on.'

The news was received with broad grins and the conversation turned enthusiastically to plans for the morrow.

The list of instructions that Leif had issued to Astrid that morning kept her occupied all day. Somewhat to her relief he didn't come anywhere near her. Once or twice she caught a glimpse of him, but he didn't look her way, and seemed entirely involved in discussion with his men. It was evening before he returned. She had been mending a torn shirt but rose hurriedly as he entered.

He surveyed her in silence for a moment and then looked around, his glance taking in every detail. The room was immaculate.

'Have you performed all the tasks which I commanded of you?'

'Almost all, my lord.' She hesitated. 'I have not quite finished mending the shirt.'

'Very well. Finish it. Then you may eat.'

She sat down and resumed work. He set down a platter of food by the hearth and then walked past her towards the far end of the room. She heard him open one of the chests and, from the corner of her eye, saw him take something out. Then he returned.

'You need not wait up for my return this evening. However, I shall rise early to go hunting. See to it that everything is in readiness.'

'Yes, my lord.'

'You'll need this when you retire.'

He held out the item he had removed from the chest. It was a woollen blanket. Astrid blinked. She took the offering somewhat hesitantly, half expecting him to snatch it back again. When he did not, hesitation became bemusement. He saw it and returned a sardonic smile.

'I don't want you succumbing to a chill. It would ruin my plans entirely.'

With that he left her. As the door closed behind him she let out a long breath. Whatever else she'd been expecting, it certainly wasn't that. Whatever his reasons for permitting her the blanket, she was grateful for it, dreading the thought of another night in the cold. She glanced at the platter of food. It was fish and bread again, but she didn't care. After working all day her appetite was sharp. As quickly as she could she finished the repair and put the sewing to one side. It occurred to her that he could have made her wait until his return before giving her any food, but he had not. Under other circumstances it might have been considered a kindness. However, she knew that was the last thing on his mind. Her well-being was important to him only because it furthered the possibilities for exacting revenge.

Chapter Eleven

When Leif woke next morning it was to find the fire lit and Astrid pouring water into a bowl for him to wash in. He rose and pulled on his breeches before bathing his face and hands. Then he finished dressing. As he did so he fired off orders.

'You will clean and tidy this room in my absence, fetch firewood and split some kindling. Then you can wash my shirt and any others that might need doing. I'll ask my men.'

Astrid's jaw tightened. 'As you wish, my lord.'

'Just so.'

With that he sauntered to the door. As she watched him go she bit back the urge to make a sarcastic reply, knowing the words had been designed to provoke. If he'd hoped she would rise to the bait he was going to be disappointed. Instead she found the broom and, to work off some of her indignation, began to sweep the floor.

However, when Leif returned a quarter of an hour later and dumped a huge armful of shirts at her feet resolution evaporated.

'What am I supposed to do with those?'

'You will wash them as I instructed you, slave. You'll find a tub of soap in the storeroom.'

'I will not.'

He raised an eyebrow. 'I beg your pardon.'

'I said I will not. If you think I'm going to act as washerwoman for your crew you're mistaken.'

'You will do as I bid you. If I have to tan your bare backside first it's all one to me.'

Outraged, she glared at him. 'Why, you utter...'

'If you're not out of that door by the count of three you won't sit down for a week.'

'How I loathe you.'

Without taking his eyes off her Leif began to roll up his sleeves. 'One...'

'Brute!'

'Two...'

Astrid paled and, with frantic haste, grabbed all the shirts, clutching them like a protective talisman. Then she backed towards the door. 'All right! I'm going.'

'I still think a good hiding would help focus your mind.'

He took a pace towards her. Astrid fled.

* * *

It took her the entire morning to launder all the shirts and hang them on bushes to dry, by which time her back was aching and her hands reddened and sore from the harsh lye soap and from kneading cloth. Then she began the other tasks still awaiting her attention, knowing full well that she wouldn't dare leave any of them undone. Leif would not only make good his threat, he'd enjoy it too. The very thought made her hot and cold by turns.

When eventually it was all done she heaved a sigh of relief. Glancing down, she eyed her makeshift costume with distaste, feeling grubby and unkempt as well as tired. There had been no chance to bathe or even comb her hair since she was brought here. She looked longingly at the fjord for a little while and then decided to risk it. Most of the men had gone with the hunting party and wouldn't be back until later. The three who remained were sitting by the large *hov* talking and playing tafl. They had barely even glanced in her direction all day. There would never be a better opportunity than this.

Astrid took the linen towel Leif had used earlier, and his comb, and made her way to the far end of the island where the shore was screened by bushes. Then she stripped off and waded into the water. It was cold but wonderfully refreshing. She washed herself all over, and her shift as well, before draping it over a bush in the sun. Having done that, she dried herself and slipped the make-shift gown over her nakedness. The woollen cloth was prickly against her skin but it was worth it just to feel clean again. Afterwards she sat down on a warm rock to let the sun dry her hair. It was peaceful here, a welcome respite from labour and from all company, and she let herself relax a little.

As the ship glided towards the mooring Leif smiled to himself. The hunt had been successful, with a fine deer to show for their efforts. They would dine well tonight; sleep well too, no doubt. That turned his mind in a different direction, and Astrid's image filtered out all other thoughts. The memory of their parting that morning raised a quiet smile. Anger suited her. She was smart too, knowing exactly how far to push her luck. In spite of himself he was amused. If she knew how close she'd been sailing to the wind she might have been a lot more worried.

When the ship was tied up he gave orders for the meat to be carried ashore, then vaulted over the gunwale on to the wooden dock and made his way ashore. He had barely gone fifty yards when he checked in surprise: every bush in sight was festooned with drying shirts. As he looked around he experienced a twinge of guilt. Had there really been that many? It hadn't seemed like it when they were bundled all together. Besides, his attention had been on Astrid rather than the shirts.

He hurried on towards his quarters. The door was open, the room beyond immaculate. It was also empty. Looking around, he saw no sign of Astrid anywhere. His smile faded. Had she somehow managed to give him the slip? Then he told himself not to be stupid: there was no way off the island other than by boat, no possible means of escape. She was here somewhere. Behind him he could hear the voices of his crew as they rejoined their remaining companions. Leaving them to it, he kept on going.

The island narrowed towards its furthest end, reducing the number of places for concealment, but when he still saw no sign of his quarry, Leif's misgivings returned. *I'll swim if I have to.* He frowned. The words had been spoken in anger; the little vixen couldn't have meant them. Then he recalled his blade at her breast and the trickle of blood as she leaned on the point, and suddenly he wasn't so sure. His gaze went to the quiet expanse of dark water. It was deep and cold, the far shore a good half-mile distant. If she'd tried that… Disquiet grew. And then, from the corner of his eye, he detected movement behind the screen of bushes nearby. His jaw tightened as he strode towards them. What he saw then took him so completely by surprise that he'd stopped in his tracks.

Astrid was perched on the edge of a low rock.

She was wearing only the length of homespun cloth he'd given her. Being open at the sides, it afforded an uninterrupted view of a slender and shapely leg that seemed to reach all the way to her waist. Above it he glimpsed the smooth curve of a breast. Her pale gold hair was unbound, flowing over her shoulders and down her back almost to her hips. He watched her re-braid it and tie off the end with a length of ribbon. It must have been there when he carried her off that night, though he didn't recall seeing it at the time. Having fastened it securely, she rose and went to retrieve her shift. When she removed the length of homespun cloth he almost forgot to breathe, his entire being caught up in the moment as reality outstripped all former imaginings. Unaware of being observed, she dressed unhurriedly, her movements as graceful as the figure beneath the folds of concealing cloth. He watched her fasten the belt that held it together. It was far too big, the spare end reaching halfway to her knees. The whole outlandish costume was an exercise in ugliness, intended to demean and humiliate. It ought to have looked ridiculous, and yet somehow she had managed to invest it with entirely different qualities.

His frown deepened and he cut off that line of thought abruptly. It was foolish and fanciful. More than that, it was dangerous. Astrid might be beautiful but she was also treacherous, something he'd do well to remember. If she sensed weakness she wouldn't hesitate to exploit it. Whatever notions he might once have entertained about her before were irrelevant now. She was just a slave; one who needed reminding who was master.

He watched her gather up the towel and comb— both his, he noticed. Then she turned towards the camp. Leif stepped out to block her path. Startled, she looked up and he heard a sharp intake of breath.

'I expected to find you in my quarters,' he said.

'I beg your pardon, my lord. It's just that I...I wanted to bathe.'

'So I inferred.' He paused. 'Who gave you permission?'

'No one, my lord, but...'

'But what?'

'I... It seemed like a good opportunity.'

'No doubt.'

'I finished all my work first, I swear it.'

He ignored that. 'Did I give you permission to use my towel and comb, slave?'

Astrid swallowed hard. 'No, my lord. Forgive me.'

'Taking my things without my knowledge could be construed as theft. The penalty for such a crime is severe.'

She paled, her gaze searching his. 'I never meant it so. You must know that.'

'I know nothing of the sort. You betrayed me before. Why would you shrink from theft?'

The violet eyes darkened with emotion. 'I was on my way to return your things, and I didn't betray you before either.'

'I may give you the benefit of the doubt on the first point. On the second there is no doubt.'

'Because you don't want there to be.'

'That isn't so,' he replied. 'Even when I was chained in the kennels I hoped against hope that I was wrong. Then you revealed the truth from your own lips.'

'No. I said what I was told to say, played the part I was commanded to play.'

'Really? Well, you were most convincing.'

'I had to be convincing. I had to make them believe me or…'

'Or what?' When she still said nothing, he took a step closer. 'Or what, Astrid?'

'Or they would have slit your nose and cut out your tongue. Even the smallest sign of disobedience in me would mean another beating for you and I couldn't bear it. So I played their game and did as I was told.'

Leif was completely still, his face as pale as hers. 'You expect me to believe this?'

'You don't want to believe it because then you would have no just grounds for your treatment of me. You don't want to believe it because you're enjoying this. Any scapegoat will serve as an excuse to vent your wrath and I am the most convenient.' Her gaze locked with his. 'You're so consumed with thoughts of revenge that you're deaf and blind to everything else.'

'And yet on your own admission your acting skills are excellent.'

'I said what they wanted to hear. I would have said anything to protect you.'

'How very moving.'

'You have no heart to move.'

'You realise it at last. How you must be regretting your efforts on my behalf.'

'No, I cannot regret that,' she replied. 'My only regret is that I ever trusted you.'

The blue-grey eyes burned. 'I came for you that night. I kept faith with you.'

'And I with you.'

'We must agree to differ on that point.'

'It doesn't change the truth.'

'This conversation is over.' He jerked his head towards the camp. 'Go.'

Astrid went without a word. For a little while he watched but made no move to follow. She didn't look back and presently was lost to view among the trees. The knot tightened in his gut and he turned away, his mind a whirl of conflicting emotions. She was lying, no question. Deception was her stock-in-trade. She excelled at it. He hadn't been able to detect so much as a flicker in those violet eyes or a note of insincerity in her voice. Her anger at least was genuine. The vixen had nerve, he'd give her that. Nor had her accusations entirely failed in their effect. For all he pretended otherwise, they had stung. *You're so consumed with thoughts of revenge that you're deaf and blind to everything else.* She had intended them to sting, of course. Words were weapons and sharper than swords. To vent his feelings he picked up a flat stone and flung it, watching it skim away across the fjord. It was followed by several more in quick succession. Astrid was skilled with words, and her words were lies.

Gradually, as some of the tension went out of him, he ceased throwing stones and sat down on a rock by the water's edge. To an observer he might have been admiring the view. In reality he saw only a pair of violet eyes, unwavering violet eyes reflecting anger and pain. He frowned and pushed the image aside. She was lying. She had to be.

Astrid marched back to Leif's quarters and returned the towel and comb to their rightful place. Unwilling to remain there, she went and retrieved all the shirts, collecting them up with indignant briskness until she had a great armful. Then she dumped the lot on a convenient boulder and set about folding them. The mechanical task at least gave her something to do other than sit around waiting to be the object of displeasure when Leif returned. His words, delivered with such cold sarcasm, had cut deep. Along with that was a burning sense of injustice, and she wondered how she could ever have thought of going away with him. She must have been mad.

Nearby, a haunch of venison was roasting over a large fire. The smell of the meat mingled with wood smoke, and a tantalising aroma drifted into the late afternoon air. Her stomach growled in response, reminding her that she hadn't eaten all day. However, roast meat was too much to hope for. Nor did she intend to ask for any, no matter how hungry she felt. That would only make his enjoyment complete.

As the pile of folded shirts grew, her mind went back a little further to the scene just before their conversation. She had just finished dressing when he arrived… Her hands paused in their task as another possibility suggested itself. How long had he been standing there before she became aware of his presence? Had he seen her dressing? Had he seen her undressed? The thought brought a flush of warmth to her face. Leif had given nothing away, but the implication was disquieting all the same.

She finished the task and, having gathered up the clean laundry, took it indoors and laid it on the bed. It could be returned to the rightful owners later. Then she turned her attention to the fire and added more wood. The sun was going down and evening coming on. Soon enough she would be shut in the lion's cage again, a prospect that was doubly unwelcome now.

* * *

It was dusk before Leif returned. Astrid was sitting by the hearth staring into the flames. She glanced up briefly as he entered, then turned back to the fire again. For a little while the only sound was of crackling logs. His gaze moved beyond her to the pile of linen on the bed.

'What in Hel's name is that doing there?'

'You gave no instruction for what I was to do with it after it was washed, my lord.'

'It should be returned to its owners, of course.'

'I do not know who they are, my lord, and I should hate to get it wrong. If one of your men were to lack his shirt I might be accused of stealing.'

He frowned. 'Take care, slave, lest you test my patience too far.'

She looked away again but made no reply. The silence grew around them. Leif crossed to the bed.

'Come here.' As she joined him he jerked his head towards the pile of linen. 'Pick it up.'

Wordlessly she obeyed.

'Now you will take it to the big house.'

Astrid's chin came up but still she made no reply and headed for the door. Leif followed after, his baleful gaze burning into her back.

As they approached the men broke off their conversation to watch. Uncomfortably aware of their attention, Astrid hugged her burden closer and kept walking. When they reached the *hov* she paused just inside the door. The silence followed them and the group of men nearby looked on with interest. Leif nodded towards a nearby bench.

'Put the shirts down there.'

She deposited the bundle carefully and then straightened, waiting. He surveyed her in silence for a moment then nodded.

'Now go back to my quarters and stay there.'

'I'll wager he won't be long,' said a voice nearby.

A second wag piped up. 'She can warm my bed any time.'

As the men chuckled Astrid's cheeks bloomed rosy pink. Leif smiled faintly and then glanced over his shoulder.

'The only bed she'll be warming is mine, Harek.'

A burst of laughter greeted this. Astrid glared at Leif and muttered, 'That'll be the day.'

He took hold of her arm and led her from the room. As the conversation resumed behind them he paused, pulling her round to face him.

'Do you imagine that because I haven't bedded you yet it means I'm not going to?' His gaze locked with hers. 'The original arrangement still stands.'

The colour deepened in her face. 'How I loathe you.'

'That will add a certain spice to the relationship.'

'Ah, yes, I'm sure you're already visualising the fun you'll have before you send me back.'

'I've been visualising that for quite a while,' he replied. 'As to the rest, perhaps I won't send you back after all. Perhaps I'll keep you for myself.'

Astrid stared at him, speechless. However, her expression was more eloquent. His eyes glinted.

'You don't seem very pleased.'

'Did you expect me to be?'

'Perhaps not.' He paused. 'I, on the other hand, find it most pleasing.'

'You would.'

He surveyed her appreciatively. 'In any event it will not be dull.'

Astrid thought that was quite certain, though she vouchsafed no reply. His words had left her mind in turmoil. Did he really mean what he said or was he just playing with her? Either way the ramifications were dire.

He released his hold on her arm. 'You may go. I'll bring you some food presently.'

She blinked, taken aback for the second time in as many minutes. Leif was confoundedly good at keeping her guessing. However, on this occasion she wasn't about to argue. It was a relief to be gone, and she was famished to boot.

Leif drew a deep breath to steady himself. How was it that she always managed to provoke him so successfully? Why was it that, every time they argued, he heard himself saying things he'd never intended to say? Astrid was courageous and quite prepared to use the same weapons as he: her wit and her tongue could be deadly, but her rebelliousness pleased him more than submission could ever have done. The truth was that, no matter what he pretended, he'd never been able to see her as a slave. He found himself looking forward to these encounters because he knew they would be stimulating for all sorts of reasons. Unfortunately they also had unintended consequences. He ought not to have implied that he would bed her without her consent. Knowing what he did, that had been a truly outrageous lie, just part of the escalating banter. Yet he did want her. He had always wanted her. That part of it had never changed. If anything, his desire for her had increased, all of which made it much harder to keep the upper hand.

The venison was delicious and he'd provided a decent portion, along with a piece of bread and a bowl of root vegetables cooked with wild garlic. Astrid ate it all and wiped the platter clean. After the earlier argument she had wondered if he would punish her by withholding the meal. She was in no doubt that her uncle would have, and Hakke too. Just why the comparison had popped into her head was impossible to say, but it was a pointed contrast. Leif's power over her was total but thus far he had exercised the kind of restraint that was foreign to them. Thus far. Was this also about keeping her guessing? He never did anything without a reason.

She wondered how it might have been between them if events had fallen out as they had planned. They would have made good their escape and he would have taken her to his bed. She would have been afraid but would not have reneged on the agreement. The Leif she had known then would likely have been gentle, even patient, and perhaps she could have grown accustomed to intimacy with him. Now his possession of her would be an act of revenge; by the sound of things a protracted revenge.

Astrid sighed. Suddenly she felt unutterably weary, wrung out physically and emotionally. Sleep would afford a welcome oblivion. Leif had not commanded her to stay up. The reed mat and blanket were lying on top of the chest across the room. She fetched them and settled herself by the fire.

When Leif returned some time later the fire was burning low and the room was still. He barred the door and then surveyed the scene in silence, listening to the sound of soft regular breathing from the figure on the floor. From the look of things Astrid had been asleep for a while.

He moved quietly past her and prepared himself for bed. However, sleep did not come easily, because his mind ran on an earlier conversation. It had haunted him all evening. Ale and good fellowship could not drive it out of his head. Nor could he forget the look in Astrid's eyes or the accusation she had flung at him. *You don't want to believe...* He sighed. The evidence of his senses had been so compelling and yet she had supplied a version of events that contradicted it spectacularly. At first the tale seemed merely fantastic but he had been unable to dismiss it since. Was it beyond belief that Einar and Hakke could have engineered such a deception? Was it beyond belief that they could have manipulated Astrid; that they could have forced her compliance in such a cruel way? Her uncle was ambitious: Hakke was ruthless and vengeful. He had lately been robbed of a bride and wanted retribution. Astrid's allegiance was to Ragnhild, and to the king who had delivered them both; by extension, then, to all those involved in that rescue. Hakke was well aware of it. Did his vengeance include the punishment of women as well? Leif frowned. Given what he knew of the man it was altogether plausible. Suddenly former certainty was open to question. Was it possible for rage to cloud judgement so completely? *Any scapegoat will serve as an excuse to vent your wrath and I am the most convenient.* Was Astrid telling the truth? Doubt nagged like toothache.

* * *

He slept ill that night and woke early as grey dawn light was seeping through the darkness. Unable to lie abed any longer he rose and dressed. The room was chill now, the fire a bed of grey ash. Astrid was still asleep. Unwilling to disturb her, he silently unbarred the door and went out. For a while he paused just beyond the threshold, his gaze taking in the scene beyond. The waters of the fjord were black and still, the far shore lost in a bank of fog. Tendrils of mist curled about the trees. From somewhere among the branches a bird called.

For a while he listened, letting the cool air clear his head. Then, having made use of the privy, he returned. Astrid stirred a little but didn't wake. The coverlet had slipped from her shoulder, revealing the fraying edges of the makeshift gown. One bare and dusty foot peeped from its lower edge. One hand was under her cheek; the other was reddened by work. As he looked he was forcibly reminded of a flower casually tossed into the dirt. It reinforced the impression of innocence and vulnerability. He frowned. Needing something to distract him from his thoughts, he began to remake the fire.

Astrid came slowly to consciousness amid a sensation of warmth and well-being. She smiled and opened her eyes, slowly taking in the details of the room in the early light. Then she turned towards the hearth. A cheerful fire was burning there. For a second or two she stared at it until its significance dawned and brought her to complete wakefulness with a jolt. Horrified, she sat up, looking around. A pile of firewood lay nearby. The pail by the door was now full of water. Her stomach lurched. She must have overslept and by some considerable time. Leif was going to be furious. He'd already given her one warning; this time her tardiness was likely to earn her a beating. The recollection of his strength made her quail inwardly. Scrambling to her feet, she hastily folded the blanket and had begun to roll up the reed mat when the door opened. Astrid froze.

Leif paused on the threshold, taking in the scene at a glance. Then he came in and closed the door behind him. She took a deep breath.

'I'm sorry, my lord. I did not mean to lie abed so late.'

'It is not late,' he replied. 'Rather I was up early.'

'Oh.'

'The rest are not stirring yet.'

'But the fire…the water…'

'I wanted something to do.'

She regarded him in astonishment. Nothing in his manner suggested imminent wrath; on the contrary, he looked quite relaxed. However, appearances could be deceptive. Half the time she never knew what he was thinking.

'I'll start cleaning right away.'

'There's no hurry. As I said, it's early yet.'

'What other tasks would you have me do today, my lord?'

He shook his head. 'None.'

Astrid blinked. 'None?'

'Just see to it that the room is tidied as usual.'

'Yes, my lord.'

Feeling somewhat confused, she fetched the broom from the corner and began to sweep. He watched her for a little while and then left her to it. Relief was so strong she could feel her knees sagging. She had no idea why he should have been so lenient but it was as welcome as it was unexpected. However, it wouldn't pay to take his new-found good humour for granted, so she set to at once.

Leif strolled away, deep in thought. It had been impossible to miss Astrid's consternation when she thought she'd overslept. It might have been amusing, except for the fleeting expression of fear he'd seen in her eyes. He sighed as the memory of a previous conversation returned. Evidently she had been expecting retribution, probably the beating he'd mentioned the previous day. He'd been angry then, made a threat which, in that instance, he had no intention of carrying out. Judging from her reaction, though, his performance had been totally convincing.

That raised another query in his mind: if he had been able to make her believe such a thing of him, was it not possible that her apparent betrayal of him had also been a convincing performance? Could he have got it so badly wrong? The more he thought about it the more the affirmative rose up to mock him. *They'd have cut out your tongue... slit your nose.* Now he was calmer he could well believe that. It would be typical of such men, and their plan was to break him. Astrid was not the culprit. It was just that he'd been so blinded by anger and resentment that he'd swallowed Hakke's lies hook, line and sinker.

'Beg pardon, my lord…'

Torvald's voice roused him from thought and he looked up quickly. 'What is it?'

'The men were wondering how long we're to remain on the island. We have enough supplies for a few more days but after that we'll need more. Then there's the matter of Hakke.'

Leif nodded. 'I hadn't forgotten. We'll leave for Agder today. There we'll have everything we need and be well placed to gather reinforcements.'

'As you say, my lord.' Torvald paused. 'Do you want me to tell the men?'

'No, I'll speak to them myself. Get everyone together.'

Now that the decision was made, Leif felt better. The island was a useful temporary refuge but the need to move on was pressing now. The sooner they reached Agder the sooner he could put his plans into action. Next time he met Hakke it would be with a sword in his hand. That day would be his foe's last. In the meantime, there was the matter of Astrid, and that was far more problematic.

Chapter Twelve

Astrid wandered to the door. Having put the room to rights she wondered how she was going to fill the rest of the day. However, as she reached the threshold she stared in surprise: the isle was buzzing with activity like an overturned beehive. Voices filled the air and men strode past carrying their sea chests. Disquiet replaced her former mood. They were evidently going somewhere and for quite a while by the look of things. Was she to go with them or was she to be left here? Either possibility gave rise to concern, but the second was worse.

She didn't have long to wonder, because a couple of minutes later Leif returned. Under her bemused gaze he fastened on his sword belt and handed her his shield and spear.

'Bring these to the ship.' When she had taken

them he picked up the wooden chest. 'I'll come back for the rest of my war gear.'

Astrid followed him to the jetty, looking on as the men stowed their possessions, the sea chests carefully placed to provide makeshift benches for the rowers. Leif handed his chest to a companion on board and then, having relieved Astrid of the shield and the spear, handed those over too. Instructing her to wait, he returned for the rest of his things. She stepped aside to avoid obstructing the others, all the while conscious of the glances that came her way. Glances in which speculation mingled with curiosity and amusement. It was evident that they regarded her as Leif's property, his slave, his whore. That was bad enough; worse was the thought that his intended revenge might take a different form from the one she had anticipated. If he left her here...

A few minutes later he was back with the rest of his things. When they too had been stowed he turned to look at Astrid.

'Come.'

'My lord?'

'We're leaving for Agder.'

'We?'

He raised an eyebrow. 'Did you think I would leave you behind?'

'You did not discuss your plans with me, my lord.'

'True. All the same, you should know that

a slave is too valuable a commodity to lose so lightly.'

Relief mingled with annoyance. 'I'm glad my worth is so great in your eyes.'

His lips twitched. 'I have yet to discover the extent of your worth, but no doubt it will be revealed by and by.'

The implication did nothing for her peace of mind and nor did Leif in this present mood. She had a strong suspicion that he was enjoying himself at her expense.

'I am flattered to be the object of such interest.'

'I did not speak to flatter,' he replied, 'and I always protect my interests.'

Without giving her time to reply he picked her up and called to one of his crewmen. Then she was tossed over the side of the ship and received with the same insulting ease before being dumped on her feet. Leif vaulted aboard and joined them. His hand closed round Astrid's arm and he led her into the stern.

'You will sit there.'

Obediently she took her place, watching the crew take theirs, conscious all the while of the man beside her, the man at whose feet she now sat. The allusion must be clear to all.

She tried not to think about what he had said before or how this removal to Agder might change things between them. *Just because I haven't bedded you yet doesn't mean I'm not going to.* Wherever they were going, Leif's power would be absolute.

'Cast off the lines!'

His voice drew her back to the present and she glanced up quickly. However, his attention was elsewhere. The command was obeyed, and moments later the ship began to slide away from the jetty.

Once in deeper water the crew shipped oars and unfurled the sail. As it bellied in the breeze the *Sea Serpent* responded, leaping forwards like an eager horse, her clean lines cleaving the water. Astrid leaned her back against the strakes and shut her eyes, breathing the smells of wood and rope, letting the men's talk wash over her. The sun was warm and pleasant and in spite of herself she relaxed a little, enjoying the illusion of freedom.

'It's peaceful out here, isn't it?' said Leif.

She looked up quickly. 'Yes, it is, almost as though we were the only beings on earth.'

'If we were we would have no worries about the likes of Hakke and Einar.'

'Are you worried?'

'Not at the moment. Even the berserkers won't follow me to Agder.' He paused. 'They might attempt to stop me getting there, of course.'

Astrid sat up. 'You think they might be lying in wait to attack the ship?'

'It's possible, but unlikely. Our stay on the island should have thrown them off the scent.'

'You have used the ploy before.'

'Once or twice.'

'It's a useful hideout.'

'The island is convenient for many reasons,' he replied.

She stopped herself from uttering the thought uppermost in mind and changed the subject. 'What will you do in Agder?'

'Raise a force of fighting men.'

'Enough to challenge Hakke?'

'Enough to be revenged on Einar. When I've dealt with him I'll find Hakke.'

'More fighting and bloodshed, then,' she replied.

'There's no other choice now. It's them or us.'

'Such a feud will not end there, my lord.'

'It will when we have no living enemies to perpetuate it.'

In spite of sun Astrid shivered. 'And yet you had a settled life once.'

'Once, in another lifetime.'

'You might again.'

'Family life proved—disappointing.'

She heard the hesitation and it roused her curiosity. 'How so?'

He frowned. 'A slave should not ask questions. You would do well to remember it.'

'I beg your pardon, my lord. I did not intend to touch a sore place.'

He made no reply and they lapsed into silence.

Astrid looked away, mentally kicking herself. *When will you learn?* In truth. her question had been almost a reflex response, spoken before she was aware. She'd had no thought of angering him and yet she had done it all the same.

Leif drew in a deep breath, annoyed with his own reaction. Even more galling was the knowledge that she was right: the past was a sore place with him, more so than he'd realised. Astrid had an uncanny knack for finding out his weak points. She had such a disarming way of leading him into conversation that he wasn't aware of danger until the ground shifted beneath his feet. His rebuke was defensive and he knew it. Some wounds never healed properly, and he had no intention of revisiting the dark memories associated with those hurts.

Astrid seemed taken aback; perhaps she hadn't intended her question to be intrusive or impertinent. Now he'd driven the wedge in deeper. It was hardly the best way to regain lost ground. He could no longer blame her for what Einar and Hakke had done, and he needed to tell her that. He could no longer treat her as a slave either. Since there was now no obvious reason to keep her captive, the most logical thing would have been to free her. Nevertheless, he knew he wasn't prepared to let her go.

* * *

Since it was hazardous to sail in the dark they put into a deserted cove that evening. Astrid glanced round the curve of the bay, taking in a short grassy slope covered with scrubby bushes, and the sheer cliff behind. It precluded all possibility of escape. Even if she had been able to scale it there was nowhere to run to. Besides, the thought of Leif's response to such an attempt sent a shiver through her.

The men gathered wood and set about building a fire. Then they broke out the rations and sat around laughing and talking. They ignored Astrid completely. Leif brought her some food and then rejoined them. Soon he was deep in conversation. She ate her portion and then looked around. The need to answer the call of nature had become pressing and, since the men's attention was elsewhere, it seemed like a good opportunity. Some fifty yards off was a likely clump of bushes. Rising quietly, she stole away.

Leif finished his food and glanced casually towards the place where he'd left his captive. His smile vanished and in seconds he was on his feet, his gaze sweeping the curve of the bay. Given the physical limitations of the place she couldn't have gone far. All the same...

Torvald glanced up and grinned. 'Lost your slave?'

Leif's gaze didn't alter. 'She can't be far.'

'You should keep that one close.'

'The closer the better, I'd say,' said Harek.

Appreciative chuckles greeted this from those nearby. Leif ignored them. Then a movement in the shrubbery caught his eye, followed by a glimpse of pale gold hair. His jaw tightened. A few moments later Astrid emerged from the screen of bushes. As the significance of her excursion dawned, some of the tension left him. He'd got so used to the company of men that he hadn't considered a woman's needs might be different. Although she hadn't complained, the incident left him feeling wrong-footed again. With a sigh he resumed his seat.

As the hour grew late the company began to turn in. Astrid eyed the proceedings uncertainly. The air was cool now and her garments ill suited to combat it; likewise her bare feet. A night in the open without as much as a blanket was an unappealing prospect. Even so, to complain was out of the question. Leif would like nothing more than to remind her of her lowly status. She threw a covert glance his way but he had his back to her, apparently in conversation with a couple of his men. A few moments later they returned to the fire; possibly to take first watch. He turned away and then, lifting his sea chest, carried it off the strand to the turf above where the others were also preparing their sleeping places. Astrid looked longingly at the fire, but the watchmen looked set to stay there. She sighed and wrapped her arms about herself in an attempt to get warm.

Pebbles scrunched nearby. She glanced up and then scrambled to her feet.

'My lord?'

'Come with me.'

'Where are we going?'

'Do as you're told and don't ask questions.'

Seeing there was nothing else for it, she followed him, stifling a yelp as a stone dug into her foot. It would give him too much satisfaction. She just had to hope her feet would toughen up eventually. As pebbles gave way to grass she breathed a sigh of relief. However, his next words banished every last trace of that emotion.

'You will sleep here with me.' He gestured to the hides spread on the ground.

Her heart leapt towards her throat. 'Here? With you?'

'That's right.'

Astrid swallowed hard, looking around for some means of escape, but the only way out of the cove was the way they had come. Suddenly she felt a lot colder. Imploring eyes met his.

'Please, my lord…'

'Lie down.'

Trembling, she lowered herself on to the improvised rug. He joined her a few moments later, pulling a sealskin coverlet over both of them. Astrid shut her eyes, hardly daring to breathe. A large hand closed over hers.

'Gods, you're cold, woman. Why didn't you sit nearer the fire?'

'I…I did not think it my place.'

'Your place is where I say it is.' He paused. 'Turn on to your side.'

'Why?'

'Just do as you're told.'

Reluctantly she obeyed. Leif shifted position too and curled himself around her. Astrid didn't move, her body as taut as a bowstring. An arm of steel drew her closer, locking her against him. Blood pounded in her ears. She closed her eyes, waiting for the coming assault. A dozen heartbeats passed and then a dozen more and nothing happened. Nothing, except for the gradual transference of warmth. She could feel it spreading through her body's core and flowing outwards towards her chilled limbs. Slowly the trembling subsided.

'Better?' he asked.

Somehow she found her voice. 'I… Yes.'

'Good. It would be most inconvenient if you were to contract the ague.'

The astringent tone rallied her as nothing else could have but she suppressed the retort that came to mind, knowing that she didn't dare offer any provocation. The lion might be in a benign mood now, but his power was unchanged. *If he chose to use it...* She took a deeper breath and tried to ignore the quivering sensation in the pit of her stomach.

However, it seemed that he had no such intent. The minutes passed without any attempt at greater intimacy, only the continued sharing of warmth. In spite of herself she began to relax a little. The sealskin cover was soft and cosy, smelling faintly of pine and salt. More disturbing was the scent of the man, a heady mingling of wool and smoke and musk that revived memories of another time when he had taken her in his arms, a time before betrayal and revenge. *There might have been a chance for us then.* The knowledge of what was lost filled her with sadness and yet here, cocooned against darkness and cold, she could almost pretend that his former feelings were not dead, that he was holding her because he cared.

Leif felt the tension ease in her but he remained still, not wanting to do anything that might revive it, knowing full well that her shivering was not just the effect of cold. His caustic remark about her catching an ague was a partial truth only. Up behind it were other reasons that were harder to explain. It was concerned with wanting to make amends; with wanting to make up lost ground; with wanting her. That last had never changed. Yet the gulf between them had widened to the point where he could hardly see the other side. Tonight had been an opportunity to do something about it. Of course, he had to let her believe she was still a slave, but this time his motives were good. He sought only to share his warmth, not to force her to do anything else. He would not be equated with that previous violation. From now on she was going to share his bed, but she would do it without fear. She would learn that he could be trusted. From now on, things were going to be different.

Astrid slept deeply and did not wake until after dawn. She stretched and smiled, enjoying the sensation of warmth and well-being, and then slowly opened her eyes. A pearl-grey sky revealed that day was not far advanced but the camp was already stirring. As memory returned she looked round for Leif but the place beside her was empty. She had no idea when he had left, or why he hadn't roused her, but was grateful all the same. Grateful too that he hadn't left her to fend for herself last night, and that he hadn't forced any more on her than warmth. If he had, no one would have tried to stop him. In their eyes she was a thrall and his rights over her absolute. Yet he had waived those rights in favour of a simple act of kindness. For all he denied it, that was what it was.

Astrid got to her feet and, having straightened her clothing, set about folding the sealskin coverlet. She didn't hear Leif approaching.

'You slept well,' he said.

'Yes, I thank you.' She paused. 'You did not wake me.'

'You looked so peaceful lying there.'

'Oh.' The thought that he had been watching her created a variety of emotions; none of them easy to identify.

'In any case I was awake particularly early.'

She resumed folding the cover. 'Will we reach Agder today?'

'If everything goes according to plan.'

'I have never been there before.'

'It's fair country; good pastureland and forest too.'

'Does it not bother you, then, to leave it for long periods of time?' she asked.

'The steading is in good hands. Aron was one of my father's crew until he lost a leg. Now he takes care of the farm and oversees the workforce. There are several other tofts round about, all belonging to various kin. From there I can draw on the support I need.' He relieved her of the cover and stowed it in the sea chest. 'In the meantime, we will be safe there.'

'Will we?'

'Have no fear. I won't let anything happen to you.'

Her gaze met his. 'Ah, yes, you always protect your interests, do you not?'

'That's right.'

'Should I find that reassuring?'

'That you should, since it means that no other man will touch you.'

The ramifications of that were enough to bring a tinge of colour to her face and neck. She ought to have been repelled, but the recollection of his arms around her, his nearness now and the expression in his eyes all contrived to create a sensation that was quite different. Unable to think of a reply, she looked away in confusion and began folding the rest of the bedding.

Chapter Thirteen

The steading in Agder was large and prosperous. As the ship entered the inlet Astrid could see several timber buildings and, beyond their shingled roofs, meadows in which cattle and horses grazed. Above the pasture, rowan and birch clad the lower shoulders of the hills before giving way to pine. After that the slopes grew steeper, leading the eye away to distant peaks of naked grey rock and patches of snow.

Their arrival had been noted. As the ship's keel crunched on shingle several men hurried to meet it. One or two called out greetings which were as warmly returned. The crew lost no time in going ashore and soon the air rang with men's voices. The atmosphere was definitely one of homecoming. Standing in the midst of the crowd, Astrid felt oddly isolated and more than ever aware of her ragged appearance which only served to underline her subservient position. She could only suppose that her life as a thrall was about to begin in earnest. It was a lowering thought.

'Well, well. What have we here?'

She looked up quickly to see a stranger. He was big and heavy set, dark of hair and beard; dark too were the eyes surveying her now. Astrid looked away. A large hand reached for her chin and forced her head round.

'Not bad,' he said. 'Not bad at all.'

Indignantly she jerked free of his hold. 'Get your hands off me.'

He chuckled softly. 'Spirited too. Better and better. I'll wager she's a lively piece in bed.'

'Speculate all you like, Gunnar,' said Leif. 'The only bed she shares is mine and you'd do well to remember it.'

Gunnar spread his hands in a gesture of resignation. 'No offence meant, my lord. Just admiring the goods.'

Broad grins greeted this and Astrid's cheeks turned crimson. However, she suppressed her anger, knowing better than to give it utterance. Leif seemed unperturbed.

'You may look,' he replied.

The rest was left unsaid. No one else ventured a comment, though the men exchanged knowing glances. Gunnar laughed and the moment passed. Presently the whole group headed towards the buildings Astrid had seen earlier. Since there was nothing else to be done she went with them.

As they drew nearer her eyes widened a little. This was indeed the house of a wealthy man. She guessed it must be at least thirty metres long. Great carved pillars flanked the main doors and carved finials projected like antlers above the shingled roof whence smoke curled up from a central hole.

No sooner had they reached the hall than a man appeared in the doorway. To judge from his grizzled hair and beard he was in his late forties, but, save for a wooden leg, he looked hale and strong. On seeing the new arrivals the man let out an exclamation of delight and hastened to meet them. Moments later Leif was embraced in a bear hug.

'Welcome back, my lord! It has been too long.'

Leif grinned and clapped him on the back. 'It's good to see you too, Aron.'

'What brings you here?'

'A series of misadventures.'

Aron's smile faded a little and he drew back looking properly now. As he took in the short hair and healing cut his eyes narrowed. 'It would seem you have much to tell.'

Leif nodded. 'That I do, but it will keep awhile.'

'As you say. Meanwhile, come in and take a cup of ale.'

They entered a large living space where several women were preparing food by a central hearth.

The smell of cooking mingled with wood smoke and the delicious aroma pervaded the whole space, reminding Astrid that she hadn't eaten for many hours. Not wishing to be seen staring, she let her gaze move on to the wide sleeping benches running down the sides of the room. The household retainers and servants would sleep there. The rear of the hall was divided off into other living quarters for the jarl and his family.

'Jarl Leif!' A woman's voice broke into her thoughts and she looked round to see a lady of middle years hurrying in via a side door. Her figure was full and her dark hair greying but her face was still handsome for all that. 'Welcome back.'

'Ingrid.' Leif smiled. 'You look well.'

'I am well, I thank you.' She returned his smile and then, as she too noticed his altered appearance, her smile faded a little. 'You have been in the wars or I miss my guess.'

'Wars enough,' he replied.

'Well, here you shall have a respite from fighting.'

'A respite only. My enemies must be dealt with.'

'Your enemies are ours, my lord.'

'Don't stand there gabbing, woman,' said Aron. 'Fetch ale for Jarl Leif and his men.'

'Of course I'm going to fetch ale,' she retorted. 'What do you take me for?'

With that she hurried off. Aron shook his head.

'I swear her tongue gets sharper with every passing year.'

Leif grinned. 'She's a fine woman and you know it.'

His companion scratched his chin meditatively. 'She has her moments.' He paused and glanced at Astrid. 'Speaking of fine women, where did you get that one?'

'I carried her off.'

'Ah, yes, of course. She'd be a welcome addition in any man's bed.'

'I didn't take her just to warm my bed. She's instrumental to my plans.'

Under the weight of the blue-grey gaze Astrid bridled. His manner towards her might have softened a little but otherwise nothing had changed.

'Is she indeed?' Aron regarded him in frank curiosity. 'Well, well. I look forward to hearing this.'

Just then Ingrid returned with two thralls carrying cups and ale, and the conversation turned to other things. When the men had refreshed themselves Aron told them where to stow their gear. For a moment or two Leif looked on. Then he summoned Ingrid and spoke some words for her alone. She heard him in silence and then nodded.

'As you wish, my lord.' She looked at Astrid. 'Come with me.'

For the space of a few heartbeats Astrid met Leif's gaze but he merely jerked his head towards the rear of the hall. 'Go.'

Taking a deep breath, she followed the older woman, wondering what her allotted tasks were going to be. They went through the rear of the hall, passing several curtained sleeping places, and out through a back door towards another smaller building. To Astrid's astonishment it was the bathhouse.

'You can wash here,' said Ingrid. 'There is water, soap and comb. In the meantime, I will fetch you some clean clothes.'

Without waiting for a reply she left again. Astrid looked around in bemusement but, nothing loath, began to remove her makeshift gown. The water was cold but she didn't care. The chance to be clean was too strong a lure. It was a luxury to have good quality soap too: beechwood ash and goat fat instead of the harsher lye. She scrubbed herself all over until her skin was pink, then combed out her hair before making use of the linen towel.

Ingrid returned with an armful of garments and a pair of leather shoes. 'Try these. They are likely near your size.'

Astrid thanked her and turned her attention to the clothing. There was a clean white shift, and a fine yellow woollen gown with a shorter russet overdress edged with green decorative binding. The shoes were slightly big but not unduly so, and a vast improvement on going barefoot.

Ingrid surveyed her curiously. 'That's better.'

'It feels better.'

'You might almost have been taken for a thrall, except of course that your hair has not been cropped.'

Astrid winced inwardly, knowing the words for truth. Thralls of both sexes had their hair cut short to demonstrate their lowly status. Leif could have humiliated her far more than he actually had.

'My clothing was the best that could be contrived in the circumstances.' It was a half-truth only but she was reluctant to go into details. Events were too recent and too raw. 'Thank you for the garments.'

'Thank Jarl Leif. It was done on his instruction.'

Astrid barely managed to conceal her surprise. She had no idea why he had done it, but she was grateful all the same. Until her recent captivity she had taken fine clothing for granted; something that was an automatic part of her status as a noblewoman. Without it there was nothing to distinguish her from the lowly. Bound up with that was the matter of self-esteem. Humiliate someone long enough and they might become the thing their persecutor wanted them to be. She shivered, trying not to think of what might have happened if Leif's crew hadn't come to find him.

Ingrid saw that tremor and frowned. 'You're cold. Come and sit outside awhile until your hair dries.'

Having directed her charge to a bench behind the hall, Ingrid departed on other errands. When she had gone Astrid shut her eyes and turned her face to the sun, enjoying the warmth and the temporary solitude. In the distance she could hear men's voices but not the words of their conversation. No doubt the new arrivals were relating their recent adventures. When her connection with those became known they would regard her with suspicion and possibly hostility. Family loyalties were strong and so was the oath that bound men to their jarl. Death was preferable to breaking it since the man who did that was a *nithing*. Betrayal of one meant the betrayal of all and vengeance was swift. *She's instrumental to my plans*, he had said. Astrid sighed. Vengeance had many forms.

'Are the clothes a reasonable fit?'

Leif's voice jolted her out of thought and she rose quickly. 'Oh! Yes, they are.'

'The colour looks well on you.' His gaze swept her from head to foot. 'It's an improvement all round, I think.'

'Very much so.' Her gaze met his. 'Apart from you, who else do I have to thank for this kindness?'

'No thanks are necessary.'

'These clothes must belong to someone.'

'Not any more. The woman who owned them is gone.'

'Won't she be back?'

'No, she won't be back.'

Astrid made a sudden leap of intuition. 'They belonged to your wife.'

For a moment she glimpsed a flicker of something like pain in his eyes. Then it was gone. 'She left them behind when the marriage…broke up. I didn't know, not for some time afterwards. When I found her things I moved the chest into storage and it's been there ever since.'

She was quietly astonished. Most men would have used them to make a bonfire, but then, he wasn't most men. Nor was his behaviour predictable. In this case, though, there seemed to be only one possible inference.

'You hoped she might come back.'

His expression hardened. 'There was no way back for us.'

'I'm sorry.'

'Don't waste your pity on the matter, and don't feel any concern about the dress either. When all's said and done it's just a piece of cloth.'

With that he turned and walked back into the hall. Astrid sank back on to the bench, her mind whirling. She hadn't meant to pry into his past but somehow the question had just come out. For all that he asserted otherwise, it was clearly a difficult and painful subject. At the same time, it left her wanting to know more, to understand what had happened. If she understood that she would be closer to understanding the man. It ought not to have mattered but she knew it did.

Leif walked through the hall and kept on going, needing a little time apart. He skirted the buildings and came to the edge of the meadow. There he stopped and leaned against the wooden rail, ostensibly surveying the cattle in the pasture beyond. In reality his mind was otherwise engaged. For all he had pretended otherwise, the recent conversation had unsettled him. Astrid was perceptive, disconcertingly so at times. He ought to have foreseen that she might ask about the origin of the dress. Of itself it didn't matter. It was what followed that had thrown him off balance, not least because the memory still had the power to hurt. He'd thought himself stronger, proof against the past. Time had helped but it hadn't entirely eradicated pain. He never spoke of it to anyone and those who knew respected his silence on the subject. It was better that way. Given the choice, he would never have returned to the steading, but he couldn't avoid it: the place was woven into his wyrd. He ought not to have been surprised: the Nornir were known to have a cruel sense of humour.

His gaze travelled on towards the edge of the trees and the small fenced area located nearby. He hadn't been back there in ten years, not since he'd buried his son. If he went, what would he find? A grassy mound and a couple of marker stones, mute witnesses to a night of horror. His gut tightened in response and for a moment he relived the griping pain and the sickness in the pit of his stomach. He closed his eyes and took a deep breath, waiting for the sensation to pass. Eventually it did, as always. He turned away. The past was done; what he needed to do now was secure the future.

When he felt sufficiently in command of himself again he went to find Aron. He was outside the hall giving instructions to one of the thralls but, on seeing Leif approach, he dismissed the slave and waited.

'We need to talk,' said Leif.

'As you wish.'

By tacit consent they walked apart a little way until they were out of earshot. Aron glanced at the younger man's face and interpreted the expression correctly.

'It cannot have been easy coming back here,' he said.

'It wasn't,' replied Leif, 'but I had little choice in the matter.'

He proceeded to give his friend a summary of events, omitting only what pertained to Astrid. Since he no longer believed in her guilt he was reluctant to implicate her. It would suffice to let his companion think he'd carried her off to be revenged upon Einar, and that chimed with what his crew believed too. Aron heard him out in frowning silence.

'You'll get the men you need, no question,' he said then. 'This treachery must be paid for in blood.'

'It will be.'

'And Einar's niece?'

'Stays here for the time being.'

'It was a shrewd move to carry her off. You have ensured that your enemies will meet you.'

'Just so.'

'What do you intend to do with her? Send them her head?'

Leif frowned. 'I will not use my sword against a woman.'

'No, or your former wife would have died long since. You would have been more than justified.'

'No, there was no justification for that.'

'Blood of Odin! The bitch tried to kill you, Leif.'

'She was not in her right mind then.'

Aron sighed. 'Well, be that as it may. Women are tricky creatures at the best of times.'

'So they are. However, as I said, this one is essential to my plans.'

'Best keep her close, then.'

'I mean to.'

His companion grinned. 'Day and night?'

'Day and night.'

'Ah. You mean to send her back with a child in her belly.'

Leif's smile faded. It was not an unnatural assumption but it jarred all the same. 'The thought had occurred to me.' Things had changed since then, but explanation was going to be difficult.

Aron eyed him closely. 'You really are intent on kicking the hornets' nest, aren't you?' He paused. 'Or is this about more than revenge?'

'What do you mean?'

'Perhaps you are not indifferent to your pretty captive.'

To his annoyance Leif felt himself redden. He opened his mouth to protest and then sighed. There was no point in lying to Aron. 'No, I want her all right. I have from the moment I first clapped eyes on her.'

'Fortunate, then, that she's in your power; now you can see your will well met. Take her and often. That way you'll soon get her out of your system.'

How simple it sounded, thought Leif, and, to an outsider, it probably was. After all, female slaves were routinely used in that way by their captors. The reasons why it wasn't going to happen in this instance were too complicated to explain.

'It's sound advice,' he said.

'Good.' Aron clapped him on the shoulder. 'As

to the rest, we must send word to Hammerstoft
and Borgshafen and convene a meeting. I predict
it won't be hard to raise men to your cause.'

Chapter Fourteen

That evening the ship's company joined the men of the steading and the hall rang with their voices. Astrid kept in the background, unwilling to draw attention to herself. Since their conversation that afternoon Leif had made no attempt to come near her. Ingrid had provided her with bread and meat and a cup of ale but, since her role had not been precisely defined, had not allocated her any tasks. At present Astrid was glad of it since it meant that she could keep apart from the company. As the night wore on the laughter had grown louder and the jests coarser. Tomorrow she would volunteer her services and find some occupation. That way she could occupy her hands and her mind and stop herself thinking too much about the future. She glanced across the hall at Leif. However, he was engrossed in male conversation and did not notice.

Her gaze moved on, taking in the whole scene. As she did so her eyes met Gunnar's. She saw him smile. Unbidden, that earlier scene returned and she looked away quickly. Not for anything would she encourage his interest.

Leif glanced across the room. He noticed Gunnar at once because, unlike everyone else, he took no part in the conversation. His attention was fixed elsewhere. Following the direction of his gaze, Leif frowned. Had his words failed to achieve their aim earlier on, or was Gunnar taking the advice and just looking? He hoped it was the latter. Astrid appeared not to have noticed that rapt gaze or else she was ignoring it. Wisely too, he decided. She belonged to him and he had no intention of allowing any trespass there. Perhaps he needed to reinforce that message.

Astrid stifled a yawn and glanced towards the open door behind her. The hall was hot, the air thick with the smells of roast meat and ale and male sweat. Everyone was engaged in conversation so it was unlikely her absence would even be noticed. Quietly she rose and stole away.

It was quiet outside, the air blessedly cool and smelling of grass and pine. A waxing moon had risen above the horizon to meet the stars. Once she would have enjoyed such a sight; tonight it only emphasised her present isolation and her weariness. Ingrid hadn't told her yet where she was to sleep but, after so long a day, the thought was becoming increasingly attractive. Probably she should go and ask.

She turned back towards the hall and then stopped abruptly to see the tall figure in the doorway.

'Leif.'

He moved closer. 'What are you doing out here?'

'It was too hot inside. I needed some air.'

'You shouldn't wander off.'

'Did you think I might run away?'

'No. I'd find you soon enough and you know it.'

'True. Therefore I will spare us both the trouble.'

'Very wise.'

Astrid remained silent, every part of her alive to him, to his nearness now and to the sudden quickening of her pulse. The very air seemed charged now as though with summer lightning; dangerous and exciting together.

'Have you eaten this evening?' he asked.

The question threw her off balance. 'Yes, I thank you. Ingrid gave me food earlier.'

'Good, I don't want you wasting away. My taste never ran to scrawny women.'

'Oh? And what is your taste exactly?'

'For soft full curves; bosom and hips in proportion, a slender waist and beautiful legs.' His gaze swept her. 'Much like yours, in fact.'

She was glad of the semi-darkness which hid the flush of colour in her cheeks. 'Am I supposed to be flattered?'

'The words weren't spoken to flatter you. I was just answering your question.' He paused. 'Of course, one cannot fully appraise a woman's figure until she's naked.'

'You would think that.'

'I'll wager most men would agree.'

The water was getting deeper by the minute and she needed to extricate herself. 'It may be so. My experience of men is limited.'

'And what you have experienced has not impressed you, has it?' he said softly.

Astrid looked away, unwilling to go there. 'It's getting late and it's been a tiring day.' She paused. 'I was about to go and speak to Ingrid and find out where I am to sleep this night.'

'I can tell you that,' he replied.

'Oh.'

'You'll be sleeping with me. Then we shall see about giving you an entirely different experience.'

Astrid felt the blood leap into her face. She opened her mouth to protest but no sound came out, only a ragged exhalation of breath. Then his hands were on her waist, drawing her closer. The touch seemed to burn. His lips nuzzled her neck, sending a tremor the length of her body. Winding her hair round his hand he tilted her head back and continued, pressing hot kisses to her neck and throat. Suddenly it was hard to think at all.

'My lord, I...'

The words were stopped with a lingering and passionate kiss that paid no heed to protest and ignored all resistance. And gradually resistance subsided and her mouth yielded to his and the kiss became deeper and more persuasive, setting every nerve alight, and she was aware of nothing except the hard-muscled body pressed to hers and the scent and the taste of him. It sent another shiver through her that had nothing to do with repugnance.

'You're beautiful, Astrid. Beautiful and very desirable.'

He bent and slipped an arm under her knees, lifting her easily; then carried her to his sleeping place. Her gaze took in his sea chest and war gear, and then the big box bed covered with furs. He set her down and drew the curtain behind them. Heart thumping, she watched him come closer until only inches separated them. His gaze never left her but he said nothing. Instead he reached for her overdress and deftly removed it before turning his attention to her gown. He removed that too so that only the linen shift remained. Then he drew her to him for another kiss, gentler this time, seeking her response. She could feel the warmth of his hands through the thin fabric and the answering shiver along her skin. Leif felt it and drew back, surveying her steadily, and she read the unspoken question in his face.

She took a step away from him. He made no move to prevent it, his expression impassive. However, the blue-grey eyes spoke for him. He wanted her but he wouldn't use force; what happened next was her decision. Her heart thumped. Slowly she drew off the shift and let it fall. The response was a sharp intake of breath. The sound was oddly empowering, like the fleeting look of surprise in his eyes. She lifted her chin. Unhurriedly she reached for the binding and unfastened her hair, shaking it loose over her shoulders.

When it was done she rejoined him. Leif reached for his belt but she caught his hands, checking him. 'No, let me.'

He let his hands fall to his sides while she unlatched the belt. Taking the bottom of his tunic in both hands, she drew it up over his chest. He lifted his arms and bent a little to accommodate its removal. The shirt followed. Her hands moved to the fastenings of his breeches and pulled them free; then pushed the fabric down over his hips. He kicked off his shoes and stepped out of the breeches.

His arms closed about her waist. Astrid slid her arms around his neck and pressed herself against his body. Almost immediately she felt him grow hard and for a moment memory reawakened. She pushed it firmly aside. This was nothing like the other time. There was no reason for fear or disgust. She wanted this. She wanted him.

Tilting her face, she invited his kiss. His hold tightened and the kiss grew more intimate. She yielded to it, letting her tongue flirt with his in a light teasing dance. He walked her backwards towards the bed, but instead of pushing her down and pinning her there, he manoeuvred her round so their positions were reversed. To her surprise he lay down first. Then he reached out a hand in invitation. She took it and joined him there. He moved over a little to give her room and then resumed where they'd left off, his hands caressing her in a leisurely exploration of her body, a firm and assured touch that set her flesh tingling. His lips grazed her neck and breast before his mouth closed over the peak, sucking lightly, drawing the nipple taut, a sensation so delicious that the breath caught in her throat.

She had thought that she knew what was going to happen, that she knew the facts of life and was therefore fully prepared. Leif wasn't going to hurt her. What she hadn't anticipated was his restraint, or the total absence of haste and coercion. She relaxed a little and tried to follow his lead, caressing him back, enjoying the play of his muscles beneath her fingers; enjoying the reciprocal touch of his hands on her body. A touch that was both skilled and seductive and arousing. No one had ever touched her like that before and it kindled something inside her that she hadn't known existed.

His hand moved over her waist and buttocks and swept the length of her thigh and slid thence between her legs. She tensed, feeling suddenly uncertain. When he continued she rebelled. Slowly, patiently he brought her back to him; then renewed the caress. This time she permitted it. When nothing terrible happened she relaxed a little, trusting him. The touch was gentle and not unpleasant, affording a glimpse of intimacies hitherto unsuspected. As he continued it created a pool of warmth in the core of her pelvis. The sensation became pleasurable. Instinctively she relaxed her thighs, wanting him to go on. Leif guided her hand to his erection. Unsure what he wanted, she closed her fingers around him and tentatively stroked. When he groaned she hesitated.

'It's all right,' he whispered. 'Don't stop.'

'I'm not hurting you?'

'No, you're not hurting me.'

Obediently she resumed and heard another sharp intake of breath. Inside her the pool of warmth expanded and her own breathing quickened. The thought of him inside her was no longer alarming; it was exciting. His fingers slid through slickness and a coil of tension formed in response. She shivered with pleasure, her body arching towards him, sensing something just beyond it, something she wanted but couldn't name.

He parted her thighs and slid into her. Astrid waited for pain but it didn't come. All she experienced was a slight discomfort. Nor was there any fear, only wanting.

He frowned. 'Are you all right, sweetheart?'

She nodded. Still he took his time, moving gently, holding back, doing nothing that might alarm or disgust her. Astrid closed her eyes, letting her body move with him, feeling the rhythm build.

'Put your legs around me.'

Again she obeyed him and it felt natural and right; natural and right to pull him closer, to surrender to his will and hold nothing back. The rhythm grew stronger and the tension coiled tighter inside her. Closing her eyes, she reached for it, willing it closer but still it eluded her, tantalisingly, teasing.

Leif let go of restraint and thrust into her deep and hard, need overtaking him, wanting full possession of her now. Astrid gasped, the blood pounding in her ears, body quivering, every fibre alive to him, revelling in submission. She felt him shudder and groan and then the spasm before the hot rush of his seed inside her.

Breathing hard, he held her there awhile as though unwilling to let her go. The blue-grey gaze locked with hers, hot, fierce, possessive. Then, slowly, the expression faded and he withdrew and rolled aside. Astrid shut her eyes. She felt boneless, sated, her entire being resonating with him. He had been considerate beyond all expectation—the entire experience had been beyond all expectation. Had that been his intention? Was her consent more satisfying to him than rape would have been? The spark between them had always been strong and once she had hoped it might develop into something more than mere physical desire. That was before she became the object of his revenge.

Leif lay still, waiting for his heartbeat to slow, every part of him conscious of the woman beside him. He had expected to enjoy her; what he hadn't anticipated was the blood-stirring thrill that he'd just experienced. His flesh tingled with it, imagination already moving ahead to other delicious possibilities. *Take her and often...get her out of your system.* He frowned. Although the first part of that injunction was simple, the second wasn't, not any more. Far from breaking the charm, gratification of desire had just made it stronger. The disenchantment that usually followed sex was conspicuous by its absence this time. Not only did he still want Astrid, he wanted to take her until she begged for mercy, until he displaced every other thought in her mind. She hadn't achieved the full height of pleasure this time but it was going to happen. She was going to be his, body and soul. It occurred to him then that there might be other outcomes. It was entirely possible that he might get her with child. What then? His frown deepened. It might have been wiser to withdraw before spilling his seed but he hadn't wanted to be wise, and anyway he wasn't sure he could have demonstrated such a degree of control. Such pleasure as he'd just experienced was rare and, far from making him cautious, it only made him hungry for more.

Astrid saw his expression and her heart sank. Had she disappointed him? Angered him in some way? Did consummation mean the end of his interest? Perhaps if she'd been more experienced she might have been able to please him better and he might have considered keeping her. It would be infinitely preferable to the alternative. Now that her value as a bride was gone, Jarl Einar would have no further use for her. Nor would he hesitate to use the quickest way to be rid of the burden she represented. He'd cut her throat and have her body flung into a pit. She could never go back. The only friend she had in the world now was Ragnhild and she was far away, unable to help. Astrid shivered.

'You're cold.' Leif shifted position and reached for the coverlet. Then he checked, staring at the smears of blood on the sheet. 'I think you're about to start your flux, sweetheart.'

'My flux?' Astrid followed his gaze and then

reddened. 'But that's not due for another ten—'
She broke off, mentally berating herself for speaking without thinking.

As the other implication dawned, his eyes narrowed. 'Then what you said before wasn't true, was it?'

'It was true, as far as it went.'

'As far as it went?'

'A man did try to force himself on me, but I managed to get away from him before he could do so.' She hesitated. 'I let you think it was rape because I was afraid that you wcrc going to...well, you were there, you know why.'

'Gods, Astrid!' His frown deepened. 'Did I hurt you just now?'

'No.'

Some of the tension left him. 'All the same, I wish you'd told me.'

'Are you angry?'

'Not angry. Surprised.'

She had no trouble believing him, but why he should attach importance to the matter now when he had not before was hard to understand.

'Don't lie to me again,' he went on, 'even by omission.'

'I'm sorry it was necessary.'

'So am I. In future I'll try not to create a situation where you'd want to resort to such a ploy.'

It was the closest he had come to an apology, but she had never expected him to unbend so far.

'All right.'

'All right, then.' He drew a cover over her. 'Here, before you catch cold.'

She summoned a smile of thanks and snuggled deeper into the bed. In spite of the awkwardness of the past few minutes, she was glad that the truth was out and that he understood why she had been economical with it in the first place. Perhaps now they could move on. After that first amazing sexual experience her imagination was alive with possibilities, knowing instinctively that there was more to discover and that he was key to that.

However, he seemed disinclined to pursue the matter. She had heard it said that men were often indifferent after desire had been sated and hoped it wasn't the case here, and that he might at least curve his body around hers and hold her as he had done the previous night.

She waited but he made no further move to touch her. It tended to reinforce the thought that, even if he wasn't angry, he was no longer interested either. Astrid turned on her side and shut her eyes, fighting disappointment.

Half an hour went by and Leif remained where he was. Surprise didn't come close to what he'd felt just now, but he'd meant it when he told her he wasn't angry. On the contrary, it pleased him to know that there hadn't been a man before him. More than ever he was thankful that he'd taken his time and hadn't hurt her. She ought to have told him the truth but he understood why she hadn't. His former behaviour was not to his credit. Of course, he had been angry then, but anger wasn't his sole motivation. The thought of her had excited him then and it still did. That was the trouble.

If he touched her now it wasn't going to stop there, not by a long way. The very thought was enough to set him alight and it was too soon to give desire free rein. Tonight was just the first step on a much longer journey, but he'd shown her that intercourse didn't have to be attended by violence, that there could also be pleasure in it for a woman as well as for a man. There was much he intended to teach her, but to do that he required a willing pupil. Next time he took her he wanted her to be eager and curious.

Imagination fuelled desire and he gritted his teeth, ruthlessly suppressing the wave of warmth in his groin. Gods! Just thinking about what he wanted to do with her was enough to make him hard. Half a minute more and resolution would be dead.

He propped himself on an elbow and dropped a kiss on her hair. 'Goodnight, vixen.'

She turned a little and glanced round. For a moment the violet eyes searched his, their expression questioning; he had almost said pleading. 'Goodnight, my lord.'

His gaze rested a moment on her naked shoulder now visible through heavy tresses of pale gold hair. He wanted to stroke it, to wrap it around his hand again and pull her head back for a long, deep kiss and then… He stopped himself there. Stroke her hair and he'd be lost faster than a ship on a reef. With a supreme effort he turned on his side and closed his eyes, mentally counting to a hundred.

Chapter Fifteen

When Astrid awoke next morning the place beside her was empty. Leif's clothes were gone and so were his sword and dagger. Hurriedly she rose and dressed and then went to find Ingrid.

'Jarl Leif rode out early with half-a-dozen men. He has gone to meet with his kin at a neighbouring steading.'

Astrid heard the news with disquiet but not surprise. 'He hopes to raise an armed force, doesn't he?'

'For sure.' Ingrid sighed. 'Always there must be fighting and bloodshed.'

'I think he has no choice now. Until he deals with his enemies he will always be looking over his shoulder.'

The older woman nodded. 'Men make war and women sit at home and wait for them to return.'

'I cannot just sit and wait,' replied Astrid. 'There must be something I can do.'

'There's work aplenty if you're willing.'

'I'm willing.'

'Very well. You could make a start on this pile of mending. I swear torn shirts breed in the night.'

'Give me a needle and thread and I'll get started.'

She took a basket of work to the bench outside where the light was good and she could work undisturbed. It was a relief to have something to do and the mechanical act of stitching was soothing in its way. However, it could not entirely keep her thoughts from drifting. She wondered what Leif was doing. Whatever it was he would have dismissed her from his mind entirely. Men satisfied their physical need and then moved on without feeling any emotional involvement. For a woman it was different. Last night Leif had made her his, an experience that would remain with her always, as indelible as a brand. She was his mistress now in good truth and he would keep her as long as it pleased him. When he tired of her he would cast her off and forget about her. That would be his revenge. How much more complete it would be if she were foolish enough to let him conquer her heart as well! That at least was within her power to prevent.

She could almost envy Einar and the rest: their fate would be found at the point of a sword, swift and sudden and soon over. Hers was likely to be long and painful. Sharing Leif's bed was going to have consequences eventually and he knew that. *Was it part of his plan to get her with child and then cast her off? Could he be so cold-blooded?* Suddenly the sunshine didn't seem quite as warm as it had.

To take her mind off the future she worked diligently all morning and gradually the pile of mended garments grew.

Ingrid returned at midday with a platter of bread and cheese and a cup of ale which she set down on the bench nearby.

'Just to keep the wolf from the door,' she said.

Astrid thanked her and laid aside her work. Her companion eyed the neat stitching with approbation.

'You sew well.'

'It is a necessary skill, like spinning and weaving.' She smiled wryly. 'My mother once told me that when she was young no man would consider taking a bride until he had ascertained her ability in those areas.'

Ingrid nodded. 'It's true, and it still holds good; at least it does in the country area where I was brought up.' She took a seat on the bench, regarding Astrid curiously. 'Is your mother still alive?'

'No. Both my parents died when I was young.'

'Aron says that your birth is good.'

'So it is.'

'He also says that Jarl Leif carried you off. Is that true?'

'It's true.'

'And he has taken you to his bed.'

Astrid knew there was no point in denying it. Likely everyone in the hall knew where she had slept last night. In such a close community it was impossible to keep the matter secret. Although the curtained sleeping places allowed a measure of privacy, sound still travelled. In all probability they had been overheard. 'That too.'

The older woman shook her head. 'I do not wonder that he should want to, but in good conscience a noblewoman should not be treated thus. He should marry you.'

Astrid's hand paused over the platter. 'I do not think that is his intention.'

'He had a bad experience before and that has coloured his view. Even so, he should do the right thing now.'

'He said that his first marriage had not worked out. That it ended in divorce.'

'So it did, although it was happy enough to begin with apparently; a match that had the blessing of both their families. From what I've been told, Thora was very attractive and Jarl Leif much in love with her.'

'What happened?'

'I don't know all the details, for I had not married Aron then and had not come to live here. It seems everything went well enough until Thora had a child. After that she changed completely, became strange in the head. Things happened…'

'What things?'

'Aron will not say, and none of the others who were here at the time are willing to speak of it either.' Ingrid paused. 'Well, I suppose sleeping dogs are best left alone.'

Astrid pondered the words after her companion had gone because they afforded an insight into Leif's past, to the events that had shaped him. Clearly he was not incapable of loving or of being hurt. Whatever had happened back then profoundly affected him though. Was that why subsequent relationships with women were always transitory affairs? If so, it didn't augur well for her. *He should marry you.* She smiled sadly, knowing that marriage was the very last thing on his mind.

It was late afternoon before she finished the mending and returned the basket of clothing.

'I've been sitting too long. I need to stretch my legs for a while.' She paused. 'And before anyone asks, I'm not going to try and run away.'

Ingrid nodded. 'As you will.'

Astrid left her and, taking care to remain in clear view, strolled to the edge of the pasture. She had no doubt that she was being watched, albeit at a distance. A glance over her shoulder revealed that her intuition was correct: there was a man by the end of the barn and another near the weaving shed. Leif wouldn't take any chances. He'd permitted her a fair amount of freedom and she wasn't about to give him a reason to change his mind.

She turned away and leaned on the wooden rail, surveying the cattle and horses grazing quietly on the early summer grass. It was a pleasant spot which made it hard to think that it had also been the scene of misfortune too. Had Leif found it hard to come back here? *I follow the whale road.* Was that because it seemed to offer a complete break with the past? She couldn't blame him for wanting that. The trouble was that the past always caught up eventually.

Her gaze moved on, surveying the wider scene. A track ran alongside the edge of the pasture and led the eye to another fenced area on the edge of the trees. Curious, she set off in that direction. On reaching the place she realised it was a burial ground. Carefully placed stones formed boat graves, three in all. In addition there were a couple of other interments, identified by simpler head and foot markers. Had these people been Leif's kin?

A shadow fell across the grass and she turned quickly to see one of the men who had been watching her before.

'You should return to the hall, lady.'

The tone was courteous but she knew that the words weren't a suggestion. Like all of Leif's men, he was tall and well made, easily able to use compulsion if he had to. However, Astrid had no intention of being combative.

'Very well.' Turning her back on the burial ground, she began to retrace her steps. 'Whose graves are those? Do you know?'

'I don't know, lady. It's the first time I've ever been here.'

'You haven't been with Jarl Leif very long, then.'

'Four years.'

'He hasn't been back here at all?'

'No, lady.'

She digested that carefully but made no reply. Even for an adventurer that was a long time to be away from home. Unless he had chosen not to return. The events Ingrid spoke of went back further than four years so this man would likely have no knowledge of them. At all events he said no more, and she was content to leave the matter there.

As they neared the hall she heard the sound of hooves and then men's voices raised in greeting. Her pace increased. She entered the building and hurried through the private quarters to the public area where Ingrid was ordering the servants to fetch ale for Jarl Leif and his men. Astrid paused at the edge of the room, her eyes seeking one man among the rest. He was in conversation with Aron and had his back to her, but the mere sight of him was enough to quicken her pulse. A servant offered both men a cup of ale and then moved on to the others. The conversation resumed. She could not hear their words but the mood seemed relaxed so perhaps the day's business had gone well.

Several more men entered through the main door and several called greetings to their friends. With them was Gunnar. He paused, looking casually round the room. As his gaze lighted on Astrid he smiled. She ignored it, hoping he'd take the hint.

'Would you mind?' asked Ingrid. She nodded to the jugs of ale she was carrying. 'An extra pair of hands would be useful.'

'Of course.'

Astrid relieved her of one of the jugs and moved away. As she filled cups some of the men acknowledged her with a smile. It was a small thing but it made her feel less of an outsider. As she approached Leif glimpsed her out of the corner of his eye and turned round.

'In good time, lady, for I've a thirst on me.'

She refilled his cup. 'I hope your journey was successful, my lord.'

'Aye, it was.' He slipped an arm around her waist. 'Did you miss me?'

'Of course. I did nothing but think of you all day.'

He smiled and raised an eyebrow. 'Much as I'd like to, I find that hard to believe.'

She pretended to consider. 'Well, now that you mention it, I did a pile of mending too.'

'If I came second to a pile of mending I'm going to have to try harder to dominate your thoughts.'

The ramifications of that created an unsettling glow of warmth in the region of her pelvis. 'I did not say that you came second, my lord.'

'No, vixen, though I'll wager it's true anyway.'

'You do me wrong,' she protested. 'I'm sure I thought of you as often as you thought of me.'

His eyes gleamed. 'I seriously doubt that.'

'You were too busy recruiting an army to think about anything else.'

'You have a way of lingering in the mind.'

Astrid shook her head. 'I still don't believe you.' She made to move away but his hold tightened, preventing it.

'Stay, vixen.'

There was no realistic prospect of doing anything else. Besides, she didn't want to. This lighter mood was a side to him that he rarely showed, like the mischievous gleam in his eyes. It was attractive on its own but when combined with his closeness and the warmth of his arm around her it became dangerously charismatic, a danger she didn't want to avoid. Nor did he seem in any hurry to be rid of her even when the men resumed their conversation. Anyone watching could have been forgiven for thinking them a devoted couple. Only the two of them knew how far that was from the truth.

Leif finished his ale and tossed the cup to a servant. Then he retired to his sleeping quarters, taking Astrid with him.

'I would wash before I eat. It feels like I've got half the dust of the road stuck to me.'

'I'll fetch you some water, my lord.'

'Presently,' he replied. 'First I want a kiss.'

'Do I have anything to say about this?'

'No.'

Reaching for her waist, he pulled her closer and brought his mouth down over hers. He tasted pleasantly of ale. It mingled with the strong masculine scents of leather and musk and horses. As if of their own volition, her arms slid round his neck and she pressed closer, kissing him back. His hold tightened and the kiss became deeper. A low growling sound rumbled in his throat and he drew back a little.

'Careful, vixen, or you're going to find yourself on that bed with your skirts around your waist.'

She smiled. 'Perhaps I'd better go and fetch that water.'

'Perhaps you had.'

She stepped away from him and picked up the empty wooden bowl. Then with a last glance over her shoulder she was gone.

Leif let out a long breath, uncomfortably aware of the partial erection swelling against his breeks.

Another minute and he'd have been past the point where he could control himself, a situation he found both erotic and disturbing. In spite of his earlier bantering tone, he had thought about her that day: both on the ride there when the recollection of the previous night was uppermost in mind, and again on the ride home when the notion of seeing her once more filled him with pleasurable anticipation. *Get her out of your system.* He shook his head, knowing that he was further than ever from that point.

He didn't linger in the hall that evening. Long hours in the saddle combined with the thought of being alone with Astrid made retiring early an attractive option. Once again he made love to her and once again he took his time, watching, listening, always paying close attention to the language of her body. This time she yielded herself without the need for coaxing, following his lead, learning the things that pleased him, but she still wasn't sufficiently relaxed for him to be able to take her to the full height of pleasure. It made him all the more determined that he would. This combination of sensuality and vulnerability was a new experience for him; it titillated his imagination and made him feel protective at the same time. Along with that was an unexpected streak of possessiveness. Her favours were for him alone.

That thought introduced darker ones and ques-

tions that needed answers. Propping himself on
an elbow, he looked into her face.

'The man who tried to rape you, Astrid. Who
was he?'

She blinked, taken by surprise and by the di-
rectness of the question. Given the choice, she'd
have preferred not to revisit the topic, but she suspected he would not be put off. She'd been the
one to mention it in the first place so perhaps if
she told him the matter could be laid to rest once
and for all.

'His name was Ozur. He was an older cousin
who came to live at my father's hall and learn the
skills of the warrior. I had little to do with him:
he was five years older to start with and close-
mouthed and sullen besides, not an easy person
to be with. But, as time went on, he began to pay
me closer attention.' She paused and took a deep
breath. 'I'd see him looking at me. He never said
or did anything that might have attracted criti-
cism or reproof; he just looked. Then, one day,
when I returned from a ride, he was waiting in
the barn. He exposed himself and then grabbed
hold of me, but I bit him and he let go long enough
for me to escape.'

'Did you tell anyone about it?'

She shook her head. 'I knew if I did that there
would be terrible trouble. In any case the whole
incident was so unpleasant that I felt ashamed to
speak of it.'

'The shame was all his, not yours.'

'I know that now, but at the time…well, I was twelve and quite unsuspecting that a man might behave in that way. I was also afraid that if I spoke, Ozur would find some way to take revenge. He was that kind.'

'What happened to him?'

'He was killed in a tavern brawl two years later, an argument over a game of dice apparently. He lost his temper with the wrong person and got a knife in the belly.'

'I cannot suppose that grieved you overmuch.'

'It didn't. All I felt was relief that I'd never have to see him again.' She sighed. 'Even so, I never forgot him.'

'Memory isn't so easy to banish, is it?' He sighed. 'I wish it were.'

The sigh was heartfelt and she would have given much to know what the memories were that troubled him so, but if she asked he might be angry and that would destroy the present mood. 'Time helps but we never forget.'

'No,' he replied, 'we never forget.'

Putting an arm around her, he drew her closer and they lapsed into silence. Although he wasn't sorry to get at the truth, Leif was conscious of conflicting emotions. He'd met one or two like Ozur in his time; brooding and dangerous brutes with the temper of pit vipers, incapable of mercy.

He hoped that whoever had plunged the knife into the snake had done it more than once, and twisted the blade as well. It disturbed him to recall how close he'd come to his own baser nature. If he'd yielded to it he'd have been no better than Ozur.

He glanced down at Astrid but her eyes were closed now, her breathing soft and regular. Taking care not to disturb her, he reached for the coverlet and drew it over them.

It pleased him that she should have confided the matter, and he felt honoured to be the recipient of that confidence. As he knew all too well, secrets long kept dark became harder to reveal. Sometimes there were no words to explain. If he could have found the words he knew that she would be the person he'd talk to; the person he'd have trusted with the truth.

Chapter Sixteen

Over the next few weeks Leif was often absent from the steading, engaged in visiting his kin and others whose allegiance he could rely on, slowly gathering the force he needed. That part wasn't hard. There were men ready and willing to fight. However, they had to be equipped and shaped into a cohesive unit. That meant discussions with blacksmiths and armourers and long days overseeing training.

In his absence Astrid occupied herself well enough. As Ingrid had said, there was plenty of work around. The heavy tasks were invariably undertaken by servants and thralls but it still left enough to keep Astrid busy. She missed Leif when he was gone and looked forward to his return. Whether it was wise or not, her feelings for him had grown strong and she could no longer deny them. She had no idea of his emotions, if indeed he felt anything for her. While he treated her well enough now he never spoke his inmost thoughts or suggested that she was anything more to him than a mistress. Along with that was a growing sense of disquiet about the preparations in hand. She understood that he had to confront his enemies eventually but what if their force proved stronger? What if it was Leif who fell in battle? The possibility filled her with cold dread. He had always seemed so much larger than life that it was impossible to visualise a world where he was not. Equally she had to face the fact that, having dealt with his enemies, he might see no reason to keep her. Essentially his revenge would be complete.

Pushing these gloomy thoughts aside forced her attention back to the loom, focusing instead on the growing length of cloth she had been working on. Late afternoon sunlight slanted through the open window and doorway. The men would be back soon, tired and hungry and ready for the meal that Ingrid was overseeing in the hall. She could probably complete another half inch of cloth before it was time to stop for the day. By then a meal and some company would not be unwelcome.

She worked on for a while until a sound behind her stopped the shuttle and she looked around to see a tall figure silhouetted in the doorway. For a brief moment she thought it was Leif. Then he stepped across the threshold and her smile faded as she recognised Gunnar.

'What are you doing here?'

'I came to see you.'

'Now you've found me. What do you want?'

'Don't you know, Astrid?'

The tone and accompanying expression set off alarm bells in her head. Suddenly she was aware of their relative isolation, of his greater size and that he was between her and the door. Her only hope was to talk her way out of this.

'I haven't the faintest idea what you're talking about.'

'I think you do.'

'I think you should go.'

'Why so unfriendly?' He took another pace towards her. 'I mean you no harm.'

'Clearly our understanding of the word differs.'

'I'm not asking for anything you haven't given a man before.'

Her skin crawled but she forced herself to meet his gaze. 'Get out. Go now and perhaps I won't mention this to Jarl Leif.'

He smiled and came on. 'Jarl Leif won't concern himself over anything as trivial as the sharing of a whore's favours.'

She edged away from him, heart pounding. 'Stay away from me.'

'Stay away?' His smile faded. 'I'm going to swive you senseless, slut.'

Without taking his eyes off her he unfastened his breeks to reveal the erection beneath. Her throat dried. She tried to dodge round him in a last desperate attempt to reach the door. With the speed of a striking snake he caught her by the waist, lifting her off her feet. Astrid shrieked. Kicking and struggling, she was borne inexorably across the room and slammed up against the wall. Her nails raked his cheek, scoring a line of red welts. He slapped her hard, rocking her head back. Warm blood trickled from her lip. As he grabbed hold of her skirts she screamed again, fighting like a cornered lynx. The scream was choked off by a hand round her throat. She clawed at his wrist, trying to break the hold, but the grip was like iron. Suddenly it was harder to breathe. Spots of colour danced before her eyes.

'Let her go.'

Gunnar froze. His hold slackened and then she was free. Astrid gasped, sucking in a lungful of air, her wide-eyed gaze moving past her assailant to the man behind him. When she realised who it was she felt almost faint with relief. She tried to speak but only a faint croaking sound came out.

Leif kept the sword against Gunnar's ribs. 'Give me one reason why I shouldn't spit you where you stand?'

'It was just a bit of fun, my lord. Nothing more.'

'Fun?' The point of the blade pressed a little deeper. 'Did you just say *fun*?'

Before Gunnar could reply, Astrid heard running feet and seconds later Harek, Ingolf and Trygg burst through the doorway. On seeing Leif, they checked abruptly, exchanging uncertain glances. Then Harek cleared his throat.

'Beg pardon, my lord, only we thought we heard a woman screaming just now and decided we'd better investigate.'

Leif nodded. 'You did hear a woman screaming. *My* woman.'

The words produced stunned silence. They looked from him to Astrid, taking in the bruises on her throat and the blood trickling from the cut on her lip. Their eyes narrowed and turned their attention to Gunnar.

He licked his lower lip. 'The woman's a whore. Where's the harm in—?'

The words broke off as the pommel of the sword struck him across the back of the head, felling him like a poleaxed steer. Leif surveyed the still form dispassionately.

'Bind him and take him to the hall.'

Ingolf eyed Gunnar's naked groin with disgust. 'Shall we cut off his balls as well, my lord? It'd be no trouble.'

'Trouble?' muttered Trygg. 'It would be a pleasure.'

Leif shook his head. 'No, just get him out of my sight. I'll deal with him presently.'

As the men moved into action, he turned to

Astrid, his gaze smouldering. She wanted to speak but the words wouldn't come. Her entire body was trembling now. He said nothing, only put his arms around her and held her close, gently stroking her hair until the shaking subsided.

When she was a little calmer he took her back to his quarters and made her sit down while he fetched water and cloth and a small pot of salve. Then he set about bathing the cut on her lip. The cold water made her wince but she made no complaint, submitting quietly to his ministrations.

'It isn't deep,' he said, 'but it'll take a couple of days for the swelling to disappear.' He laid down the cloth and dipped a finger in the salve. 'This will take the sting out of it.'

'What is it?'

'Honey. It's good for healing.' He applied it carefully, the touch feathering along her skin. Then he scrutinised his handiwork. 'That's better.'

'It feels a little easier already. Thank you.'

'You're welcome.' He paused, surveying her critically. 'You still look pale. Lie down for a while and rest.'

'I'm all right now, truly.'

'When will you learn to do as you're told, vixen?'

A smile robbed the words of any sting but the look in his eyes was all too familiar. Knowing it was pointless to argue, Astrid gave in.

'All right. Just for a while.'

When she had lain down he pulled a cover over her and kissed her lightly on the cheek. 'Rest now.'

She watched him move away but when he reached the threshold he paused.

'I'm sorry for what happened today. Rest assured, Gunnar will be punished for his crime.'

'What will you do to him?'

The blue-grey eyes glinted. 'That need not concern you.'

Astrid started up on one elbow. 'Leif?'

'Gunnar was warned. He chose to ignore that.'

'What he did was wrong but surely...'

Leif's expression was as hard and cold as frosted steel. 'No man challenges my authority with impunity,' he replied, 'and no man touches what is mine.'

With that he departed. Astrid fell back on the bed and shut her eyes, her mind in turmoil. Her lip throbbed and her bruised throat hurt. The memory of Gunnar was keen and the knowledge of what he had been about to do to her. *If Leif hadn't arrived when he did...* The thought wouldn't finish itself. The whole business made her feel queasy. Even so, would she have demanded a man's life in payment for the crime? She let out a ragged breath, knowing that such hesitation would be seen only as weakness. Gunnar had broken a taboo and he would pay for it with his life. Leif would have no mercy and nor would his men respect him for showing any. By now everyone on the steading would know what had happened and they would expect their jarl to dispense swift and summary justice. That expectation would be met.

However, it was about more than discipline and authority, she realised. By acting thus Leif was also sending out a clear message to the rest. *No man touches what is mine.* After this, no one else would lay a hand on her. It wasn't just a protective move either: to enact his revenge he needed to keep her safe. In the meantime, she was reserved for his pleasure alone. The knowledge did nothing to raise her spirits.

The atmosphere in the hall was sombre that evening, the conversation muted. Those who glanced in the jarl's direction registered his mood and left him to his thoughts. Thorvald was less reticent.

'You did what you had to. No one questions that.'

Leif nodded. 'I know. The matter leaves a bad taste though.'

'It could have been much worse.'

Leif didn't care to think about how much worse it might have been; what would have happened if he'd returned to the steading just a little bit later. The sight that greeted him in the weaving shed created a surge of fury unlike anything he'd known before. *She's just a whore.* His jaw tightened. He'd never been able to see Astrid in that light any more than he'd been able to see her as a thrall. That another man should think her available for his entertainment was intolerable. Until then Leif hadn't concerned himself too much with the reactions of others; today's events had revealed a fundamental shift in his thinking that had happened a while ago without him even being aware of it.

'The fact that it wasn't a lot worse is the reason Gunnar got a quick, clean death,' he replied.

'Some might think he got off lightly in that respect.'

'People may think what they like, but if they're wise they won't mention his name again.'

Thorvald took the hint and changed the subject. For a while they talked of military matters but Leif was not in the humour for protracted conversation of any kind, and after a while he rose and took his leave.

Instead of returning directly to his quarters though, he went outside, needing some fresh air. The night was cool and when he glanced up the stars were hidden by cloud. A breeze was blowing in from the west and it smelled of rain. He took a deep breath and exhaled it slowly, letting some of the tension go with it, and then strolled to the edge of the pasture. The quiet was welcome because it allowed him to order his thoughts. Events that day might have been unexpected and unpleasant but they had also concentrated his mind on a problem that had been teasing him for weeks. He'd been letting matters drift but that would no longer serve: he was going to have to make a decision.

When he retired some time later it was to find Astrid fast asleep so he undressed and slid into bed without disturbing her. She looked remarkably peaceful. In a few days the bruises would be gone and there would be no outer signs of the assault. Whether it had done lasting damage in other ways remained to be seen. It wouldn't have been surprising if she'd fallen into a fit of hysterics after what had happened, but she'd proved more resilient and more courageous. It was only when he put his arms around her that he'd realised how much she was shaking. It reinforced his sense of her vulnerability and his own protective instincts. Along with that was a streak of jealousy he hadn't known he possessed. At the time anger was too great for words. Besides, what could he have said that would not sound like a platitude? He couldn't change what had happened but he could ensure it never happened again, not to her or any other woman. Gunnar had got off lightly, all things considered.

Chapter Seventeen

For a few days after her ordeal, Leif made no attempt to force himself on Astrid when they retired. Instead he seemed content just to hold her. If he kissed her it was on the cheek or the forehead, thus avoiding the cut lip. That patient consideration did him no disservice in her eyes, or his gentleness either. It was a side to him that she found both unexpected and compelling. In so many ways he was a paradox, and yet the warlord and the lover were indisputably the same man. Except, she reflected sadly, that he didn't love her and never had; he'd always been honest about that. A degree of consideration was the best she could hope for from him.

His present mood encouraged her to think she might broach a subject that had been much on her mind; the matter of what he meant to do with her in the end. In all the time they'd been together Leif had never done her physical injury or permitted anyone else to either. That being so, might he not let her go to Ragnhild rather than sending her back to her uncle which would mean almost certain death? Having taken his pleasure, would he be prepared to show her that much mercy? She could only pray he might. In any event it would be better to know than to live in uncertainty and that meant asking him. Not just yet perhaps, but soon. It was just a matter of finding the right moment.

Leif and Aron stood at the edge of the meadow where half-a-dozen mares were grazing quietly.

'They're fine animals. They'll improve the bloodline, no question.'

Leif nodded. 'That they will.' He looked around in silent approbation at the well-kept fences and growing crops and healthy livestock. 'You've looked after the place, Aron, and I thank you.'

His companion smiled faintly. 'It's all I'm good for now that my sea-faring days are done.'

'The whale road is not the only way of making a living.'

'No, but it's the most exciting.'

'You miss it.'

'Sometimes: usually when Ingrid is nagging or one of the horses has colic or a fox has got into the henhouse.' Aron paused. 'But you know all this. You were a homesteader before you went a-viking.'

'In another lifetime.'

'Would you not settle down again one day?'

'Who knows?' replied Leif. 'The Norns weave as they will.'

'True enough. I didn't think I'd ever marry again but circumstances change.'

'I didn't know you were married before.'

'Well, I was—for eight years. We had three sons. Then the fever came one summer and took them all and my wife with them. After that there was nothing to stay for so I took to the whale road and followed it for twelve years until I lost my leg in battle.'

'And my father gave you charge of the steading in his absence.'

'He was a good jarl and he kept faith with his oath men. Then, one Yuletide, I met Ingrid. Her husband had died so she was alone too.' Aron paused. 'Loneliness does things to a man after a while; makes a stone of his heart, twists his mind if he lets it. I've seen it happen. I should not like it to happen to you.'

'It won't.'

'You are still young enough to start again, to take another wife and have a family—fine sons to continue your line.' Aron met his eye and held it. 'I will never have that now, but you can.'

'If anyone sires fine sons it will be Finn, or Erik perhaps.'

'And yet you take the Lady Astrid to your bed.'

'That's different.'

'Ah, yes, of course. You're just getting her out of your system before you send her back.'

Leif shot him a piercing look. 'You were the one who said I should get her out of my system.'

'So I did, and with good reason. She'll have your child in her belly by then so you'll need to feel quite indifferent, won't you? Especially when Einar cuts her throat.'

The words hit Leif with the force of a punch in the gut and rendered him speechless. His eyes were more eloquent, though, searching the other man's face, seeking his motive. Aron's expression remained bland. Then, apparently noticing his companion's discomfiture for the first time, he raised an eyebrow.

'What? It can't be news to you. You've always known what Einar would do to her. It was all part of your revenge, right?'

Leif's stomach spasmed and he gritted his teeth, fighting a wave of sickness. Had he really entertained such thoughts? Could hatred and anger run so deep that they no longer distinguished between justice and brutality? His enemies were Hakke and Gulbrand and Einar and their followers, mercenaries whom he would meet and slay in combat. Either that or they would slay him, in which case he would enter Valhalla and feast with the gods. That was the warrior's path. No man worthy of the name made war with women. Astrid was not the enemy and never had been. He knew that. He'd known it for some time. How could he ever have considered condemning her to such an end? He had spared a woman once even though she had tried to kill him, but he had known what mercy was then. He closed his eyes for a moment, trying to regain some sense of balance.

'I had not finally decided,' he replied. It was a lie and he knew it. Unconsciously his decision had been made long since but the reasons for it were still too complex to explain.

Aron nodded. 'It seems like a waste to me. Besides, it would gall Einar far more if you kept her. Of course, it's your decision.' He looked away across the field to where a thrall was rounding up the cattle for milking. 'Ah, there's Ulf. I need to have a word with him about the brindle cow. Cracked udders. Would you excuse me?'

Without waiting for a reply he walked away. Leif watched him for a moment or two and then slowly retraced his steps. The conversation had unsettled him. Until then he had looked no further ahead than achieving revenge. Aron's words had shown him all the years that lay beyond that. *How were those to be filled?*

His steps brought him to the fence so he vaulted over the rail and then followed the track down the slope. He could stay on the whale road. It was exciting, but it was also a hard life—a young man's life. He was not yet thirty, in his prime, but it wouldn't always be so. Eventually the years would catch up with him. *What then?* Once he had been certain of the answer. He would watch his sons grow to manhood and he would teach them how to tend the land and how to fight. However, the gods laughed when men spoke of certainties.

He was so engrossed in thought that he didn't notice the burial ground until he was almost on top of it. His first reaction was to walk on past but as he drew level with the place his pace slowed. For a moment or two he hesitated. He'd vowed never to return here. He'd vowed never to return to the steading either and yet it had happened. The strand was woven into the fabric of his destiny. He could almost hear the Norns' laughter. How the old hags must be enjoying this. He set his jaw. Then, taking a deep breath, he stepped off the track and walked through the narrow gateway.

The grave seemed even smaller now, the original mound of earth almost flattened by the elements and passing years. Grass had grown over the bare soil and round the marker stones. It was a small enough space, he thought, yet it contained the better part of his life, a part he had buried deep in every sense of the word. Not deep enough to lay the ghost though. In spite of his best efforts, the small, pale fetch had drawn him back. His journey had not been linear after all, only a vast circle which brought him back to the place he'd started from. What had it all been for? Just then he had no idea.

Slowly he sat down beside the grave and closed his eyes, trying to recall his son's face. It was like trying to clutch mist. The harder he tried, the more it eluded him and in the end he gave it up, aware only of irreparable loss and an increasing sense of weariness and desolation.

Astrid finished mending the ripped seam in the tunic and bit off the thread. Having folded the garment and laid it with the rest, she got to her feet, glad to stretch her limbs again. She had been sewing since noon and her eyes were tired from looking at tiny stitches. It was time to stop for a while.

'I'm going for a stroll.'

Ingrid glanced up from her work. 'As you will. I'm almost done myself.'

Astrid wandered away from the hall towards the pastureland. It was quiet and pleasant with only the sound of the breeze and the songs of birds for company. Considering that she was a captive, she'd been permitted considerable freedom and the buildings and lower fields that comprised the steading had become familiar to her now. Her movements were watched of course but that was only to be expected. Leif's trust only went so far.

She reached the fence and continued on along the track a little way. Once or twice she glanced at the horses grazing in the fields beyond, thinking that it would be good to ride again, to explore a little further afield. Perhaps she could put it to Leif. The very thought brought a smile to her lips, for it wasn't hard to visualise his response. No way would he let her anywhere near a horse. She wasn't going anywhere.

Glancing along the track, she saw that she was nearing the burial ground. When she reached it she'd turn back. In any case her guards would soon intervene if she tried to go any further, and pushing her luck might result in being allowed less freedom. The thought of being locked up held no appeal.

Another thirty paces brought her to the end of her walk. She smiled ruefully and was about to turn back when she noticed the figure sitting beside the small grave she had seen earlier. Then she saw who it was. His presence here was so unexpected and so incongruous that she felt at a total loss. Moreover, something in his very stillness suggested that she had inadvertently intruded on something that was both personal and private. Wincing inwardly, she backed off.

It might have been motion or the sound of leather on stone that warned him he wasn't alone but he looked up quickly and saw her. His brow creased and he came to his feet in one fluid movement.

'Astrid. What in Freya's name are you doing here?'

She swallowed hard. 'Walking, my lord.'

'Walking? You're a little far from the buildings, aren't you?'

'I was just about to turn back.'

'Indeed.'

'I beg your pardon, my lord. I didn't mean to intrude. I didn't know anyone was here.'

He surveyed her in silence and then his features relaxed a little. 'Well, no matter.'

Astrid glanced back along the track and backed another pace. 'I'll leave you in peace.'

'Stay.' His voice checked her. 'There's no harm done, at least not by you.' He left the graveside and came to join her. 'We'll go back together.'

They fell into step and for a while strolled in silence. More than ever aware of him, she darted a covert look his way, but his expression gave no clue to his thoughts. Curiosity strove with caution and lost.

'Whose graves were those, my lord?'

'My kin. Three generations of them: my grandfather, my father and my son.'

'The one you spoke of before?'

'He.'

'What was his name?'

'Sigurd.'

'How old was he?'

'Eleven months.'

The tender age caused Astrid no surprise: infant mortality was commonplace. Grief and loss, however, were intensely personal, and they were not limited by time.

'Had he lived he'd have been ten this summer.' Leif paused and shook his head. 'Children should not die before their parents.'

'No, they shouldn't,' she replied. 'Though I think Sigurd will never be dead to you.' *Nor will your wife. Was the child's death the reason she left? She couldn't bear it either.*

'Laying someone in a grave doesn't end it.'

They lapsed into silence again and she made no attempt to probe any further. His pain was almost palpable. It was like a hurt that had never healed and, glimpsing the extent of it, she realised that he was not invulnerable. That he could have loved a child so much spoke of something in him that was far removed from the persona of ruthless warlord that he presented to the world.

'I grieved for a long time after I lost my sisters,' she said.

He threw her a swift sideways glance. 'What happened to them?'

'My uncle married them off to old men in order to further his political ends. They wept, pleaded with him not to make them go through with it, but he took no notice.' She paused. 'Their husbands took them far away. I never saw either of them again and probably never will.'

'It is the way of things,' he replied.

'So it is, but the grief was no less real for that.'

'Your uncle has much to atone for.'

Astrid rested a hand lightly on his arm. 'Don't send me back to him, Leif. When this is over, I mean. Let me return to Ragnhild instead.'

He stopped and his gaze locked with hers. 'You're not going back to Ragnhild or to your uncle.'

Her mouth dried. 'You mean to kill me yourself?'

'If I'd wanted to kill you, I'd have done it already.'

With a sinking feeling she realised what form his revenge was going to take. 'I would rather die at the point of your sword than be sold as a slave.'

'Quite possibly,' he replied. 'As it happens I have no intention of doing either of those things.'

Something in his expression set the skin prickling along her spine. 'What, then?'

'You stay with me.'

Astrid stared at him, speechless. Once those words would have gladdened her beyond measure, because he of all men was the one she would have chosen to be with. It would have meant that he felt the same way, that he believed there was a chance for them, a future. Under the present circumstances the suggestion was monstrous. When she'd tried to imagine all the forms his revenge might take, this one hadn't occurred to her at all.

'You can't be serious.'

'Never more so,' he replied.

'I knew you to be angry and vengeful but I never thought you deliberately cruel.'

He raised an eyebrow. 'I'm sorry you think it now.'

'Neither had I realised your hatred ran so deep.'

'I don't hate you, Astrid. On the contrary, your company is becoming most congenial to me—in bed and out of it.'

With an effort she held on to her temper, suspecting now that he would enjoy seeing her lose it. 'You've already taken what you wanted. You could let me go.'

'You're wrong, on both counts.'

'Leif, think…'

'I have, and that's my decision. I shall not alter it.'

Her hands clenched at her sides. 'It may be *your* decision but *you* are only half of this…this relationship.'

'Yes, but I'm the half with the power.'

It was the truth, but no more palatable for that. Astrid's chin tilted to a militant angle and her violet eyes darkened with suppressed fury.

'Do you have any idea how insufferably arrogant you are?'

'Do you have any idea how attractive you are when you're angry?'

The reply was a strangled growl in her throat. With that she turned on her heel and marched away. Leif watched her go and smiled to himself.

Chapter Eighteen

Astrid paced up and down behind the hall, quietly fuming. He had enjoyed every bit of that last conversation; had enjoyed delivering the killer blow. The brute had been playing with her. He'd once said something about keeping her but she'd taken it as a taunt. How long ago had his decision been made? How long had he been maintaining silence, letting her sweat and think he would send her back to her uncle, when privately he was planning something quite different? While she had dreaded the former she viewed the latter with total shock. The enormity of it took her breath away. To enter into a lifelong relationship was one thing; to enter into it motivated only by thoughts of revenge was quite another.

As her anger began to cool it was gradually replaced by sadness and dread. It was clear now that he'd never entertained any doubts about her complicity in the plot to destroy him: he not only believed her guilty but intended to make her pay for the rest of her life. The plan was chilling. It wasn't physical punishment he intended but something much subtler and infinitely worse. He must already have guessed that her emotions were involved. Had he intended to make her fall for him in order to demonstrate complete indifference later? Was he so cold-blooded? It seemed so much at variance with the man she had glimpsed before, a man she could have learned to love.

For the remainder of the afternoon and evening she avoided him, finding a host of reasons to stay away. However, as the hour grew later it brought with it inevitable reunion.

Astrid was already in their sleeping quarters when he returned, but spoke no word as he entered or made any acknowledgement of his presence beyond a glance. Leif did not speak either, only began to undress. Astrid pulled off her overdress and gown and laid them aside but instead of climbing into bed she approached only long enough to remove the top cover.

Leif raised an eyebrow. 'What do you think you're doing?'

'I'm sleeping on the floor tonight.'

The blue-grey eyes glinted. 'You will be sleeping with me, vixen—tonight and every night.'

'Of course, I was forgetting. You have the power in this relationship.'

'So I do.' He confiscated the cover and tossed it back on the bed; then stepped closer and reached for her waist.

Astrid made a fruitless attempt to disengage herself from his hold. It didn't alter. 'Let me go, Leif.'

'I have already said I will not.'

She renewed the attempt but with no more success. 'How I detest you.'

'No, you don't.' His lips nuzzled her neck and throat. 'However much you might want to.'

She shivered and tears pricked behind her eyes because she knew the words for truth and they merely served to enhance the sense of his power over her. 'I do want to. I want to hate you as much as you hate me, every last cold calculating inch.'

Leif frowned and drew back, looking into her face. 'I don't hate you, Astrid. I thought I'd made that clear.'

'Then why are you doing this? Why won't you let me go?'

'Because you belong with me.'

'You mean I belong *to* you.'

'If you want to put it that way. It doesn't change anything.' His gaze bored into hers. 'Even if I did let you go, do you seriously think Ragnhild could protect you once your uncle got wind of your whereabouts?'

'It's a chance I'm prepared to take.'

'Well, I'm not.'

'No, it would destroy your long-term plans for revenge, wouldn't it?'

'What are you talking about?'

'You know very well. Did you not recently describe the punishment you mean to inflict? Should I be grateful that death and slavery don't feature, that it's only going to be a lifetime with you, to be destroyed slowly, a day at a time?' Her gaze met his. 'You know I'm not indifferent to you. I wish I could be. As it is, your task is likely to be quite easy.'

Leif paled and his hold slackened. 'Is that what you think?'

'What else is there to think?'

'That I might want to keep you for yourself.'

'A woman whom you believe to have betrayed you? Hardly.'

'It wasn't you who betrayed me. I know that now.'

She stared at him in frank astonishment. 'When did this come about?'

'Some time ago.'

It was hard to take in, and when she did it was with mixed emotions. 'You never told me.'

'I thought it was obvious.'

'Not to me.'

'Well, now we've cleared up that misunderstanding.' His frown deepened. 'And while we're on the subject of misunderstandings, you can forget about murder, slavery, torture, maiming or any other forms of brutality that your overactive imagination may have suggested to you.'

Astrid's eyes became a deeper shade of violet. 'Why should you be surprised if I did imagine such things?'

'I admit you may have had grounds at first.'

'May have? You told me yourself that I was your slave; forced me to undertake all manner of menial tasks and spoke to me as if I were dirt.'

He cleared his throat. 'Yes, well, I was angry at the time.'

'So that excuses your behaviour?'

'I do not excuse it. What I'm saying is that it's in the past and it's staying there. And you're staying with me.'

'Whether I want to or not.'

'That's right.' He reached for her waist again. 'Besides, you're not indifferent to me. You just said so.'

Astrid resisted his hold. 'It's not enough, Leif.'

'Why? What else is there?'

'If you don't know then you certainly don't want me for myself. You have no idea who I am.'

'I know all I need to—all that matters.'

'Keep telling yourself that. You may come to believe it.'

'What's that supposed to mean?' he demanded.

'It means I want to be more than just the woman you sleep with.'

'You are more than that. If you weren't I wouldn't be keeping you with me.'

'You're keeping me because it suits you and because you hate to be thwarted.'

'Question my motives if you wish. It won't change the outcome.'

'Probably not.'

She moved away from him and climbed into bed, pulling the covers over herself. Leif made no reply, though his face was thunderous. He finished undressing and doused the lamp. A few moments later the bed creaked and she felt the mattress shift beneath his weight. Although he made no move to touch her, she could feel anger flowing off him. Silence thickened around them until she could hear the blood beating in her ears. Her throat tightened. Once she would have given anything to hear those words from him, to believe he really did want her for herself, but that was wishful thinking. The woman he really wanted was lost and his anger was rooted in that knowledge. She could only ever be second-best. To fall for glib assurances would be naïve indeed. He already had too much advantage; she wasn't about to hand him that one as well.

Leif lay awake for a long time, staring into the darkness. He hadn't expected Astrid to be overjoyed by his decision to keep her with him but he'd never imagined the construction she would put on his words. Did she really believe him to be such a monster? That he wanted to spend the rest of his life destroying hers? His jaw tightened. Somehow he was going to have to disabuse her of that notion. It was his fault for allowing a note of teasing to creep into their earlier conversation. He shouldn't have done that but, at the time, hadn't been able to resist it. It had never occurred to him that she would swallow it whole. As to the rest, she was staying with him whether she liked it or not: his enemies couldn't touch her here.

He sighed. It wasn't just about her safety, important as that was. It was more that he couldn't imagine being without her. After the disaster of his marriage he'd never imagined he might one day come to feel such a depth of attraction again. But, from the day he'd met her, he hadn't been able to put Astrid out of his mind. Marriage was not his intention and he'd said so, but he had wanted more than a brief casual liaison. Back then he'd believed that the surest way to quench passion was to satisfy it. Yet far from getting her out of his system it had only deepened desire. She was under his skin, in his blood. He wanted hers to be the first face he saw when he woke and the last one he saw before he slept. Somewhere along the line desire had become fused with need. He would keep her because he had to. She belonged with him. *You mean I belong* to *you.* He grimaced. Both were true and, eventually, he would make her understand that.

The hangings were pulled aside and a gust of cool night air swirled into the tent as the man entered. The lamplight shone softly on his helmet and the naked sword in his hand. Astrid started up on to one elbow, her heart thumping as he advanced nonchalantly towards the bed. When he reached it he stopped, looking down at her for a moment. Her throat dried. She wanted to run but the fur coverlet was all that lay between her and intruder. Beneath it she was naked. Wide-eyed she watched him sheathe the blade and remove the helm, tossing it aside, but with the light behind him his face was in shadow, familiar but unidentified. Without taking his gaze off her he unfastened his sword belt and let it fall. The studded leather tunic followed and then, unhurriedly, the rest of his clothing before he joined her beneath the furs. She slid away from him to the far side of the bed but he reached for her waist and drew her back again. Her protest was silenced by a kiss. Gradually her mouth yielded to his, opening to receive his tongue. Strong warm hands caressed her skin, hands whose touch both alarmed and aroused. She stirred restlessly but he continued to explore her, the touch bolder, moving to her sex. He drew a finger lightly through the slickness there. She gasped as, deep inside her, warmth flared into being...

She opened her eyes to grey dawn light. The tent was gone, and the shadows, but not the man. This time when she looked into his face she knew who he was.

'Leif.'

As memory began to return, it was accompanied by confusion as her mind tried to separate dream from reality. The hard-muscled body was present in both, like the bed and the fur coverlet against her skin. She frowned. When she had retired last night she had been wearing her shift; now she wasn't. As she glanced at her nakedness confusion was replaced by indignation.

Leif had no trouble interpreting the expression. 'The shift was in the way so I removed it.'

'Why, you...'

The words ended on a sharp intake of breath as his mouth closed over the peak of her breast and sucked gently.

'Leif?'

'Mmm?'

'It's not going to work.' She suppressed a shiver as the nipple hardened under his tongue. 'If you think I'm going to...that I'll...' She gasped and the rest of the sentence became incoherent.

His mouth travelled a little higher, kissing her neck and throat. Where his lips touched the skin seemed to burn. Meanwhile the delicious stroking sensation continued.

She swallowed hard. *The man was outrageous, utterly without conscience. He couldn't be allowed to get away with this.* He gently tugged the lobe of her ear, sending a shiver through her flesh. *She ought to resist, make him stop.*

His fingers found the nub they had been seeking, and stroked gently. Her breathing quickened and suddenly she didn't want him to stop. Deep in her body's core the warmth intensified and became heat with a coil of tension at its heart. Her blood raced. She closed her eyes, reaching for the elusive sensation she had felt before. The tension increased and rippled outwards, sending a tremor the length of her. It was followed by another, stronger this time. She gasped as her body shuddered beneath his hand.

'Merciful gods!'

He entered her then, slowly, letting the length of him slide into her, but she was impatient now, hungry for what she sensed was almost within reach. Instinctively she closed her legs around him, pulling him deeper. Still he made her wait, teasing, tantalising, building the fire inside her, taking her with him. Astrid writhed, arching against him, her nails raking his back.

'Leif, please…I beg you…'

The words caught in her throat but her gaze spoke what she could not, the violet eyes darkened now with desire and with aching need. The rhythm increased and he thrust deeper and the coiled heat in her pelvis became exquisite, lifting her, carrying her with it to the edge of a precipice. Leif let go of restraint and the tension exploded outwards in shock waves of pleasure—and with a cry she went over the edge with him into free fall and heart-stopping delight so intense she thought she would die. For a moment the blue-grey gaze burned into hers, fierce and ardent. Then she felt him shudder and heard him cry out before the last deep rush of release. Panting, overwhelmed, she closed her eyes, every part of her resonating to him, sated yet burning too, stunned by the response he had drawn from her. This time it went far deeper than mere physical possession; this time he had stolen her soul and she was now irretrievably lost. Mingled with that was the knowledge that he would take this in his stride; that she was just another conquest in every sense of the word. His emotions were not engaged. He loved someone else and she wished with all her heart that it were not so.

Leif glanced down at the woman drowsing in his arms and then closed his eyes too, surrendering to temporary physical torpor. He'd long since recognised the inherent sensuality in her nature and had set himself the challenge of arousing it. By catching her off guard and totally relaxed he'd finally been able to overcome all resistance as he'd hoped. Nevertheless, the experience had been beyond his wildest expectation. His entire being reverberated with it and yet satiety had not displaced desire. *On the contrary...*

Some time afterwards Astrid was woken by a hand stroking the small of her back. She opened her eyes to see Leif watching her, the expression in his eyes unmistakable. The look set her flesh tingling but in her mind all the old doubts reawakened. He was an experienced lover, and if he had gone to so much trouble to give her pleasure it had been for a reason. He must have known what the result would be, the mental turmoil it was going to create. It could not have been accidental.

'Why are you doing this, Leif?'

'You must have guessed by now.'

The words reinforced all her former suspicions. 'Have you no mercy?'

The blue-grey eyes glinted. 'None,' he replied.

Astrid stiffened and would have pulled away but the hand on her back prevented it. He surveyed her in surprise.

'What is it? What's wrong?'

'I'm not doing this, Leif.'

He smiled. 'Would you care to wager on that?'

'I mean it.' She sat up, clutching the coverlet close. 'You've had your fun.'

His smile faded a little. 'I was under the impression it was fun for you too.'

'That's not the word I was going to use.'

'Oh? Then what word would you choose?'

'I could give you quite a few: incredible, wonderful, heart-stopping…it was all of those things.' She turned to look at him. 'It was also cynical and ruthless.'

Leif propped himself on an elbow. 'I beg your pardon?'

'Don't try to deny it. You did it on purpose.'

'Of course I did it on purpose. It was intended to give you pleasure. Why is that cynical and ruthless?'

'You know why.'

'No, I don't. Explain it to me.'

'Stop this, Leif.'

She tried to turn away but he caught hold of her shoulders, holding her fast. 'Stop what? What is this about?'

'Can you pretend you didn't know what the effect was going to be? That the whole thing wasn't just an exercise in emotional manipulation?'

'The effect was exactly what I hoped it would be,' he replied, 'though I've never heard it described in that way.'

Astrid tried unsuccessfully to free herself. 'You wanted my feelings to be more deeply engaged and you deliberately set out to do it.'

'That's right.' He tipped her backwards, pinning her there, his gaze locked with hers. 'And before I'm done your feelings will be so deeply engaged you'll never look at another man or think of one either. You'll belong to me, body and soul.'

Astrid struggled, fighting his hold. 'You'd like that, wouldn't you?'

His grip didn't alter. 'Above all else.'

'Of course you would.'

He frowned. 'I think you'd better explain that.'

'How delicious it must be to have your captive fall for you; how very gratifying. Yet it won't stop you from breaking her heart later.'

He paled and the expression in his eyes caused a host of winged creatures to take flight in her stomach.

'I'd like to think I had the power to break your heart, but I'm not so deluded.'

'You're not interested in my heart. The one you want is lost.'

'What are you talking about?'

'Your wife. She's the woman you can't forget.'

He released his hold abruptly. 'You're quite right. I can't forget her no matter how hard I try.'

Astrid sat up. 'She's the reason you've never remarried, isn't she? Why you avoid all but temporary involvement with women?'

'It's not your concern.'

'Ten years is a long time.'

'Not long enough.'

'Why did she leave you, Leif?'

'Let it go, Astrid.'

'Was it after Sigurd died?'

'You speak of what you don't know.' He swung his legs over the side of the bed and, retrieving his clothing, began to dress.

'Have I come too near the truth?'

His expression was chilling. 'Not another word.'

She fell silent, wanting to pursue it and knowing she'd better not. It had already gone too far. He finished dressing and, pausing only to give her a last icy stare, he departed.

Astrid collapsed on to the bed, her heart thumping unpleasantly fast. She'd never meant to goad him so far, but somehow hadn't been able to help herself. All the same, she derived no pleasure from his reaction. It was like probing a wound, and she knew it caused him pain. It had also confirmed what she'd suspected: his wife was the only woman ever to have won his heart. She shared it with their dead son. That would never change and that was what hurt.

Until now she had never known what it was to be jealous, but then, she had never loved before. She'd spent so long fighting the attraction that she had failed to call it by its right name. Self-deception was no longer possible. Last night had stripped away the last shreds of pretence. It had also left her more vulnerable than she had ever been.

* * *

Leif quit the hall and went out into the early morning air. It was fresh and cool and peaceful, unlike the bed of thorns he had just left. How was it possible to share such soul-shaking intimacy one moment and then be at daggers drawn the next? The accusations she had made were still ringing in his ears. It had stung to know that she really believed him capable of the kind of ruthless, emotional manipulation she had described. Mingled with that was a twinge of guilt. His earlier motivation had been highly questionable but it had been informed by red-hot anger. He'd also been so certain of the justice of his actions. So much had changed since then, changes so gradual he'd scarcely been aware of them but they'd taken place and they were profound.

As for the rest... The vixen was so skilled at finding all the chinks in his armour. She seemed to know just where to thrust the knife. He sighed. The wounds were only superficially closed, which was why he'd overreacted. Old habits became ingrained. His had been to bury the past and never to speak of it, but doing so had not laid the ghosts. Astrid had recognised that, even though she was wrong about so many other things.

He let out another long breath. This whole situation was beginning to spiral out of control and allowing himself to get angry and defensive would solve nothing. *You have no idea who I am.* The charge she had levelled at him not so long ago was also applicable the other way round. However, he could do something about that. He hadn't found the words before, but now they were welling up thick and fast and he was good and ready to spit them out. Perhaps then he could put an end to this situation once and for all. Making up his mind, he strode back into the hall.

Astrid was still abed, although she wasn't asleep. She looked up as he entered, evidently startled. He noted it with satisfaction. It wouldn't hurt to have the vixen on the back foot for a change. At least he might get a chance to say what needed to be said before she leapt in with more accusations. He picked up her shift and gown and tossed them over.

'Get up.'

Chapter Nineteen

Astrid eyed him with misgivings. He had rarely seemed more forbidding than he did now, his anger the worse for being cold. It was tempting to ignore that arrogant command, but she knew she didn't dare. She donned her shift and slid out of bed, keenly aware of his scrutiny the while. The gown and overdress followed in short order and she slid her feet into shoes. Her hair was still loose but he seemed not to notice or at least not to heed it. Taking hold of her arm, he hustled her out of the sleeping quarters.

When they got outside Astrid darted a covert look at his face. 'Where are we going?'

'You'll see.'

The reply was not calculated to inspire confidence, nor was the grip on her arm. His stride was so long that she was compelled almost to run to keep up. He led her away from the buildings towards the pasture and thence along the track to the burial ground. Apprehension prickled.

'Leif, what are you about?'

He vouchsafed no reply but strode on. By the time they reached the place she was panting and her heart hammering. Without a word he drew her through the gateway and thence to the edge of Sigurd's grave. She shivered.

'Why have you brought me here?'

'Because I have things to say and you're going to hear me out.'

Astrid licked dry lips. 'What things?'

'It's time to straighten out some of your misconceptions about the past. My past.'

'Leif, I didn't mean...'

His gaze burned into hers. 'You wanted to know about my wife and son, did you not?'

She nodded, dumbly aware now of having trespassed in a dangerous place. At the same time, she wanted to hear what he had to say, wanted to understand. Besides, they'd come too far to retreat now. Slowly some of the fire went out of his eyes and he slackened his hold on her arm.

'I told you my marriage was a love match and so it was, at first. For a year or so we were as happy as any two people could be. When Thora told me she was carrying our child I was overjoyed.' He paused. 'It seemed as though the gods had favoured us in every way. She was delivered of a beautiful, healthy boy.'

'Sigurd.'

'Yes, Sigurd. He was…perfect. I thought no man ever had so fine a son.'

Astrid smiled wistfully. The domestic happiness he described was what she had once wished for herself.

'But, after the baby was born, everything began to go wrong. Thora sank into a deep melancholy. The older women said that it sometimes happened after the birth of a child and that she would come out of it. Only she didn't.' He sighed. 'Nothing I could do or say made any difference. Indeed she developed an aversion to me and to our marriage bed. She couldn't even bear me to touch her. She also resented the child.'

'The child?'

'She didn't want to pick him up when he cried or change his cloth or talk to him or play with him or do any of the other things a mother usually does with her baby. She hated feeding him. She asked why he should demand her milk when he'd already had her blood.'

Astrid stared at him, appalled. 'What did you do?'

'Some of the other women rallied round to help where they could. The child drank goat's milk in the end but he seemed to thrive on it well enough.'

'I have heard of this,' she said.

'I still hoped that all might yet be well and that Thora's dark mood would pass, but instead it grew deeper, blacker.' He took a deep breath. 'I did not know how black until one night she put poison in my food.'

'Poison?'

'When the stomach cramps began, I took them for indigestion. But they quickly got worse. Then Thora told me what she'd done. I managed to fill a large jug with salt water and drank it down. I did it several times. I was as sick as a dog but it got rid of most of the poison. Thora fled the house.' He let out a shuddering breath. 'It was only then that it occurred to me to check on the baby...'

Astrid paled. 'Oh, no.'

'Unfortunately the poison had acted faster on him.'

'Dear gods!'

'I took my sword and went after Thora. In spite of the pain and sickness, the gods gave me strength and I caught her up. It was in my mind to slay her, but when it came to the point I could not, for it was even more apparent that she was not in her right mind. Besides, I have never used my sword on a woman.'

'So you divorced her instead.'

He nodded. 'Her kin took charge of her and sent her to relatives in the north. I have not set eyes on her since. Nor do I ever wish to.' He glanced down at the small grave. 'I buried my son and then I left, for good as I thought. However, the Nornir had other plans for me.'

Her throat tightened and tears pricked her eyelids. 'Leif, I'm so sorry.'

'Why should you be?'

'For making arrogant assumptions and for jumping to conclusions,' she replied.

For the space of several heartbeats he was silent. Then he sighed. 'You only had part of the story.'

'I wish you had told me. Although I understand why you did not.'

'It was not a subject I wanted to discuss ever again. My only thought was to take up a new life and leave the past behind me.' He smiled mirthlessly. 'I should have known better.'

'I think we can never leave the past behind; all we can do is come to terms with it.'

'Perhaps. That remains to be seen.' He surveyed her steadily. 'In the meantime, there's something else we need to get straight.'

The intensity of that look made her feel distinctly uncomfortable. 'Something else?'

'You made some other remarks that I didn't much care for.'

'What remarks?'

'The ones about emotional manipulation.'

Warmth swept from her neck into her face. 'Are you telling me I was wrong?'

'Yes, I am telling you that.'

'Yet until recently all your talk was of revenge.'

'My revenge is concerned with men and swords,' he replied.

'You were going to rape me, Leif, or had you forgotten?'

A muscle jumped in his cheek. 'I haven't forgotten, or ceased to be ashamed of it. I let anger cloud judgement and it shouldn't have happened.'

'You also spoke of a different kind of possession: body and soul, I believe you said.'

'So I did. I still want that, but I also want them to be freely given.'

Astrid's gaze searched his face but what she found there looked like sincerity. Confusion mingled with guilt and self-doubt. Was it possible to have got things so badly wrong? How was she to reconcile this with what had gone before?

'I want to believe you.'

'And I wanted to believe you, to believe *in* you. It's why I gave you the benefit of the doubt.' He paused. 'Will you do as much for me?'

She felt her throat tighten. 'If I trust you, am I going to regret it?'

'There will be plenty of time for you to find out, won't there?'

The implications of that were disturbing on several levels, not least because the thought of a future spent in an atmosphere of doubt and suspicion filled her with dread. If they were to have any hope of emerging from this mess it would only be on the basis of trust.

'Yes, I suppose there will, always assuming that your enemies don't kill you.'

'I'm not easy to kill. In the meantime, you and I need to come to a better understanding.'

'A truce, then?'

'Something like that.' His gaze held hers. 'We can start by dismissing the charge of emotional manipulation. I won't touch you again until you ask me to.'

Whatever else she might have expected, it wasn't that. Along with surprise was a host of other feelings that weren't so easy to decipher.

'What if I never ask you to?'

'That would mean I was wrong about last night,' he replied. 'But I don't think I was wrong. I think you want me every bit as much as I want you. The only difference between us is that you haven't admitted it yet.'

Much to her annoyance she could feel her face turning pink again, not least because she knew he was right. All the same, saying it was harder than knowing it, and physical desire was only part of the truth, at least so far as she was concerned. If he ever guessed the rest, if he ever discovered how deeply her feelings were involved, his hold on her would be complete.

'Desire burns out eventually,' she replied. 'Any meaningful relationship requires more than that.'

'Clearly our understanding of *meaningful* differs. As far as I'm concerned this relationship has already achieved that status. Otherwise we wouldn't be having this conversation.'

'I see.'

'I told you at the outset what to expect from me. It still holds good, but do not entertain hopes of any more than that.'

'You will not make false promises. I remember.'

'It is well. It was never my intention to deceive you in that way.'

Suddenly doubt evaporated and she had no trouble believing him at all. Their relationship was as meaningful as it was ever going to get for him.

'I understand that now,' she replied.

'I'm glad to hear it.'

For a short space they lapsed into silence. Unable to follow his thoughts and uncomfortable with her own, she wanted only to be gone now.

'Was there anything else, my lord?'

'No, nothing else.'

She nodded and turned away. Leif remained where he was, though she could feel his gaze following her down the path. Tears pricked her eyelids. Just then she didn't know who they were for: herself, a deranged mother, a murdered boy or the father whose heart was in the grave with him.

For the next two days, Leif was away from the steading for the majority of the time and when he returned he spent the evenings with his men and with Aron. By the time he came to bed Astrid had already retired. She stirred a little as he climbed in with her but didn't wake. He watched her for a while, then sighed and doused the light. For some time he lay awake in the darkness, every part of him aware of her, aware of her nearness and her warmth. That last astonishing lovemaking session was etched on his memory and the temptation to renege on his promise was strong. With an effort he resisted it. The next time he took her it would be at her invitation. A few days' space would do them no harm. If he was right she would soon be feeling the lack as much as he.

However, three more days came and went without any invitation forthcoming. Astrid was courteous and did his bidding without argument but she gave no sign of wanting further intimacy. When a week had gone by he began to experience doubt. *What if I never ask you?* The words returned to mock him. Was this another form of revenge? If so, he had to admit it was powerful, more so than he could have anticipated.

Frustration found an outlet in hard physical exercise; in riding and in practice bouts with his men. At the end of it he was sweating, filthy and aching so he stripped off the rest of his clothing and plunged into the fjord in the hope that the water would cool his blood. He swam for a while and then climbed out on to a flat rock to dry off.

Then his mind went back to the island and the day he'd watched Astrid getting dressed after bathing and he suppressed a groan. Lately she was all he could think about. Somewhere along the line desire had undergone a transformation to become a great aching need. Moreover, he didn't know what he was going to do about it.

Astrid sat down to help Ingrid prepare vegetables for the pot. For the most part they worked in silence, methodically slicing and chopping, working their way through the pile in front of them. From time to time the older woman threw a sideways glance at her companion but Astrid was too deep in thought to notice. She had been too caught up in events to notice the absence of her moon blood at first, but when that was combined with other changes its significance had eventually impinged on her consciousness. The realisation left her feeling stunned, uncertain whether to laugh or cry. Eventually she had done both.

For some days her mood had swung between elation and sorrow: the first because she was carrying Leif's child and the second because she dreaded his reaction. Coming so soon after the revelation about his past, she could not suppose he would receive the news with gladness. Furthermore, a man's interest in his mistress was confined to the pleasure she could give him in bed. It did not extend to her pregnancy, not usually anyway. Sometimes men did acknowledge their bastard offspring and provide for them, but without a husband a woman was vulnerable. *I told you at the outset what you could expect from me.* That had never included the possibility of marriage. At the same time, he had a right to know about the child, and she would need to tell him before its existence became obvious. She wanted to speak to him alone, away from the hall and the possibility of being overheard.

When she had finished the vegetables she went outside and looked around for Leif. A quiet word with Aron elicited the information that the jarl had gone off in the direction of the fjord. Accordingly she directed her steps that way. On first glance the place seemed to be deserted but a closer look revealed a figure sitting atop a large flat rock. He was naked, a pile of clothing beside him. She wondered if he were asleep and was unwilling to wake him so she sat down to wait on the turfy slope above.

She had been there about ten minutes before there was any sign of movement. Then he got to his feet. Her breath caught in her throat. His body was magnificent: broad across the shoulders, narrow in the waist and flanks, and long in the legs. There wasn't an ounce of fat in evidence, only hard muscle. She saw him reach for his breeks and pull them on, followed by the shirt, tunic and belt. Finally he retrieved his socks and slid his feet into leather boots. Then he turned to make his way back up the path. It was only at that point he noticed Astrid for the first time. He checked in mid-stride, clearly surprised to see her there, but he recovered soon enough and came on. Astrid took a deep breath and rose to her feet, waiting for him to join her.

'This is a surprise,' he said. 'How long have you been here?'

She smiled. 'Oh, a little while.'

He raised one eyebrow. 'How little a while exactly?'

'Long enough to admire the view. The scenery hereabouts is really quite compelling.'

The blue-grey eyes glinted. 'Is it indeed?'

'Oh, yes.' She returned an innocent look. 'I think it's the combination of rocks and trees and water.'

He grinned. 'But you did not come here just to admire the landscape.'

'No, I was hoping to find you.'

'This is encouraging. I was beginning to think my company had palled on you.'

'What?' She stared at him blankly. 'Why should you think that?'

'Never mind. What was it you wanted to see me about?'

Astrid took a deep breath and told him. For several seconds he was quite still, his face unreadable. Her heart thumped in her breast as fear and hope wrestled for supremacy.

'Well,' he replied, 'I suppose that was bound to happen eventually.'

'You knew it would. How could it not?'

He clearly assumed the question was rhetorical, because he made no answer. Instead he looked at the front of her gown but as yet there was no sign of the new life in her belly.

'You are sure about this?'

'Quite sure.'

'When will the child be born?'

'Next spring.'

'I see.' He paused. 'You're not so far along yet.'

'No. Why?'

'If the thought of bearing the child displeases you there are ways of preventing it. There are wise women who can provide certain potions.'

Astrid recoiled as though he had struck her. 'What?'

'I only meant…'

'I know what you meant, Leif, and the answer is no. This child may be an inconvenience to you but it will come to no harm at my hand.'

'I am not talking about inconvenience.'

'Aren't you?'

'Childbirth does things to a woman, Astrid. It twists her mind until she becomes a total stranger even to those who knew her best.'

Just for a moment the mask slipped and she

glimpsed the pain in his eyes. Recognising its source, she let go of her anger and sought for the words she needed.

'What happened to Thora was terrible, and so was what she did, but that doesn't mean it's going to happen again. Her case was unusual and tragic. Most women give birth and rejoice in their babies.'

'It may be so. I wouldn't know.'

'But you will know eventually, if…'

'If what?'

'If you still wish me to stay.'

He frowned. 'Of course I still wish it. This makes no difference to that.'

'It is going to make a great deal of difference, Leif. I want our child to know its father.'

'I will acknowledge it.'

The words afforded her considerable relief, but one matter was still unresolved. Her gaze held his. 'I would not have our child born into bastardy, Leif. Will you make me your wife and give us both an honourable place in the world, in your life?'

'Do you really think that it is marriage which makes a relationship honourable?'

'Past experience does not have to dictate the future. I would like to prove that.'

'There is nothing you can teach me about marriage,' he said, 'and they are fools who do not learn from past mistakes. I shall not repeat mine.'

Her heart sank. 'You don't have to decide now.

All I ask is that you should consider what I have said.'

'I told you how it would be, Astrid, and that is how it will remain. So far as the rest of the world is concerned you're my woman and I will acknowledge the child as mine. Let that content you.'

'How can it? I have more than just myself to think of now, and the child should not have to suffer for something it didn't do.'

'The child will not suffer.'

'That's nonsense, Leif, and you know it. The stigma will remain for its entire life.'

'A man makes his own fame. That is what lives after him, not the details of his birth.'

'It might be a girl. What then? What will be her fame?'

'A good dowry,' he replied.

'I had not thought you so cynical.'

'It's not cynicism. I know how the world works.'

'Oh? I think you don't know much at all, at least not about what really matters.'

She turned away from him and hurried off towards the steading.

Leif watched her go and swore softly, his mind in turmoil. In spite of his earlier assertion, the news had taken him by surprise. It re-awoke a raft of painful memories and with them fear. One part of his mind knew that what she had said was true: what happened before was not typical. Just for a moment he had a mental image of a beautiful healthy child smiling up at him from the cradle. It was replaced by another image, this time a limp and lifeless form with blue-tinged lips that resisted all his efforts to awaken or revive it. A familiar spasm of pain cramped his stomach and he closed his eyes, waiting for it to pass.

He told himself those things were in the past; what had happened then was unlikely to happen this time. But what if it did? He couldn't discount the possibility. What if Astrid became estranged from him? What if she too began to look at him with hatred? What if she too avoided his touch and his bed? She had denied him her body for the past week. Perhaps this was the start of it. His stomach cramped again and he retched.

When his stomach was empty he lay down on the grass until the pain went away. By that time he felt calmer, better able to think. It was early days yet; too soon to hope or to fear. What would be would be. In the meantime, he had other matters to deal with, things that would keep him occupied and hold the darkness at bay.

Chapter Twenty

The interview with Leif left Astrid with a strong desire to weep but she refused to give in to it. Tears wouldn't change anything and they wouldn't help either. Her bid to regularise their relationship might have failed dismally but it could have been worse. At least he hadn't cast her off and refused to acknowledge the child. All the same, he hadn't been able to conceal his true feelings either. The suggestion that she might abort the foetus had come as a real shock. The very thought was abhorrent. If it had been made in a callous attempt to rid himself of a problem she could never have forgiven him, but that had not been his intention. What lay behind the words was fear. Until that moment she hadn't understood how badly the past had scarred him.

In the light of that her request was foolish. Of

course he wasn't going to marry her. His fear ran too deep for that; too deep to see anything other than a repeat of former disaster. While he intended to keep her with him, it would be on his terms. She sighed. He'd told her that from the start. It had been naïve to think she could sway him, that anything had changed. While she had his protection that was all very well, but what if she lost it? What if, in the forthcoming confrontation with his enemies, he were killed? For all sorts of reasons it didn't bear thinking about.

She had no idea how to deal with the situation. Tears and pleas wouldn't serve. Anger and coldness would only alienate him and make the situation worse. Having been so cruelly rejected by the person he'd loved most, Leif had armoured his heart against further injury. Somehow he had to be persuaded to trust again, to love again. Yet love could not be commanded, nor would it grow in a climate of coldness and recrimination. To receive love one had to give love, at least that was the theory. Failing that, she was going to need enough for the two of them.

Somewhat to his surprise, when Leif rejoined her that evening Astrid made no mention of their earlier conversation and nor could he detect any coldness or resentment in her manner. When he entered their sleeping place, she acknowledged him courteously. He saw that she had already undressed in preparation for bed and was just then combing her hair. It hung over her shoulder like a fall of pale gold. The linen shift afforded an uninterrupted view of shapely calves and ankles and hinted at the curves of the figure above. He gritted his teeth and began to undress.

He had been in bed awhile before she finished her grooming, time enough for his belly to grow taut with anticipation and desire. He was strongly tempted to go and fetch her and then pin her to the bed and see his will well met. However, he had promised. Not only that, she was now with child. To yield to his baser nature might mean harming one or both of them.

Finally Astrid put down the comb. He watched her cross the room to extinguish the lamp and then felt the mattress shift as she climbed into bed. As she did so her leg brushed his, a fleeting contact but more than enough to increase the tension in his groin. He shut his eyes and suppressed a groan.

She turned on her side. 'Goodnight, my lord.'

His jaw tightened and somehow he mumbled a reply. It was evident now that she had no intention of issuing the invitation he sought, but at least he knew the reason for it now. It wasn't capriciousness or pique or a desire for revenge. It was because she was pregnant. There hadn't been any overt hostility yet, but it would come. In the meantime, her rejection of him had begun.

He lay awake for a long time listening to her quiet breathing before he eventually sank into uneasy slumber.

When Astrid woke it was early and the place quiet, save for the distant sound of snoring coming from the main body of the hall. She turned her head to look at her companion but he was still asleep. His face was peaceful now, almost boyish. Her gaze drank in the strong planes of his cheeks and jaw, the firm sculpted mouth, the light stubble on his chin. The bruises had faded now and the cut on his head healed to a pale scar. Even his hair was beginning to grow out. Eventually he would be as he had been before he fell into Hakke's clutches, outwardly at least. If only memory could be as easily erased.

She let her gaze travel on a little further to the place where his neck joined his shoulder, a place that might have been made for her lips to kiss. That thought engendered others, not least that last incredible coupling, and a flicker of warmth licked into being deep inside her. Suddenly all the preoccupations of the past week began to diminish until there was only the man beside her. *I won't touch you again until you ask me.*

She eyed the sleeper speculatively. She wanted to rouse him. No, not just rouse him, she amended mentally, *arouse* him. Did she still have that power? What would happen if she gave rein to the thoughts currently rioting in her head? She had never done anything so bold in her life. Would he be angry if she disturbed his sleep? Would he still want her even though she was with child? She bit her lip, torn between doubt and desire. Then she reminded herself that they hadn't made love for a week or more and if she hoped to break through his defences she would need to use every available opportunity. She had no idea what his reaction was going to be but there was only one way to find out...

Leif smiled and stirred between sleep and wakefulness, caught in the throes of a delightful dream. His belly was taut and heat flared through his loins under a gentle but persistent caress. He drew in a sharp breath, feeling himself grow hard. In moments he was erect. The stroking intensified. He opened his eyes to find himself under intense scrutiny.

'Good morning, my lord.'

He blinked. Then he tried to speak but all that emerged was a faint croaking sound. Before he had time to gather his wits Astrid's body was pressed the length of his, her hands caressing his back and buttocks, her mouth kissing his breast and neck. He felt her teeth gently tug the lobe of his ear, sending a delicious shiver the length of him. Her tongue probed deeper and the shiver became a tremor.

Somehow he found his voice. 'Have a care, vixen, you play with fire.'

Astrid made no reply except to push him on to his back and then straddle him. However, instead of letting him slide into her as he'd anticipated she leaned forwards, letting herself brush against him, her breasts sliding over his chest. He stifled a groan as his heart performed a series of erratic manoeuvres. Heat flared through his belly where a coil of tension was tightening fast. She repeated the motion and he caught his breath.

'For the love of all the gods, have you no mercy?'

Astrid surveyed him steadily and returned a decidedly wicked smile. 'No, my lord, none.'

His body arched towards her, every part of him aching with need. She smiled and straightened, adjusting her position to take him inside her. He shuddered and she heard him groan. Thus encouraged, she began to rock slowly. Leif caught his breath. Reaching for her hips, he was about to pull her deeper, then hesitated.

'Am I hurting you?'

'No, you're not hurting me.'

Even so, he was careful, moving gently, controlling desire, savouring the moment. He felt her muscles clench around him, creating a sensation so exquisite he almost forgot to breathe. He lifted his hands to her breasts and brushed his thumbs across the peaks. Astrid gasped and he felt her shudder. He moved deeper, letting the tempo increase, letting pleasure have a little more rein. It elicited a series of shudders which found an answering response in him. And then further restraint was impossible and he swept her with him to climax.

Heart pounding, he closed his eyes for a moment, trying to reconcile his former fear with what had just happened. Never in a thousand years would he have anticipated this. It was astonishing, wonderful. The experience made him feel whole again, complete. He felt her hair brush his skin and then the light touch of her lips on his before she lay down beside him. He smiled and opened his eyes, drinking her in. Her character had always been multifaceted; it was part of her attraction, like unpredictability. The violet-eyed seductress, the gentle handmaid and the wildcat were one. No matter how much he learned about her there was always something new to be discovered. It intrigued and delighted him.

She smiled and snuggled closer, her head on his breast. Now that he had more leisure to reflect, it occurred to him that this seduction had had an ulterior motive. Had it been intended just to reassure or did she have a longer view in mind? Both perhaps. Whatever her motives, she had beguiled him completely. The man would have to be dead who was not beguiled by that. However, it was still early days yet. Would her passion survive pregnancy and childbirth? His heart constricted. He didn't know which was more painful, hope or dread.

However, in the weeks that followed Astrid's manner did not change nor could he detect any signs of the mental disturbance he had seen in Thora. During the day while he was busy Astrid occupied herself as well. In the evenings they would talk; he would tell her how he had spent his time and she listened with close attention, occasionally asking questions. Pertinent questions too, he realised. Moreover, she remembered the answers. It reinforced the notion that she had a quick and clever mind. She was a good listener too, and he discovered anew that it was disarmingly easy to talk to her. When they retired he made love to her and she returned his passion. She attended quietly to his comfort as well, ensuring that his shirts were washed, his clothing neatly mended, their sleeping quarters clean and tidy. He knew that she contributed her share to other chores as well, taking some of the load off Ingrid. Although she had never adverted to the matter again, Astrid was quietly adopting the role of a wife. It did not displease him, since it indicated that she had accepted his decision. The arrangement was good. Vows wouldn't improve it, especially not when they might prove impossible to keep.

* * *

A distraction arrived in the form of a trading knörr from Sogn. Compared to the sleek lines of a sea dragon, the knörr was like a fat beetle. Powered primarily by sail, she had decks fore and aft and a deep open space amidships which served as a cargo hold. The vessel belonged to Ingrid's brother, Harald, who plied his trade along the coast and was bound for Vestfold with a cargo of furs and iron and amber. He and his crew of six were frequent visitors to the steading and were greeted warmly. Quite apart from the goods they carried to trade, they also brought news of events from elsewhere.

Leif hoped he might hear word of Finn and Erik, but when questioned Harald said he knew nothing of them.

'No news is good news,' said Aron.

Leif nodded. 'Likely you're right.'

'If Steingrim or Thorkill had caught up with them we'd hear about it soon enough. Such a confrontation would not escape notice.'

'Confrontation?' asked Harald. 'Did I miss something?'

His brother-in-law summarised briefly.

'If I learn anything you'll be the first to know,' said the trader.

'I'd appreciate it,' replied Leif.

'I hope your kin send the bastards to the bottom, my lord. There's plenty of folk would celebrate if they did; me among them. Steingrim and his crew stole a cargo of iron from me a couple of years back, so it would be a fitting payment.'

Knowing the high price that iron commanded, Leif could understand his reasoning. It was a rare commodity and thus highly prized. Such a loss must have been serious.

'My lads are handy with weapons,' Harald went on, 'but we were seven against thirty. We had no choice but to give up the cargo, but it went against the grain, I can tell you.'

'I'm surprised they let you live.'

'They might not have done, only another vessel came into sight so they cleared off before anyone could challenge them.'

Aron nodded. 'Steingrim and his ilk won't fight unless they're pretty sure of winning.'

'They'll get their dues,' replied Leif, 'just like the rest of our enemies.'

'I'll drink to that,' said Harald.

Apart from undertaking routine domestic chores, Astrid turned her attention to sewing clothes for the baby. She hadn't given much thought to the sex of the child until now. Although she would be happy with a healthy child of either sex, she knew that men set more store by sons. Leif had loved his first child but would he love this one? Would a boy help to heal the hurts of the past or would his presence be a constant reminder of them? What if

the child were to be sent away to be raised elsewhere? The possibility was chilling. Leif had said
he would provide for it, but providing for was not
the same as loving. Furthermore, the babe would be
born out of wedlock. That would have far-reaching
repercussions. She wondered how she could ever
have been naïve enough to think that an informal
relationship with a man could ever replace the se-
curity of marriage. She was older and wiser now.
And yet, if it were all to do again, would she have
wished to marry Gulbrand? It didn't take long to
know the answer. For better or worse, it was Leif
who had her heart. Love ought to be a joyful passion but when unreciprocated it caused only pain,
a hurt worse than a physical wound.

Her present occupation with baby clothes hadn't
escaped notice in other quarters. Ingrid surveyed
the work in silence and then fixed Astrid with a
penetrating look.

'You're carrying his child.'

'Yes.'

'Then he should do the honourable thing. There
is nothing to prevent him.'

Astrid had no intention of explaining the obstacles in that particular path. It was too complicated, and anyway the matter was private.

'He says he will acknowledge the child.'

Ingrid snorted. 'So he should. Not that that
helps you overmuch. A woman needs the secu-
rity of wedlock.'

It was an echo of Astrid's former thought. 'He means to keep me with him.'

'That is shameful behaviour. He's seen his pleasure well met: now he must live up to his responsibilities.'

'I have no power to bring that about, and no male kin to act on my behalf. At least none who would see me wed to Leif.'

'Then he should pity your condition.'

Astrid bit her lip. It wasn't his pity that she wanted. 'I can only hope he will change his mind.'

'He must be made to change it.'

'I don't want him to marry me out of compulsion. I want—' She broke off, embarrassed.

'You're in love with him, aren't you?'

'Yes. I think I always was.'

Ingrid sighed. 'Love puts one at a terrible disadvantage.'

'I know. But there's nothing to be done about it now.'

'Well, he's not indifferent to you either. I've seen the way he looks at you. The fool just doesn't know his own heart, that's all.'

Astrid could only wish it were that simple.

Before either of them could say more they heard the sound of hoofbeats. The horse was being ridden at a gallop and was heading in the direction of the steading. The two women exchanged glances and by tacit consent laid down their sewing and went to investigate. They cut through the hall and reached the front door in time to see the horseman pull up his lathered and blowing mount, and leap down from the saddle. The men who had been standing nearby broke off their conversation and then Aron approached the stranger.

'What is your business here?'

'I must speak with Jarl Leif at once,' the man replied.

Astrid eyed the proceedings dubiously. This boded no good, she was certain of it. A few moments later Leif appeared and took the man aside. She could not hear the words but their expressions only served to reinforce her misgivings.

Chapter Twenty-One

I was late evening before she learned the substance of the news. Leif had remained in the hall until then, deep in conversation with his men. Astrid had stayed up, awaiting his return.

'I thought you would be in bed by now,' he said.

'I could not have slept. What's happening, Leif?'

'It seems that Gulbrand intends to be revenged for Vingulmark's former shame. He has raised a force and challenged Halfdan to meet him.'

'He has challenged the king? Is he mad?'

'Berserker madness,' he replied.

'Vingulmark's forces were badly depleted at the Battle of Eid. Gulbrand can't possibly have enough men.'

'If he's confident enough to issue a challenge,

it's because he's expecting reinforcements from elsewhere.'

Astrid paled. 'My uncle.'

'Among others. I fear he'll be sadly disappointed there.'

'Why so?'

'My preparations are complete; my force is ready. I'm going back to Vingulmark.'

Her stomach lurched. 'To Vingulmark? Please tell me you're not serious.'

'Of course I'm serious. What in Hel's name do you think I've been doing these past weeks?'

The feeling of foreboding intensified. She knew full well he had been planning and making preparations but the timing of his revenge had always been unspecified, until now.

'What do you mean to do?'

'To slay Einar and all his crew and burn his hall to the ground.'

Astrid shivered inwardly, her mind trying to assimilate the news. Suddenly everything was threatening to turn awry.

'You don't know how many men he has, Leif.'

'I have more than enough to deal with him. Besides, I'm the last person he'll be expecting to see.'

'You're planning a surprise attack.'

'Just so.'

'When do you mean to go?'

'We leave at dawn.'

She shut her eyes for a moment, fighting panic. 'What if my uncle slays you?'

'Have you so little faith in my fighting skills?'

'I know your reputation in battle and it is well earned, but Einar is treacherous and cunning. He will not hesitate to use dirty tricks if they serve his ends.'

'I'm well aware of that,' he replied. 'I've had first-hand experience of it, remember? Nevertheless, I shall put paid to Einar's trickery once and for all.'

'His men are mercenaries, Leif. They kill for pleasure.'

'And on this occasion, so shall I.'

Goosebumps prickled along her arms. This was an aspect to his character that she had not witnessed before, and it didn't make for comfortable viewing. Nor did the depth of his hatred. She had no idea how to deal with it either, except by open appeal.

'Please don't do this.'

'I know this isn't easy for you, and that Einar is kin. However, his insults to me cannot be forgotten or forgiven.'

'I do not speak out of kinship to Einar. He is vile and loathsome and he did you great wrong. So did he me, and in ways I cannot forgive either.' She laid a hand over her belly. 'I speak because I don't want my child to be fatherless before he is even born.'

His gaze softened a little. 'I will return, Astrid. I have good reason.'

'But not good enough to keep you from going in the first place.'

'I don't intend to spend the rest of my life looking over my shoulder. To prevent that, Einar and his confederates must die.' He paused, 'And when I've dealt with him I'll go after Gulbrand.'

Astrid felt her heart constrict as the implications of that remark sank in. 'You mean to join Halfdan.'

'That's right.'

'The king is capable of dealing with the problem, Leif.'

'I don't doubt his capabilities in any way, but I mean to be there all the same. Gulbrand was complicit in the plot against me and he'll pay for it. His death will not be swift but he's going to wish for it more than anything in his life before, and I mean to look him in the face while it happens. He's going to know the author of his doom.'

She swallowed hard, fighting queasiness. 'This is more than revenge, Leif. It has become an obsession.'

'It became an obsession with me the day I was shorn and beaten and chained in that kennel. Gulbrand will die all right. So will Einar, and then I'll feed his stinking carcass to his own dogs.'

'And when you have done it, what then?' she asked. 'What will you have become?'

'Victorious. My revenge will be complete.'

'But then you will become little better than they.'

Leif's frown deepened. 'You would equate me with them?'

'A man cannot enact such deeds without consequences to himself. Some part of that foulness will remain like a taint on his soul.' Her hand rested on his arm. 'Don't do it, Leif. Don't let that happen. There's a different kind of future within your grasp: a home, a family and the chance of happiness. All you have to do is seize it.'

He made no reply but the look in his eyes spoke for him. Astrid recoiled as though from a slap.

'You don't want to seize it, do you? That's the real reason you're so eager to go.'

'I must fulfil my vow. I will not be forsworn.'

'How very convenient.'

'It's not about convenience.'

'Isn't it? The truth is that you'd rather brave battle than stay here.'

A muscle jumped in his cheek. 'When this is over I'll be back.'

'But for how long?'

'My destiny is to follow the whale road. You've always known that.'

'I know it's a useful escape route.'

'I'm not trying to escape.'

'You've been trying for the past ten years. Perhaps it's time to stop.'

'The whale road is my life now.'

'And more important than any life you could have with me and your child.'

'That's not what I meant. Stop putting words into my mouth.'

'There's no need. Your mouth is doing well enough on its own.'

Astrid turned away, knowing she had lost. He had long since explained the conditions upon which their relationship was based, and time had done nothing to change it. Whatever he felt for her, it wasn't love and it never would be. The knowledge was bitter.

Sick at heart she undressed and climbed into bed. Leif followed suit and for a while they lay in silence. Then he turned towards her.

'I would not have us part at odds, Astrid.'

Her throat tightened. 'Nor I, my lord.'

'Then I would say farewell in my own way.'

He reached for her then and she closed her eyes. She would not think of the coming confrontation or anything else, only of being here with him, and, for a little while, in the concealing darkness, she could pretend that he loved her.

Next day he rose before dawn and collected his war gear: mail byrnie, sword belt, helm, shield and spear. Astrid watched in silence: she had no more words and he would not have been dissuaded anyway. Nor would tears move him. He was resolved upon this course and would follow it to the end. It was his wyrd.

When he was ready he turned to look at Astrid. 'Go well, vixen. I'll see you again soon.'

'Go well, my lord.'

'If the gods so will.'

He bent and kissed her soft mouth. She closed her eyes, savouring the moment along with the memory of his lovemaking, and wishing that she had the power to hold him. All too soon he drew back. For a second or two the blue-grey eyes held hers. Then he smiled faintly and turned to go.

Astrid followed the men out into the cool, grey dawn and thence down the track to the cove where the *Sea Serpent* waited. Just offshore another vessel was waiting too, crewed by those he had recently recruited to his cause. Most would be kinsmen or oathmen, or both. She estimated about a hundred and twenty in all. Greetings and laughter rang out on the quiet air as *Sea Serpent*'s crew climbed aboard and stowed their sea chests. Then they sat and took up their oars. Slowly the ship began to move, the blades dipping and rising, barely ruffling the dark water as she headed out of the cove.

Astrid stood motionless, watching the progress of the vessels along the fjord, her heart like lead in her breast. How many of the men who set out would return? Vengeance was the preserve of Vidar, a powerful and ruthless god who could only be appeased by blood. Against that deity she had no power. No power either to bind Leif with love. Her life had touched his for a while, a strand woven into his wyrd, but no more than that. The effect would be brief and soon forgotten. In time other women would claim his attention for a while and he would pleasure them well and move on, but the passage of years would strengthen the armour around his heart. Once she had thought she might reach him, that he might come to feel about her as she felt for him. It was forlorn hope. Better to be alone than to be with a man who could not love.

She remained at her vantage point until the ships were out of sight. By then she was resolved upon her own course of action. Slowly she retraced her steps to the hall. Then she found Ingrid and, drawing her aside, came straight to the point.

'I need your help.'

'In what way?'

'I want you to speak to your brother and arrange a passage for me on the knörr when it returns to Vestfold.'

Ingrid stared at her. 'What will you do in Vestfold?'

'I have a friend there who will help me.'

'It is no small thing that you ask.'

'I know that and would not implicate you if it were possible to avoid it. As it is, I cannot do this alone.'

Ingrid nodded, though her eyes were troubled. 'Are you sure this is what you want?'

'I did not come to the decision lightly.'

'Jarl Leif will be sorely displeased if you are not here when he returns.'

'He'll get over it soon enough,' replied Astrid, 'if he returns at all.'

'He will. He's a survivor if ever I saw one.'

Astrid sighed. 'I pray you're right and that the gods may bring him through this conflict unscathed. However, that will not change things between us and I will not go on as they are.'

'Men can be such fools. He should have taken you to wife long since.'

'He would not, any more than he would listen when I urged him not to undertake this latest enterprise. Revenge rules his heart now, and it has killed what the past did not.'

'I wonder if he truly knows his own heart.'

'There is no place in it for me or for his unborn child. He will tire of us both eventually and I would rather end it now than see that happen.'

Ingrid nodded slowly. 'I can understand your reasoning but, all the same, I wish you would stay.'

'I cannot.' Astrid laid a hand on her arm. 'Will you help me?'

'Very well. I'll speak to Harald.'

When the knörr left later that morning Astrid was on it. She boarded the vessel at the last moment and ensconced herself in a corner with the cargo, making herself as inconspicuous as possible. Ingrid had provided her with a warm cloak and food and a little money for the journey. Their leave-taking had been confined to a brief, heartfelt hug. Fortunately there were few people around to witness Astrid's departure since most of the men had departed with Leif and the majority of those who remained were thralls who had long since gone about their work. All the same, her heart thumped as the vessel moved away from the cove and her gaze scanned the track for signs of pursuit. None came. Even so, it wasn't until the knörr rounded a bend in the fjord and the steading was lost to view that she breathed a little easier.

At any other time she might have admired the wooded hills and green meadows, but all she could see now was Leif. He would be angered by her going. Being used to command and to being obeyed, he would take it amiss that a mere woman should take such a decision upon herself. Nevertheless, self-respect demanded it. She was not a thrall to do his bidding without question and she was not his wife. A lump formed in her throat. She suppressed it. It was no use wishing for something you could never have. Leif belonged to the past and she needed to look ahead now, both for herself and her child.

Chapter Twenty-Two

Leif halted his force at the edge of the trees and let his gaze move ahead through the grey gloom to the buildings that comprised Einar's holding: hall, bower, barn, stables, kennels and storerooms were islands in a sea of stillness. The time between night and morning was when sleep was deepest, but for those who watched it afforded light enough. Leif turned to his companions.

'Our quarrel is not with servants and thralls. Provided they offer no resistance let them go unharmed. Our business is elsewhere.' He looked at Harek and the four men nearest to him. 'Let's smoke these vipers out.'

Harek moved forwards, carrying a lighted brand. His four companions carried skins full of oil. Like wraiths they slipped from cover and ran silently towards the hall. Leif and the rest followed after.

While the main host formed a cordon of steel around the building, the others doused the base of the timber walls with oil. When it was done Harek touched them with the brand and then retired. The dry wood caught in a whoosh of billowing flame. The waiting host regarded it with quiet satisfaction.

For a little while nothing happened. The blaze took hold and grew louder, filling the air with dark, acrid smoke. From inside the hall they heard a shout of alarm and then a confusion of other voices mingled with oaths and coughing. Bewildered and frightened servants ran out through the side door and then checked in horror as they saw the armed men in front of them. They cowered, caught between the flames and the swords. A woman screamed. Leif shouted to them over the din.

'Go! It's not your lives we want!' He turned to his men. 'Let them through.'

The cordon opened. For a moment or two the fugitives hesitated, torn between hope and disbelief.

'Bloody fools!' bellowed Thorvald. 'Are you going or not?'

One man, bolder than the rest, ran for the gap. When no one tried to stop him the others followed and then they were all through and running for their lives. The ring of steel closed up behind them.

Inside the hall someone raised the bar on the

main entrance and flung it aside. The portal
swung open and the first figures appeared through
the smoke.

'Here they come,' said Thorvald.

Leif nodded. 'Kill all you can. Just remember,
Einar is mine.'

More men poured out through the burning
doorway and then, understanding the true nature of the danger, shouted a warning to the rest.
Most had grabbed their swords on the way out but
the rest of their war gear was still in the building which was rapidly filling up with smoke.
For a brief space they hesitated, then, seeing no
other choice, launched the attack. The fighting
was fierce and brutal. Einar's mercenaries fought
with the courage born of desperation as Leif had
known they would. However, he had no intention
of losing his own men if he could avoid it. Full
war gear and the element of surprise gave them
the edge and he intended to press the advantage.

The walls were well alight now and the heat intensified, driving the fugitives towards the waiting enemy. Leif's sword arm rose and fell until the
ground around him was littered with bodies, and
Foe Bane's blade smoked with blood. He fought
tirelessly, fed by the swift surge of energy that always came in battle. It flowed through him, hot
and fierce and exhilarating, lending strength to
his arm, sharpening reflex and instinct until he
and the sword were one. As he despatched an-

other opponent he darted swift looks around for the man he sought. When at last he saw him his heart leapt.

'Einar!'

The shout tore from his throat, carrying over the din of the fire and the fighting, and the warlord looked round, seeking the source of the voice. Then he found it. Leif bared his teeth in a smile.

'Remember me?'

Einar vouchsafed no reply save a snarl and then hurled himself into the fray. For all that he was twenty years older, he was still strong and quick, laying on with savage zeal, intending to slay his opponent swiftly. However, Leif's guard was impenetrable and unflagging, meeting and returning blow for blow, denying Einar the opening he sought. Gradually the older man began to tire, perspiring profusely with effort and the heat of the fire behind him. Sweat ran into his eyes and down his face and his breathing grew ragged. For a moment his gaze met Leif's and what he read there changed defiance to desperation. He licked dry lips.

Still Leif kept up the pressure, untiring, relentless. Einar stumbled and then swore as Foe Bane slashed his arm. Blood welled through the torn fabric, staining shirt and tunic scarlet. Another slash opened a rent across his ribs. He grimaced and clapped his free hand to the wound, reeling as the blood dripped through his fingers.

Still Leif came on. Einar fought wildly, his face a mask of hatred.

'I should have killed you while I had the chance.'

'Aye, you should,' replied Leif.

'What have you done with my niece?'

'I took her to my bed and pleasured her well. Now she carries my child.'

'Then she's rightly paid out for her defiance.' Einar swore as Foe Bane carved a parallel cut in his arm. 'I hope the bitch dies in childbed.'

Leif's eyes glinted and he lunged past Einar's guard, thrusting the point of his sword into the warlord's shoulder. Einar sank to his knees, dropping his weapon in the dirt. A hand in his hair jerked his head back and then Foe Bane was against his throat.

'What defiance?' demanded Leif. 'Did she not lure me into your trap?'

For a moment Einar's gaze slid away. Then he smiled maliciously. 'Aye, she did and willingly too. In fact she rejoiced when Hakke told her of the plan.'

'Just as she rejoiced in the thought of marriage to Gulbrand, I suppose.'

'That's right.'

'You lying bastard.'

Einar laughed. 'You'll always wonder, won't you?'

Leif drew back his sword arm and Einar's

laughter ended in a choking wheeze amid bubbles of blood. 'No,' he replied, 'now I'm certain.' Then, releasing his hold, he let the body fall, surveying it with anger and disgust.

'My lord?'

He glanced up to see Thorvald. 'Well?'

'It's finished.'

Leif looked around at the strewn bodies and the burning hall and then at the silent waiting men. Then he nodded.

'Any losses?'

'Not on our side. Half-a-dozen injured is all and none of the wounds mortal.'

'It's well.'

'What now?'

'We dig a pit and bury the slain.'

Thorvald blinked. 'We're not leaving them for the foxes and crows?'

'No. If we do that they'll breed a pestilence, and we're going to need this place since I'm quite certain that Steingrim and company have destroyed ours.'

'I see your point.'

'This will serve us well while we rebuild what they destroyed,' said Leif. 'We'll leave a small contingent to take care of things while the rest of us deal with Gulbrand.'

'Right.'

'In the meantime, when we've buried the dead, I'll go and find out what's left of my holding.'

* * *

He was quite correct in his assumptions about that. All that remained of his hall and the other buildings were piles of cold black ash. Weeds and tall grasses had sprung up all around them and the bones of slaughtered cattle lay nearby, the carcasses picked clean by scavengers. Only the land endured, untouched and unchanged.

'Steingrim was thorough,' said Thorvald, surveying the devastation.

'He'll pay for it,' replied Leif, 'if he hasn't already. It will all be paid for.'

Soon enough they would reach the palace at Mørkestein. He calculated on a day or two at most. Then his force would combine with the king's and smash Gulbrand once and for all. *A man cannot enact such deeds without consequences to himself.* He frowned. The consequences to himself would be freedom from his enemies. They would die honourably in combat like Einar, a nobler end by far than the one they'd planned for him. When he'd spoken of those other excesses he had been angry, letting his baser nature have a voice. If he'd meant the words Astrid's dismay would have been well founded.

The thought of Astrid induced sharp pangs of guilt. Indeed he couldn't remember when he'd last felt so wrong-footed. He couldn't deny that there was truth in some of the things she had said, and when he returned they were going to have to talk.

He didn't know what the answers were, but somehow he would find them. He didn't deceive himself that it would be easy.

Once Harald had disposed of his cargo he left his men with the knörr and accompanied Astrid on the last short leg of her journey to Halfdan's hold at Mørkestein. As she had anticipated the king had elected to leave his wife in a place of safety while he went to deal with the rebels.

Ragnhild received her friend with pleasure and surprise and lost no time in taking her aside for private conversation. Then she listened without interruption while Astrid related her story. She stuck to the facts, omitting only those details that were too intimate to share. In any case the revelation of her pregnancy spoke for itself. The queen's expression registered both sympathy and indignation.

'When your uncle came for you, I thought we should never meet again. I cannot be sorry that the marriage with Gulbrand did not take place.'

'Nor I. It's the one positive aspect of the whole business.'

'Gulbrand's fate is as good as sealed now. Better for him that he dies in battle: the king has a short way with those who oppose him.'

Astrid nodded. In truth, it was not Gulbrand's fate that interested her. Her thoughts were with another man altogether.

'But Hakke still lives?' Ragnhild continued.

'Yes, and as long as he lives there will be a legacy of revenge.'

'After all that you have told me Leif Egilsson can not do other than avenge the insults he suffered. His honour demands it.'

'I know,' replied Astrid, 'and I understand his anger, but it has gone beyond that.'

'Some deeds must be paid for in blood. It is the warrior code, and nothing will content a wronged man until he has exacted the price from his enemies. My lord husband has taught me that.'

'It is a lesson I have but lately learned. I tried to talk Leif out of going.'

'As well tell the wind not to blow.'

'It was foolish, I admit. It's just that I couldn't bear the thought of anything happening to him.'

Ragnhild regarded her keenly. 'You care for him very much, don't you?'

'Much good may it do me. His heart is out of reach.'

'Yet he is not indifferent.'

'Not entirely, but he does not care enough to marry me and give our child a name.' Astrid sighed. 'The settled life no longer has any attraction for him.'

'No longer?'

'His first marriage ended in disaster.'

Briefly Astrid outlined the circumstances.

Ragnhild heard her in appalled silence and then shook her head.

'He's afraid, isn't he?'

'Too afraid to commit himself again.'

'Only he can overcome his own fear, and if he's not prepared to do that you're better off without him.'

'I know,' said Astrid. 'I just wish it didn't hurt so much.'

Chapter Twenty-Three

Leif and his men arrived in Mørkestein two days later. He went directly to the king's hall to ask for an audience. However, it wasn't Halfdan who received him. Instead he found himself face-to-face with Ragnhild. She greeted him courteously and listened with close attention as he explained his mission. Then she shook her head.

'I regret that you are too late, Jarl Leif.'

His heart sank. 'Too late?'

'My lord husband set out a week since,' she explained. 'I have lately received word that he and his men met the rebels in the field and won.'

Leif was silent for a moment, torn between pleasure and disappointment. Then he recollected himself. 'And Gulbrand?'

'Dead, along with most of his force.'

'I'm pleased to learn of the king's victory, although I had hoped to play a part in it.'

Ragnhild smiled. 'Your loyalty does you credit, my lord. It has also cost you dear. We heard of the attack upon your estate.'

'My lady is well informed. However, the perpetrators are dead.'

'It is well. Perhaps now order may be restored to the land.'

'That is a hope I share, my lady.'

'My lord sends word that he expects to return very soon. I have no doubt he will be most pleased to see you and to learn your news. Until then, you and your men are welcome to remain here. Accommodation and food will be provided for you.'

'My lady is gracious.'

The queen smiled and inclined her head. 'Farewell for the time being, Jarl Leif.'

He bowed and retired, his brain assimilating what he had just learned. As he had anticipated, the news caused a stir among his men too.

'Well,' said Thorvald, 'I'm delighted to hear that Gulbrand's dead. All the same, it's a pity we missed the battle.'

'Especially when we'd just got warmed up and all,' replied Ingolf.

'That's life for you.'

'There's still Steingrim and Thorkill to deal with. If Finn and Erik don't kill them first, that is.'

'Chances are they will though,' replied Thorvald.

Ingolf frowned. 'There must be someone left to fight.'

Leif smiled ruefully and strolled away, leaving the men to talk. While it was disappointing that they hadn't been present for the final confrontation, he couldn't regret Gulbrand's demise either. No doubt they'd learn all the details soon enough. The skalds would sing of it at the feast when the king returned. It promised to be a lively affair. Afterwards the *Sea Serpent* would set sail for Agder. Leif sighed. The battle might be won but his problems were far from over.

Astrid looked at her friend in astonishment. 'Leif is here, my lady?'

'That's right. I've just spoken with him,' said Ragnhild.

She related the gist of the conversation. Astrid received the news of her uncle's demise with little surprise and even less regret. Her dominant emotion was relief. Einar's power over her was at an end. More importantly, Leif was alive and well.

'He and his men are to stay awhile,' the queen went on. 'Halfdan will certainly wish to speak with him.'

Astrid's stomach fluttered. 'Oh, yes, of course.'

'You need have no fear. You don't have to see him unless you wish to.' Ragnhild paused. 'It's your choice.'

'I wish I didn't want to see him. I wish I could feel as detached about him as he feels about me.'

'Perhaps we should test this apparent detachment.'

'Test it how, my lady?'

'Don't reveal your presence here. Let him return to Agder and find you gone.'

Astrid's eyes widened. 'Merciful gods! He'd be furious.'

'Furious is a good start,' replied Ragnhild.

'Is it?'

'Of course. No man who is truly detached would react like that, which means he'll come after you.'

'Any anger he feels will be a consequence of being thwarted, nothing more.'

'It's good for men to be thwarted occasionally. It stops them from getting complacent. Anticipate a great deal more than anger from Jarl Leif. One powerful emotion is like to engender others, the ones I suspect he conceals even from himself.'

'And if it doesn't?'

'Then you've lost nothing. Either way you'll know the truth.'

Astrid was silent for a moment. If she agreed to this plan the truth would come out, but she had to face the possibility that it might not be what she hoped for. However, Ragnhild was right. There was nothing to lose now.

'I'll do it.'

The queen smiled. 'Good. It's time this man was brought to his senses.'

The king's return was greeted with great acclaim and his victory celebrated with feasting and drinking. Astrid remained in the women's quarters throughout. In accordance with Ragnhild's instructions no one spoke of her presence, and particularly not to Jarl Leif. As the queen had expected, Halfdan received his friend warmly and expressed his regret that Leif had missed the battle.

'You'd have enjoyed it. The rest of us did.' Halfdan grinned. 'Especially the part where I cut off Gulbrand's ugly head and stuck it on a spike.'

Leif smiled in quiet appreciation. 'I'm truly sorry to have missed that, my lord. Unfortunately my men and I were delayed...'

He gave the king a summary of recent events. Halfdan listened attentively and his grin widened. When the tale concluded he clapped Leif on the shoulder.

'So Einar's dead as well, eh? This calls for a drink.'

In fact the drinking and feasting went on for the rest of that evening and all of the following day. Leif and his men participated in the celebrations, the latter with considerable enthusiasm, but, while the jarl was sincerely pleased by the recent victory, he also felt a curious sense of anticlimax. His enemies were slain, with the possible exceptions of Steingrim and Thorkill, and when Finn and Erik had enough men they'd take care of the matter. Leif was content to let them. He'd achieved his aim and his revenge was complete.

He'd once thought that the accomplishment would leave him with an overwhelming sense of satisfaction, and in some ways it had, but it also left a gaping hole in his life.

For the first time he began to think about what he was going to do next. He had a ship and a crew and the whale road offered plenty of new adventures. He had a holding which needed to be rebuilt. There was timber aplenty and enough skilled hands to do the work. His imagination supplied the image of a fine new hall and a barn and fields of growing crops. It would be a fresh start, a place far removed from Agder and its attendant memories. He could take Astrid with him.

In many ways the thought pleased him, but there was still the matter of her pregnancy.

Most women rejoice in their babies. What if that really happened? What if her words proved true? After all, she had spoken the truth about everything else. That knowledge revived his guilt and he frowned. As soon as he returned to Agder they were definitely going to talk. It wouldn't be an easy conversation but it was necessary; without it they couldn't move forwards and he realised he wanted that. Somewhere along the line she had become necessary to him. He knew he couldn't just sail away and forget her but there were other ways to lose a woman, ways that could not be seen or fought or helped. The dark shadow was stealthy and insidious in the way that it overtook its victims, but its grip was sure and terrible and far-reaching. If it happened a second time... *It wouldn't happen a second time. It couldn't. Surely even the three hags wouldn't be that cruel.* He found himself clinging to that hope because the alternative filled him with dread.

He and his men departed a few days later. Astrid heard the news with a heavy heart. Living in such close proximity and not being able to see him or speak with him had been torment and for the hundredth time she wondered whether that course of action had been the right one. Only time would tell now. She laid a hand over her belly and closed her eyes, trying not to think of all the long, empty years ahead without him.

Ragnhild had been kind, doing her best to keep up her friend's spirits. Astrid was grateful for it. Without that the days would have been bleak indeed. She tried to keep herself occupied and silently prayed to every god she knew. If things did not turn out as they hoped then eventually another husband would be found for her.

'You are fair and nobly born,' said Ragnhild,

'and you are now an heiress. My husband has confirmed that Einar's estate in Vingulmark shall pass to you. With so fine a dowry there will be no lack of suitors. You need have no fear of the future.'

Astrid summoned a smile. For such a reward she had no doubt there were men who would take her, bastard child and all. Among them there might even be one or two who would use her with kindness, but they would never have her heart. That belonged to one man only and it always would.

As the cove and the steading came into view Leif felt a pleasant sense of anticipation. The voyage had afforded him leisure to clear his mind. He still didn't know exactly what he was going to say to Astrid; all he knew was an overwhelming desire to see her again. With every day that passed it grew stronger. This wasn't like the other times. Familiarity with her had not bred contempt, only a sense of rightness and belonging.

The steading was quiet and basking in the same atmosphere of peaceful prosperity. Leif smiled to himself. He'd only been away a few days yet it felt much longer. Once it would have been impossible to think that he might look forward to coming back here. As the arrivals approached the hall Aron appeared to greet them, clearly surprised to see them so soon.

'I thought you'd be gone longer.'

'We came too late for the battle,' explained Thorvald. 'By the time we'd dealt with Einar, the king's forces had already defeated the rebels.'

'Do I take it, then, that Einar and Gulbrand are dead?'

'You do.'

Aron nodded. 'Well, that's good.'

They all trooped into the hall and the men put down their sea chests and called for ale.

Aron eyed his jarl uneasily.

'Is something wrong?' asked Leif.

'The woman has gone.'

Leif frowned. 'Astrid? Gone where?'

'I think you'd better speak to Ingrid.'

The ensuing conversation removed every last trace of Leif's good humour. 'You connived in this?' he demanded. 'You allowed her to leave?'

Ingrid paled but she met his gaze. 'It was not for me to forbid her. Astrid is not a thrall. She's a free woman and entitled to go where she will.'

'Her place is here. She belongs with me.'

'Perhaps you should have told her that.'

His jaw clenched. 'She knew it well enough.'

'Did she?'

'What's that supposed to mean?'

'You carried her off, got her with child and yet had no intention of marrying her. Why ever would she want to stay?'

Leif's face turned pale too. 'Where did she go?'

'To a friend.'

He took a step closer. 'Where, damn it?'

Ingrid swallowed hard. 'To Vestfold. To the queen.'

He stared at her, dumbfounded. 'To Ragnhild?'

'She said the two of them were old friends.'

'I last spoke with the queen only two days ago. She said nothing to me of Astrid's presence.'

'Perhaps Astrid asked her not to.'

His mind reeled. Had Astrid been at Mørke-stein all the time without his knowledge? The palace was large and rambling. Concealment would not be hard, especially with the queen as an ally. Her orders would be obeyed without question. Moreover, she would not have given those orders unless Astrid had requested it. *She's my best friend.* Suddenly it didn't seem so incredible. He ran a hand through his hair, trying to think. She timed her flight well, waiting until he was safely out of the way and could not prevent it. Then she had deliberately avoided him in Mørkestein. It could not have been through fear of his anger, because she knew he wouldn't physically harm her. That argued she really didn't want to see him.

He cast his mind back. They had quarrelled on the night before he left but then made it up afterwards. He didn't want them to part at odds with each other and she had agreed that they should not. In retrospect her reply implied a different kind of parting. She must have been planning her departure even then. His frown deepened.

'No woman likes to be taken for granted,' said Ingrid. 'Astrid has no need to. She's beautiful and nobly born and not without friends.'

He glared at her. 'Astrid is mine, and if she thinks I can be so easily shaken off, she's mistaken.'

'She has the queen's protection. You can't remove her by force.'

'We'll see about that. Tomorrow I leave for Vestfold. When I return, Astrid will be with me.'

Anger smouldered through the rest of the evening until he retired. Then, as he lay alone in his bed, other feelings began to creep in. Not least were loss and pain. He'd once thought that achieving revenge had left a gap in his life but it was as nothing compared to the gap that Astrid's absence left. Losing her was like losing his right hand. He had to get her back. In spite of what he'd said earlier, he realised that force was not the answer. He didn't want to hold her against her will; if she stayed with him it had to be because she wanted to. *You carried her off, got her with child and yet had no intention of marrying her. Why ever would she want to stay?* He winced inwardly. His treatment of her had left much to be desired, but he could make it up to her if only she would let him. Somehow he was going to have to persuade her, make her understand how much he needed her.

Chapter Twenty-Four

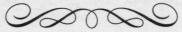

On his return to the palace he was received again by Ragnhild. She greeted him courteously as before and then enquired of his business. Leif came straight to the point.

'I think you know why I'm here, my lady.'

'Perhaps. Would it have anything to do with Astrid?'

'It would.'

'I will enquire whether she will see you.'

'I'm not leaving until I do.'

She raised an eyebrow. 'Then you may be here some time.'

Leif drew a deep breath, fighting impatience. 'I must speak with her, my lady.'

'Must? I think you are in no position to make demands, Jarl Leif.'

For a moment he was sorely tempted to ignore

her and go straight to the women's quarters and find Astrid himself. Of course, if he did that the resulting uproar would bring the guards running, and at the very least he'd find himself ejected on his ear. Common sense prevailed.

'I beg your pardon. I did not intend it so, my lady. It's just that the matter is urgent.'

'Urgent? How so?'

He controlled the urge to shake her. 'I'll explain that to Lady Astrid.'

'If she agrees to see you.'

Leif put his hands behind his back. 'Perhaps you would be so gracious as to ask her, my lady.'

Ragnhild inclined her head in acquiescence and then left him. Several minutes passed. He paced the floor slowly, frustration suddenly replaced by anxiety. What if Astrid still refused to see him? If she did agree to see him what was he going to say? All the speeches he'd prepared had gone right out of his head.

As more minutes passed, his anxiety increased. She wasn't going to see him. She *had* to see him, even if it meant turning the palace upside down to find her and taking on every damned guard in the palace...

He heard a light footstep behind him and turned quickly, only to stop in his tracks. She was wearing a pale blue gown with a darker over-dress edged with red embroidery. It was fastened at the shoulders with fine enamelled clasps. Her golden hair hung loose down her back. She might have been the daughter of a king. He watched her cross the room towards him. Although he could not yet detect any sign of her pregnancy, he could not deny that she was blooming.

With an effort he found his voice. 'You look wonderful.'

'Thank you.'

For a moment or two they lapsed into silence. Her expression was contained and thus hard to interpret.

'I have missed you, lady.'

A hint of some deeper emotion flickered into the violet eyes. 'Have you?'

He sighed. 'I wish you had not left, Astrid.'

'I thought it for the best.'

'I'm sorry you did.' He paused. 'In truth, I'm sorry for many things.'

'As am I,' she replied.

'You have done nothing to apologise for.'

'Yes, I have. It was wrong of me to try and talk you out of avenging yourself when your honour demanded it. I see that now.'

'I understand why you did it.'

'Well, you have your revenge in any case. Your enemies are dead and you can move on.'

'I want that very much,' he said.

'So you mean to return to the whale road.'

'No, I mean to rebuild the steading in Vingul-

mark, the one that Steingrim and his men burned
down.'

Now that he'd voiced the decision he knew it
was the right one, and that it came from a place
deep inside him.

'I see.'

'There has been enough killing and destruc-
tion. I thought it might be good to build something for a change.'

She smiled faintly. 'It would be a novelty, at
any rate.'

'That it would.' He returned the smile. 'I was
hoping you might help me there.'

'Help you how?'

'Come with me, Astrid.'

For a moment she had the uncanny sense of
history repeating itself. She wanted to say yes,
wanted it so much that it hurt, but if she did that
nothing would change. Having found the courage,
to leave she couldn't weaken now and allow the
old pattern to be re-established. She wasn't just
fighting for her own future any more.

'I know I behaved badly but things will be different from now on,' he continued. 'I'll make it
up to you, I swear it.'

'If I come with you things will have to be different,' she replied, 'because I won't be your mistress any more, Leif. I need more than that, for
my child as well as for myself.'

'I have already said I'll acknowledge the child.'

His gaze locked with hers. 'I want you with me, Astrid. I need you with me, but...'

'But not badly enough.' She shook her head. 'Any woman can warm your bed at night.'

'I don't want just any woman. I want you, damn it.'

'There's only one way that's going to happen now.'

A muscle jumped in his cheek. 'I won't have my arm twisted over this.'

'Nor would I wish to do so. I hoped that your feelings for me were as strong as mine for you, but they're not.'

'In ten years I have not felt this strongly about anyone, but what you're asking isn't possible. Not yet.' He hesitated. 'Let's wait and see what happens once the child is born. Perhaps after that we might talk about this again.'

Astrid shook her head. 'Perhaps? And perhaps not too.'

'It's the only undertaking I can give.'

'What undertaking? It commits you to nothing.'

'This isn't fair, Astrid. You know my reasons.'

'Yes, I know them, and I know you hide behind them as well.'

'What?'

'They provide you with a convenient way of avoiding commitment.'

'That isn't true.'

'It *is* true. You may be brave on the battlefield, my lord, but when it comes to facing your demons you're a total coward.'

Leif's face went white. 'That's enough.'

'Have I struck a nerve?'

'A nerve? Your tongue lets blood.'

Her gaze never wavered. 'If you really want to move on stop using the past as a shield.'

'I have never done so.'

'You've done nothing else. The hurt won't heal because you won't let it. It has turned your heart into a cold and unresponsive thing and you've allowed it to happen because you lack the courage to offer it again. Thora's poison works on you still.'

He froze, every muscle taut, and for the space of several heartbeats he was silent. Then, with an effort, he controlled his voice.

'For the last time, Astrid, are you coming with me or not?'

'No.'

'So be it. I'm done with this. I was a fool to have come here at all.' His gaze burned into hers. 'Rest assured, I won't come running after you again.'

With that he turned on his heel and strode away, flinging the door wide. He didn't look back. Astrid remained where she was, her gaze following his departing figure, her heart leaden in her breast. She had lost him, and her hopes of happiness were ashes.

* * *

As Leif marched towards the outer doorway, the guards took one look at his savage expression and got out of his way. In fact he didn't even see them, oblivious to everything but rage and the words echoing in his head. There were many kinds of revenge, but a woman's cut deepest. He'd expected the conversation to be difficult but he'd underestimated her completely. Astrid had always been skilled at finding an opening for her knife, unfailingly locating the place that could be exploited and cause the greatest hurt. And it had hurt. More than he could ever have anticipated.

He stalked out of the building into the courtyard beyond and paused awhile in the fresh air, pacing to and fro while he tried to order his thoughts. He was sorely tempted to go back and fetch the contrary little witch, and take her to Vingulmark by force. Once he had her there he'd damned well ensure she didn't leave again. *Astrid is not a thrall. She's a free woman and she goes where she will.* His jaw clenched. Much as it irked him, he knew Ingrid had spoken the truth. He had no right to compel Astrid to go anywhere against her will. Nor could he compel her to share his bed. The very thought of a pretended passion was abhorrent. It was better to end it now than to have that happen. *Any woman can warm your bed.* He let out a long breath. He knew which woman he wanted, but the price was just too high.

* * *

Ragnhild took one look at her friend's desolate expression and guessed the rest. 'I'm so sorry, Astrid. When he returned I was convinced...'

'So was I, my lady. At least I hoped.' Astrid made an empty gesture with her hands. 'But all hope there is at an end.'

'Men can be such fools at times.'

'I was a fool to think he would marry again. The damage has gone too deep with him.'

'He has just thrown away his chance of mending it.'

Astrid made no reply. Just then she felt too numb even to cry. Even the enormity of her predicament receded in the face of present loss. Likely she would never see Leif again, or if she did they would meet as distant strangers. In the meantime, she had no idea what she was going to do next.

Realising that her friend needed a little time alone, the queen withdrew. As the door closed behind her the silence settled around Astrid like a shroud. She had never felt so empty or so alone in her life. It was hard even to think, but she had to think, for the sake of her child if nothing else. No matter what happened it would be loved and wanted by one of its parents at least.

'Leif Egilsson! What in the name of the All-Father are you doing back here?'

Leif turned to see Halfdan striding towards him and with a concerted effort recovered his poise enough to bow. 'My lord.'

'I thought you'd left for Agder.'

'I did,' replied Leif, 'only I discovered that there was unfinished business here.'

The king smiled. 'Ah, Lady Astrid.'

'Yes, Lady Astrid.' Was everyone involved in the conspiracy to keep her hidden?

'I trust everything has been concluded to your satisfaction.'

'It is concluded, my lord, though it does not afford me any satisfaction.'

Halfdan's smile faded. 'I'm sorry to hear that. I thought the two of you had an understanding.'

'So did I, but it seems not.'

'But she's carrying your child, is she not?'

'She is. I shall acknowledge it and provide for it too when the time comes, but all else is at an end between us. She has made that quite clear.'

'She's refused to marry you? That's crazy.'

Leif frowned. 'I... No, she didn't refuse. It's marriage she wants but...'

'But what?'

'I cannot offer her that.'

'Why not?'

'It's complicated, my lord.'

'How is it complicated?' demanded Halfdan. 'Lady Astrid is no common trollop. Her birth is as good as yours and she's fair to boot. She is more than fit to be your wife.'

'I do not dispute her breeding or her qualities.'

'Then why in the name of the gods will you not marry her as you should?'

'I have my reasons. She knows what they are.'

The king's gaze grew cool. 'Up until this moment I had always believed you to be a man of honour, Jarl Leif, but this is shameful. I will not have the lady treated in this manner.'

'It was never my intention to treat her ill.'

'Well, what do you think this is? Must she bear disgrace because you will not live up to your responsibilities?'

Had it been any other man his teeth would have been halfway down his throat. As it was, Leif contained his anger. 'I said I had my reasons.'

'Perhaps you'd care to explain them to me.'

The words were quietly spoken but Leif knew better than to think they implied a choice. His gut tightened as he mentally sought for the composure with which to frame his reply. Then, drawing a deep breath, he furnished the king with a succinct and factual explanation. However, the words sounded strangely distant, as though they had been spoken about someone else. Of course, he had been someone else back then.

Halfdan heard him out in silence, and although his gaze never wavered, it lost some of its former coldness. 'It's time to move on, Leif. You've got a chance to make a fresh start, but you're using the past as an excuse not to.'

It was an uncanny echo of what Astrid had said before and he frowned. The king continued to regard him keenly.

'If you will not marry Lady Astrid, I'll find her another husband. It won't be hard to do.'

Leif frowned. 'Astrid belongs to me.'

'Then you'd better claim her and soon, or someone else will.'

With that Halfdan walked away, leaving him alone. Leif remained where he was for a moment or two then made his way back to the outer gate, deep in thought. If the king found a husband for Astrid she would be lost for good, and the baby too. The realisation was accompanied by a sharp spasm in his stomach. Halfdan's reaction didn't help matters either. He'd been a shield brother and a friend, one whose good opinion Leif had valued highly. The thought of forfeiting that regard was bitter indeed. What made it worse was that, deep inside, he knew his friend's anger to be justified. Astrid was all he had said and more. She was worthy to be his wife and yet...

He left the royal compound and paused, looking around. He had no desire for company just then so instead of going back to the ship to join his men he turned off the road and, having found a convenient rock, sat down awhile. Events this day had left him feeling shaken, as though he had lost all sense of himself. *Thora's poison works on you still.* The accusation cut deep and suddenly all the foulness of the past burst to the surface like pus from an infected wound. Leif stared at it in disgust. Yet he couldn't disown it: he'd carried it with him these past ten years. In part it had shaped who he'd become and found expression in blood and fire and war—and in revenge. Revenge in which guilty and innocent alike had been punished.

Astrid had always been innocent. She had spoken the truth and he had refused to listen. *You won't listen because you don't want to.* He closed his eyes but it only brought his mistreatment of her into sharper focus and he was sickened. Fortunately she'd had the courage and the will to rise above it and to fight on her own terms. He might have possessed her body but in the end she had conquered by taking possession of his heart. It was a victory he had feared to acknowledge. *When it comes to facing your demons you're a total coward.* She had spoken the truth about that too. He had been cowardly, so much so that he had been about to throw away everything that really mattered. Now he just had to hope that self-knowledge hadn't come too late.

Chapter Twenty-Five

Leif strode back to the palace and retraced his steps to the small audience chamber where he'd spoken to Ragnhild and Astrid before. It was empty so he kept on going. Startled servants regarded him in astonishment. One bolder than the rest attempted to protest. Leif ignored that too.

'Where is Lady Astrid?'

'These are private quarters, my lord. You cannot just—' The sentence ended on a yelp as Leif grabbed the front of his tunic and dragged him closer.

'Where is she?'

The man gulped and pointed to a doorway at the end of the passage. 'Y-yonder, my lord.'

Leif shoved him aside and strode on, oblivious to the babble of voices in his wake. When he reached the door he paused long enough to take a deep breath and then flung it wide.

Astrid was standing by the window but turned quickly. Then her heart missed a beat and she smiled tremulously. 'Leif. What are you…?'

That was all she had time to say before he crossed the room and drew her into his arms for a long and passionate kiss. When they eventually paused for air he drew back a little, his gaze searching her face.

'I'm so sorry, Astrid. Can you ever forgive me?'

'You came back.'

'I came to my senses. I love you, lady. I always have—only I was too afraid to admit it, even to myself.'

A lump formed in her throat. 'Do you mean that?'

'Yes, I mean it. I should have told you long ago.' He hesitated. 'It's not the only thing I've been afraid to admit. When first you told me that you were with child I was terrified.'

'I know.'

'That why I said those things about terminating the pregnancy. I thank all the gods that you didn't.'

'I could never have done such a thing. I want this child, Leif.'

'So do I, with all my heart, but…' He took a deep breath. 'I couldn't bear it if I lost you as well.'

'You're not going to lose me.'

'If I had a fraction of your courage my fame would be great indeed.'

'It is great enough already.'

'And yet in some things I am a coward.' He sighed. 'Could you ever love such a man?'

'I do love you, Leif. I thought you knew that.'

'I've been such an almighty fool but I will make it up to you if you'll let me. Will you do me the honour of becoming my wife?'

His image blurred through the water welling in her eyes. 'Willingly, my lord.'

There followed another lingering kiss.

From outside the sound of footsteps and voices grew louder. Two armed guards halted on the threshold with half-a-dozen servants hovering in the background. As they took in the scene beyond, the guards exchanged glances and then grinned broadly.

'What is the meaning of this?' demanded a voice behind them.

The men's grins disappeared and they sprang to attention as the crowd parted to let the queen through. When she saw what they were staring at she stopped in her tracks and for a moment or two there was a pregnant silence. Ragnhild smiled. Then she waved all the onlookers away and quietly closed the door.

Leif and Astrid were married the following day. As there hadn't been time to make a new gown for the occasion, the queen had lent her one, a beautiful creation in violet and gold that suited her colouring and enhanced the colour of her eyes. Even now she found it hard to believe that what she'd most wanted had come about. Oddly it was she who stumbled over the words and he who spoke with firm, clear assurance. When he sealed their agreement with a kiss it drew a roar of approval from the crowded hall. Astrid's cheeks turned a deep shade of pink.

The king smiled. 'Long life and happiness to you both.'

Ragnhild added her congratulations and then other well-wishers crowded round. Astrid was scarce aware of what she said or did, for her whole being was attuned only to Leif. It seemed to her that he had never looked so handsome. The black-and-gold tunic enhanced every line of his powerful frame and acted a foil for the mane of gold hair. It had grown out considerably over the past months. More than ever he reminded her of a lion—no longer predatory, only virile and dangerously exciting. It seemed that she was not alone in thinking so, to judge from the female attention directed his way. Astrid smiled, her heart full with the knowledge that he was hers.

Leif smiled too. 'Happy?'

'Most happy, my lord. More than I ever dreamed possible.'

'I will try my best to be a good husband.'

'And I to be a good wife.'

'Goodness comes more naturally to you,' he replied. 'You are an improving influence.'

'I seriously doubt it. Besides, I would not seek to change you in any way.'

'And yet you have, whether you know it or not.' He let his hands rest lightly on her waist. 'There is no going back now and nor would I wish to.'

'There's too much to look forward to.' She kissed him softly.

The blue-grey eyes gleamed. 'Have a care, wife, lest I forget all recent improvement and give rein to my desire.'

'Such a lapse would be truly shocking—if it occurred in public.'

'Hmm. I can see it's going to have to wait until I get you alone.'

'Are you planning a seduction, my lord?'

He grinned. 'That's one way of putting it, I suppose.'

The thought of being alone with him filled her with eager anticipation, but first there were social obligations to fulfil since a feast had been prepared in their honour. However, laughter came easily now and they relaxed into the conviviality all around them, letting themselves be borne along on the current. None of those present could miss the glow of happiness emanating from the newly wed pair.

* * *

The eating and drinking went on for several hours until the company was in various stages of intoxication. Leif had deliberately limited his intake of mead and ale so that while he was pleasantly mellow he was very far from being drunk. All around the jests grew bawdier. He smiled and looked at his bride, letting his mind move ahead a little. Mentally he began to strip away her clothing. The result was a rush of heat to his loins. Desire increased. He set down his cup and rose from the table, drawing Astrid with him. Then he picked her up and carried her from the hall to the accompaniment of cheers and raucous laughter and the resounding din of fists and cups pounding on wood.

A chamber had been prepared for them. Leif set Astrid down and barred the door securely. He had no intention of being disturbed by drunken revellers this night. Having ensured privacy he took his wife in his arms.

'Now where were we?'

She smiled and slipped her arms around his neck, pressing close. 'Somewhere around here I think.' Her lips met his, warm, inviting and seductive.

His hold tightened and the kiss became intimate, arousing. Leif groaned. 'I have missed you, lady.'

'And I you, my lord.'

He undressed himself and then her, letting his gaze travel the length of her body. It was still slender but, now that the concealing drape of the gown was gone, he could see the gentle swelling beneath. His throat constricted and he was filled with love and pride and tenderness. Tentatively he reached out and placed a hand over her belly, feeling the rounded warmth that spoke of the new life within. It seemed so small and fragile. His son? His daughter? It didn't matter what the sex was, just as long as the child was healthy; as long as Astrid was safe. That thought led to others and suddenly he was uncertain.

'Sweetheart, are you sure this is all right? I'll not press you to make love if you don't wish to. It's your choice.'

'My choice?' She stepped closer and placed a hand lightly on his breast. 'Let me think about that.' Her hand moved lower across his stomach and abdomen.

His muscles tightened in response. 'And?'

'Hmm.' Her fingers closed around him and stroked. 'It's a difficult decision.'

Leif caught his breath. 'Any more, vixen, and you'll have no say at all.'

'Dear me.' She smiled mischievously. 'I think we'd better go to bed at once. I'll be able to concentrate better there.'

* * *

His lovemaking was considerate and tender, taking his time, delighting in relearning every line and curve, breathing the sweet familiar scent of her. It mingled with the smell of clean linen and fragrant herbs, heady and exciting. Absence had only increased his desire but he controlled it, wanting to savour each moment and draw the moments out; wanting to please her as much as himself.

Afterwards he held her in his arms, aware of both contentment and belonging. He hoped with all his heart that this time the feeling would last, that they might really have the happiness she had once described. Before that there were practical matters to attend to.

'It will be necessary to return to your uncle's estate for a while, until such time as I can raise a new hall.'

Astrid looked up at him. 'I have no fondness for the place but it is likely to be harder for you, I think.'

'The memories are unpleasant, but it's a means to an end. Besides, Einar is dead and gone now.' He paused. 'The other possibility is for you to remain here until the hall is ready.'

'I would not be parted from you again. Where you go, I will go also.'

He kissed her bright hair. 'Then we will face the ghosts together.'

Of necessity the journey was slow out of consideration for Astrid's tender condition. Ragnhild had provided a wagon for the purpose and filled it with every conceivable comfort and a generous supply of provisions. Leif rode alongside while his men brought up the rear.

Their presence ensured that the trip was trouble free: no robber band would be foolish enough to attack a large group of seasoned warriors. Thus the time passed pleasantly enough.

Their arrival was greeted warmly by the men whom Leif had left to oversee things in his absence. Astrid looked around. The place looked much the same, save for an ash pile where Einar's hall had once stood. Given the scenes that had taken place there she could not lament its passing. Since that shelter was no more she guessed that Leif's men would have made use of the *hovs* that Einar's troops had vacated.

Leif helped her down from the wagon. 'Welcome back, if that's the right expression to use.'

She smiled ruefully. 'As you said, it's a means to an end.'

'And an incentive to get our home rebuilt as soon as possible.'

'I'll second that.'

'In the meantime, I need to speak to my men. Will you excuse me for a little while?'

She kissed his cheek. 'For a little while.'

Leif grinned. 'It would be impossible to stay away longer.'

She left him to it and strolled away towards the women's bower. Several figures stood outside, watching the proceedings from a respectful distance, but now one of them hurried forwards to greet her. Recognising the woman at once, Astrid smiled.

'Dalla! I'm so glad to see you.'

The servant's delight and relief were unmistakable. 'And I you, my lady. The gods have heard my prayers.'

'The gods have heard all our prayers,' said Astrid.

'After you disappeared I feared the worst.'

'There is much to tell you.'

'I long to hear it but you must be tired after the journey. Come in and rest awhile.'

Astrid gave a concise version of events since their last meeting and then listened while Dalla recounted what had occurred on the night that Einar had died. Leif's revenge had been thorough but it had been confined to those able to defend themselves, and he'd allowed his enemies to die in combat. There was honour is such a death, and magnanimity too, considering the end they'd planned for him. The recollection of it made her feel cold. It only reinforced the view that the world was well rid of such men. Even so, there was one question left, one that she dreaded asking.

'What was done with my uncle's body?'

'Jarl Einar is buried with the others, my lady.'

Astrid was deeply thankful. Burial was practical but, more importantly, it was honourable and far removed from the news she had feared to hear. Leif had not given in to the evil thoughts that anger had suggested, although she was in no doubt that, had their positions been reversed, Einar would not have hesitated.

'I can show you the place,' Dalla continued, 'if you so wish.'

The burial site was some distance from the buildings and marked by a long strip of bare earth that covered the trench where the slain had been interred. Astrid regarded it in silence. She could not regret Einar's passing. Indeed her dominant emotion was relief. The grave served as an affirmation that he and his henchmen were really gone.

Leif came to join her there a few minutes later. 'I was not inclined to afford them an elaborate funeral,' he said.

She shook her head. 'They were lucky to get a funeral at all. You could have left them to the carrion birds.'

'I was tempted. But for the threat of disease I might have done it.'

'It would be just like my uncle to cause a plague.'

'Quite.'

'He was my kin and yet I loathed him. There was no kindness or mercy in the man, only ravening ambition.'

'Forget him.' Leif put an arm about her waist. 'His ambition cannot hurt us now. We'll shape the future we want.'

Astrid smiled. 'It'll be a good future, Leif. I know it.'

He bent and kissed her softly. Then together they turned and walked away from the grave.

Chapter Twenty-Six

The months that followed were filled with intense activity. Leif and his men discovered a large pile of seasoned timber behind the barn which they put to good use. The saw pits were busy and a steady stream of wagons carried planks and beams to the ruined steading. Astrid stole a couple of hours to climb aboard one of the carts and ride over to take a look and see how the work was progressing.

From her vantage point she surveyed the site with interest. The framework of a new hall was already in place and the walls were going up around it. Some distance off, men were digging out the post holes for a barn. The air rang with the sound of hammering and sawing. Noting her arrival, Leif broke off his discussion and came to meet her. Like most of the men he had stripped off to the waist while he worked. Exposure to the sun and wind had tanned his skin and streaked his hair with strands of paler gold. It rendered the blue-grey eyes more vivid. He was altogether an arresting figure and her heart filled with pride that he was hers.

He smiled and lifted her down from the wagon. 'This is a pleasant surprise.'

Astrid tilted her face to receive his kiss. 'I wanted to see how you were getting on.'

'We've made good progress but there's plenty more to do though.'

It was no exaggeration. Apart from all the re-building work, there were also two farms to tend. Late summer had meant a pause to bring in the harvest. That would be followed by burning off the stubble and then ploughing. Soon enough there would be cattle and pigs to slaughter and meat to be salted. The women servants were kept busy making cheese and churning butter. Others spun wool and wove and dyed cloth. The men fished and hunted and trapped. From dawn until dusk the work went on.

'When winter comes we must be ready for it,' he went on. 'I'll not have our people starve or freeze.'

She could well understand the sense of urgency. Winter would be long and hard and by the end everyone would be longing for the spring. She rested a hand lightly on the mound of her belly. Spring would see the birth of their child too, an event that filled her with eager anticipation.

'We'll be ready,' she replied.

He put an arm around her waist. 'It'll be next year before we can move into our new home though.'

'It'll be something else to look forward to.'

'Yes.'

Although he never said so, she knew that he did not view the coming birth with unqualified joy. His manner was unfailingly courteous and considerate and, as her pregnancy advanced, he did not press her to make love as often. Sometimes, though, she looked up to find him watching her and once or twice caught the fleeting expression of anxiety in his eyes before he had time to conceal it. Although he never gave voice to his thoughts, she sensed the underlying tension in him. She also understood it. No matter how loving she was now, this would not be resolved until after the child was born. Only then would Leif realise that his fears were unfounded. In the meantime, she could only offer reassurance.

'It will be all right,' she said. 'You'll see.'

Leif wanted to believe it. He wanted the dream she had described: a thriving family of handsome, healthy children who would grow up here in the home they had built. His rational mind told him it was possible; almost certain. Almost. Try as he might, he could not entirely rid himself of the last lingering traces of apprehension. Work kept it at bay for the most part but, sometimes, at night, the shadow returned. It crept up on him unawares and clouded his thoughts. Then he would feel angry with himself for letting it happen. Astrid was beautiful and loving and kind, in every way a wife to be proud of. She deserved better from him.

He bent and kissed her soft mouth. 'Of course it will be all right.'

Epilogue

Astrid's labour began on a cold and blustery spring morning. It went on all afternoon and into the evening. Leif had taken Dalla's advice at first and tried to occupy himself with chores, but, as time wore on, it became impossible to do that and he was reduced to pacing up and down outside the bower, occasionally glancing at the timber wall with misgivings. Although he'd had repeated assurances that everything was proceeding normally, he could not suppress his anxiety. Childbirth was dangerous. Women died. The thought of losing Astrid filled him with fear. Underneath that was the deeper dread that even if she gave birth normally it might mean the end of the happiness they'd known together.

Recognising the shadow, he made a determined effort to repel it. Thus far, there had been no sign that her feelings for him had altered in any way. She was just as loving as she had always been. As for the child, it was lusty. He'd felt it kick on many occasions. Astrid was sure it would be a boy, a warrior in the making.

A cry of pain stopped Leif in his tracks and his stomach lurched. In spite of the cold air, a light sheen of sweat broke out on his forehead. Going into battle against overwhelming odds would have made him less nervous than he was now. Instinctively his hand went to the amulet he wore around his neck: the likeness of Thor's hammer, Mjollnir. Previously it had always brought him luck... Another cry issued from the bower. His hand clenched around the amulet. Then he squatted down with his back to the wall and he prayed.

The cries of pain grew more frequent, the women's voices more urgent in exhortation. Leif put his head in his hands. And then, over it all, he heard a baby cry. It was followed by a variety of exclamations impossible to distinguish apart. He froze, chest as tight as a drum. The baby yelled again. The other voices fell silent. It was several minutes before Leif found the courage to move. Slowly he eased himself upright. Then, taking a deep breath, he made his way to the door of the bower.

It was Dalla who eventually found him there. Leif tried to speak but no sound came out. He cleared his throat and tried again.

'Astrid?'

'Is well, my lord. And you have a son, a fine healthy boy.'

He stared at her, trying to take it in. 'A boy?'

'Yes.'

'And Astrid is well?'

'She's tired but otherwise perfectly well.'

'Can I come in?'

'Of course.' Dalla stood aside to let him pass.

The other women smiled and melted into the background. Leif paused on the threshold and licked dry lips, his gaze taking in the quiet scene beyond. The room was warm and tidy. Astrid was lying on the bed, propped against cushions, holding the child in her arms. She looked up as he entered and then she smiled; a warm and gentle smile in which he saw both pride and joy.

'Come and meet your son.'

He moved forwards and sat down by the bed and stared. The baby stared solemnly back.

'Isn't he beautiful?' she continued.

Leif swallowed the lump in his throat. 'He's wonderful. Perfect, in fact.'

'He takes after his father.'

'His father is very far from perfect.' His gaze met and held hers. 'However, he'll try and mend his ways.'

'I would not change him,' she replied. 'I love him exactly as he is and I always will.'

As he looked into her eyes the last remnants of

shadow dissolved and vanished. It was replaced by joy and relief so intense that he felt almost light-headed. He understood then that, this time, everything really would be all right.

* * * * *

A sneaky peek at next month...

HISTORICAL

IGNITE YOUR IMAGINATION, STEP INTO THE PAST...

My wish list for next month's titles...

In stores from 1st November 2013:

☐ Rumours that Ruined a Lady — Marguerite Kaye

☐ The Major's Guarded Heart — Isabelle Goddard

☐ Highland Heiress — Margaret Moore

☐ Paying the Viking's Price — Michelle Styles

☐ The Highlander's Dangerous Temptation — Terri Brisbin

☐ Rebel with a Heart — Carol Arens

Available at WHSmith, Tesco, Asda, Eason, Amazon and Apple

Just can't wait?

1013

A Royal Mistress!

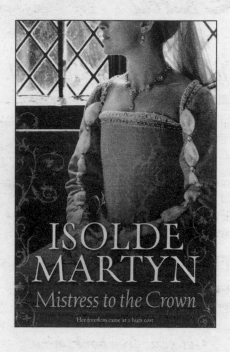

ISOLDE
MARTYN
Mistress to the Crown

Her freedom came at a high cost

Elizabeth Lambard was to become known as the
notorious whore 'Jane Shore'——lover of King
Edward IV. Facing scandal and a damaged reputation
can Elizabeth's beauty keep her out of trouble?
Or will it lead her to the hangman's noose?

Available from:

www.millsandboon.co.uk

oin the Mills & Boon Book Club

Want to read more **Historical** books?
Ve're offering you **2 more** absolutely **FREE!**

e'll also treat you to these fabulous extras:

- 🌹 **Exclusive offers and much more!**

- 🌹 **FREE home delivery**

- 🌹 **FREE books and gifts with our special rewards scheme**

Get your free books now!

visit www.millsandboon.co.uk/bookclub
r call Customer Relations on 020 8288 2888